THE HIDDEN HAND

LECTOR HOUSE PUBLIC DOMAIN WORKS

THE HIDDEN HAND

EMMA DOROTHY ELIZA NEVITTE SOUTHWORTH

ISBN: 978-93-5342-833-4

First Published: -

LECTOR HOUSE

LECTOR HOUSE LLP
E-MAIL: lectorpublishing@gmail.com

THE HIDDEN HAND

BY

MRS. E. D. E. N. SOUTHWORTH
AUTHOR OF THE CURSE OF CLIFTON

CONTENTS

THE HIDDEN HAND

CHAPTER I.

THE NOCTURNAL VISIT.

* * * Whence is that knocking?
How is't with me when every sound appals me?
* * * I hear a knocking
In the south entry! Hark!—More knocking!

—SHAKESPEARE.

Hurricane Hall is a large old family mansion, built of dark-red sandstone, in one of the loneliest and wildest of the mountain regions of Virginia.

The estate is surrounded on three sides by a range of steep, gray rocks, spiked with clumps of dark evergreens, and called, from its horseshoe form, the Devil's Hoof.

On the fourth side the ground gradually descends in broken, rock and barren soil to the edge of the wild mountain stream known as the Devil's Run.

When storms and floods were high the loud roaring of the wind through the wild mountain gorges and the terrific raging of the torrent over its rocky course gave to this savage locality its ill-omened names of Devil's Hoof, Devil's Run and Hurricane Hall.

Major Ira Warfield, the lonely proprietor of the Hall, was a veteran officer, who, in disgust at what he supposed to be ill-requited services, had retired from public life to spend the evening of his vigorous age on this his patrimonial estate. Here he lived in seclusion, with his old-fashioned housekeeper, Mrs. Condiment, and his old family servants and his favorite dogs and horses. Here his mornings were usually spent in the chase, in which he excelled, and his afternoons and evenings were occupied in small convivial suppers among his few chosen companions of the chase or the bottle.

In person Major Warfield was tall and strongly built, reminding one of some old iron-limbed Douglas of the olden time. His features were large and harsh; his complexion dark red, as that of one bronzed by long exposure and flushed with strong drink. His fierce, dark gray eyes were surmounted by thick, heavy black brows that, when gathered into a frown, reminded one of a thunder cloud, as the flashing orbs beneath them did of lightning. His hard, harsh face was surrounded by a thick growth of iron-gray hair and beard that met beneath his chin. His usual habit was a black cloth coat, crimson vest, black leather breeches, long, black yarn stockings, fastened at the knees, and morocco slippers with silver buttons.

In character Major Warfield was arrogant, domineering and violent—equally loved and feared by his faithful old family servants at home—disliked and dreaded by his neighbors and acquaintances abroad, who, partly from his house and partly from his character, fixed upon him the appropriate nickname of Old Hurricane.

There was, however, other ground of dislike besides that of his arrogant mind, violent temper and domineering habits. Old Hurricane was said to be an old bachelor, yet rumor whispered that there was in some obscure part of the world, hidden away from human sight, a deserted wife and child, poor, forlorn and heart-broken. It was further whispered that the elder brother of Ira Warfield had mysteriously disappeared, and not without some suspicion of foul play on the part of the only person in the world who had a strong interest in his "taking off." However these things might be, it was known for a certainty that Old Hurricane had an only sister, widowed, sick and poor, who, with her son, dragged on a wretched life of ill-requited toil, severe privation and painful infirmity in a distant city, unaided, unsought and uncared for by her cruel brother.

It was the night of the last day of October, eighteen hundred and forty-five. The evening had closed in very dark and gloomy. About dusk the wind arose in the northwest, driving up masses of leaden-hued clouds, and in a few minutes the ground was covered deep with snow and the air was filled with driving sleet.

As this was All Hallow Eve, the dreadful inclemency of the weather did not prevent the negroes of Hurricane Hall from availing themselves of their capricious old master's permission and going off in a body to a banjo breakdown held in the negro quarters of their next neighbor.

Upon this evening, then, there was left at Hurricane Hall only Major Warfield, Mrs. Condiment, his little housekeeper, and Wool, his body servant.

Early in the evening the old hall was shut up closely to keep out as much as possible the sound of the storm that roared through the mountain chasms and cannonaded the walls of the house as if determined to force an entrance. As soon as she had seen that all was safe, Mrs. Condiment went to bed and went to sleep.

It was about ten o'clock that night that Old Hurricane, well wrapped up in his quilted flannel dressing-gown, sat in his well-padded easy-chair before a warm and bright fire, taking his comfort in his own most comfortable bedroom. This was the hour of the coziest enjoyment to the self-indulgent old Sybarite, who dearly loved his own ease. And, indeed, every means and appliance of bodily comfort was at hand. Strong oaken shutters and thick, heavy curtains at the windows kept out every draft of air, and so deadened the sound of the wind that its subdued moaning was just sufficient to remind one of the stormy weather without in contrast to the bright warmth within. Old Hurricane, as I said, sat well wrapped up in his wadded dressing-gown, and reclining in his padded easy-chair, with his head thrown back and his feet upon the fire irons, toasting his shins and sipping his punch. On his right stood a little table with a lighted candle, a stack of clay pipes, a jug of punch, lemons, sugar, Holland gin, etc., while on the hearth sat a kettle of boiling water to help replenish the jug, if needful.

On his left hand stood his cozy bedstead, with its warm crimson curtains festooned back, revealing the luxurious swell of the full feather bed and pillows, with their snow-white linen and lamb's-wool blankets, inviting repose. Between this bedstead and the corner of the fireplace stood Old Hurricane's ancient body servant Wool, engaged in warming a crimson cloth nightcap.

"Fools!" muttered Old Hurricane, over his punch—"jacks! they'll all get the pleurisy except those that get drunk! Did they all go, Wool?"

"Ebery man, 'oman and chile, sar!—'cept 'tis me and coachman, sar!"

"More fools they! And I shouldn't wonder if you, you old scarecrow, didn't want to go too!"

"No, Marse——"

"I know better, sir! Don't contradict me! Well, as soon as I'm in bed, and that won't be long now, you may go—so that you get back in time to wait on me to-morrow morning."

"Thanky, marse."

"Hold your tongue! You're as big a fool as the rest."

"I take this," said Old Hurricane, as he sipped his punch and smacked his lips—"I take this to be the very quintessence of human enjoyment—sitting here in my soft, warm chair before the fire, toasting my legs, sipping my punch, listening on the one hand to the storm without and glancing on the other hand at my comfortable bed waiting there to receive my sleepy head. If there is anything better than this in this world I wish somebody would let me know it."

"It's all werry comfortable indeed, marse," said the obsequious Wool.

"I wonder, now, if there is anything on the face of the earth that would tempt me to leave my cozy fireside and go abroad to-night? I wonder how large a promise of pleasure or profit or glory it would take now?"

"Much as ebber Congress itse'f could give, if it give you a penance for all your sarvins," suggested Wool.

"Yes, and more; for I wouldn't leave my home comforts to-night to insure not only the pension but the thanks of Congress!" said the old man, replenishing his glass with steaming punch and drinking it off leisurely.

The clock struck eleven. The old man again replenished his glass, and, while sipping its contents, said:

"You may fill the warming-pan and warm my bed, Wool. The fumes of this fragrant punch are beginning to rise to my head and make me sleepy."

The servant filled the warming-pan with glowing embers, shut down the lid and thrust it between the sheets to warm the couch of this luxurious Old Hurricane. The old man continued to toast his feet, sip his punch and smack his lips. He finished his glass, set it down, and was just in the act of drawing on his woolen nightcap, preparatory to stepping into his well-warmed bed when he was suddenly startled by a loud ringing of the hall-door bell.

"What the foul fiend can that mean at this time of night?" exclaimed Old Hurricane, dropping his nightcap and turning sharply around toward Wool, who, warming-pan in hand, stood staring with astonishment. "What does that mean, I ask you?"

"'Deed, I dunno, sar, less it's some benighted traveler in search o' shelter out-en de storm!"

"Humph! and in search of supper, too, of course, and everybody gone away or gone to bed but you and me!"

At this moment the ringing was followed by a loud knocking.

"Marse, don't less you and me listen to it, and then we ain't 'bliged to 'sturb ourselves with answering of it!" suggested Wool.

"'Sdeath, sir! Do you think that I am going to turn a deaf ear to a stranger that comes to my house for shelter on such a night as this? Go and answer the bell directly."

"Yes, sar."

"But stop—look here, sirrah—mind I am not to be disturbed. If it is a traveler, ask him in, set refreshments before him and show him to bed. I'm not going to leave my warm room to welcome anybody to-night, please the Lord. Do you hear?"

"Yes, sar," said the darkey, retreating.

As Wool took a shaded taper and opened the door leading from his master's chamber, the wind was heard howling through the long passages, ready to burst into the cozy bedroom.

"Shut that door, you scoundrel!" roared the old man, folding the skirt of his warm dressing-gown across his knees, and hovering closer to the fire.

Wool quickly obeyed, and was heard retreating down the steps.

"Whew!" said the old man, spreading his hands over the blaze with a look of comfortable appreciation. "What would induce me to go abroad on such a night as this? Wind blowing great guns from the northwest—snow falling fast from the heavens and rising just as fast before the wind from the ground—cold as Lapland, dark as Erebus! No telling the earth from the sky. Whew!" and to comfort the cold thought, Old Hurricane poured out another glass of smoking punch and began to sip it.

"How I thank the Lord that I am not a doctor! If I were a doctor, now, the sound of that bell at this hour of night would frighten me; I should think some old woman had been taken with the pleurisy, and wanted me to get up and go out in the storm; to turn out of my warm bed to ride ten miles through the snow to prescribe for her. A doctor never can feel sure, even in the worst of weathers, of a good night's rest. But, thank Heaven, I am free from all such annoyances, and if I am sure of anything in this world it is of my comfortable night's sleep," said Old Hurricane, as he sipped his punch, smacked his lips and toasted his feet.

At this moment Wool reappeared.

"Shut the door, you villain! Do you intend to stand there holding it open on me all night?" vociferated the old man.

Wool hastily closed the offending portals and hurried to his master's side.

"Well, sir, who was it rung the bell?"

"Please, marster, sir, it wer' de Reverend Mr. Parson Goodwin."

"Goodwin? Been to make a sick-call, I suppose, and got caught in the snow-storm. I declare it is as bad to be a parson as it is to be a doctor. Thank the Lord I am not a parson, either; if I were, now, I might be called away from my cozy arm-chair and fireside to ride twelve miles to comfort some old man dying of quinsy. Well, here—help me into bed, pile on more comforters, tuck me up warm, put a bottle of hot water at my feet, and then go and attend to the parson," said the old man, getting up and moving toward his inviting couch.

"Sar! sar! stop, sar, if you please!" cried Wool, going after him.

"Why, what does the old fool mean?" exclaimed Old Hurricane, angrily.

"Sar, de Reverend Mr. Parson Goodwin say how he must see you yourself, personable, alone!"

"See me, you villain! Didn't you tell him that I had retired?"

"Yes, marse; I tell him how you wer' gone to bed and asleep more'n an hour ago, and he ordered me to come wake you up, and say how it were a matter o' life and death!"

"Life and death? What have I to do with life and death? I won't stir! If the parson wants to see me he will have to come up here and see me in bed," exclaimed Old Hurricane, suiting the action to the word by jumping into bed and drawing all the comforters and blankets up around his head and shoulders.

"Mus' I fetch him reverence up, sar?"

"Yes; I wouldn't get up and go down to see—Washington. Shut the door, you rascal, or I'll throw the bootjack at your wooden head."

Wool obeyed with alacrity and in time to escape the threatened missile.

After an absence of a few minutes he was heard returning, attending upon the footsteps of another. And the next minute he entered, ushering in the Rev. Mr. Goodwin, the parish minister of Bethlehem, St. Mary's.

"How do you do? How do you do? Glad to see you, sir; glad to see you, though obliged to receive you in bed. Fact is, I caught a cold with this severe change of weather, and took a warm negus and went to bed to sweat it off. You'll excuse me. Wool, draw that easy-chair up to my bedside for worthy Mr. Goodwin, and bring him a glass of warm negus. It will do him good after his cold ride."

"I thank you, Major Warfield. I will take the seat but not the negus, if you please, to-night."

"Not the negus? Oh, come now, you are joking. Why, it will keep you from catching cold and be a most comfortable nightcap, disposing you to sleep and sweat like a baby. Of course, you spend the night with us?"

"I thank you, no. I must take the road again in a few minutes."

"Take the road again to-night! Why, man alive! it is midnight, and the snow driving like all Lapland!"

"Sir, I am sorry to refuse your proffered hospitality and leave your comfortable roof to-night, and sorrier still to have to take you with me," said the pastor, gravely.

"Take me with you! No, no, my good sir!—no, no, that is too good a joke—ha! ha!"

"Sir, I fear that you will find it a very serious one. Your servant told you that my errand was one of imminent urgency?"

"Yes; something like life and death— —"

"Exactly; down in the cabin near the Punch Bowl there is an old woman dying— —"

"There! I knew it! I was just saying there might be an old woman dying! But, my dear sir, what's that to me? What can I do?"

"Humanity, sir, would prompt you."

"But, my dear sir, how can I help her? I am not a physician to prescribe— —"

"She is far past a physician's help."

"Nor am I a priest to hear her confession— —"

"Her confession God has already received."

"Well, and I'm not a lawyer to draw up her will."

"No, sir; but you are recently appointed one of the justices of the peace for Alleghany."

"Yes. Well, what of that? That does not comprise the duty of getting up out of my warm bed and going through a snow-storm to see an old woman expire."

"I regret to inconvenience you, sir; but in this instance your duty demands your attendance at the bedside of this dying woman— —"

"I tell you I can't go, and I won't! Anything in reason I'll do. Anything I can send she shall have. Here, Wool, look in my breeches pocket and take out my purse and hand it. And then go and wake up Mrs. Condiment, and ask her to fill a large basket full of everything a poor old dying woman might want, and you shall carry it."

"Spare your pains, sir. The poor woman is already past all earthly, selfish wants. She only asks your presence at her dying bed."

"But I can't go! I! The idea of turning out of my warm bed and exposing myself to a snow-storm this time of night!"

"Excuse me for insisting, sir; but this is an official duty," said the parson mildly but firmly.

"I'll—I'll throw up my commission to-morrow," growled the old man.

"To-morrow you may do that; but meanwhile, to-night, being still in the commission of the peace, you are bound to get up and go with me to this woman's bedside."

"And what the demon is wanted of me there?"

"To receive her dying deposition."

"To receive a dying deposition! Good Heaven! was she murdered, then?" exclaimed the old man in alarm, as he started out of bed and began to draw on his nether garments.

"Be composed; she was not murdered," said the pastor.

"Well, then, what is it? Dying deposition! It must concern a crime," exclaimed the old man, hastily drawing on his coat.

"It does concern a crime."

"What crime, for the love of Heaven?"

"I am not at liberty to tell you. She will do that."

"Wool, go down and rouse up Jehu, and tell him to put Parson Goodwin's mule in the stable for the night. And tell him to put the black draught horses to the close carriage, and light both of the front lanterns—for we shall have a dark, stormy road——Shut the door, you infernal——I beg your pardon, parson, but that villain always leaves the door ajar after him."

The good pastor bowed gravely, and the major completed his toilet by the time the servant returned and reported the carriage ready.

It was dark as pitch when they emerged from the hall door out into the front portico, before which nothing could be seen but two red bull's-eyes of the carriage lanterns, and nothing heard but the dissatisfied whinnying and pawing of the horses.

CHAPTER II.

THE MASKS.

"What are these,
So withered and so wild in their attire
That look not like th' inhabitants of earth
And yet are on't?"

—MACBETH.

"To the Devil's Punch Bowl," was the order given by Old Hurricane as he followed the minister into the carriage. "And now, sir," he continued, addressing his companion, "I think you had better repeat that part of the church litany that prays to be delivered from 'battle, murder and sudden death,' for if we should be so lucky as to escape Black Donald and his gang, we shall have at least an equal chance of being upset in the darkness of these dreadful mountains."

"A pair of saddle mules would have been a safer conveyance, certainly," said the minister.

Old Hurricane knew that, but, though a great sensualist, he was a brave man, and so he had rather risk his life in a close carriage than suffer cold upon a sure-footed mule's back.

Only by previous knowledge of the route could any one have told the way the carriage went. Old Hurricane and the minister both knew that they drove, lumbering, over the rough road leading by serpentine windings down that rugged fall of ground to the river's bank, and that then, turning to the left by a short bend, they passed in behind that range of horseshoe rocks that sheltered Hurricane Hall—thus, as it were doubling their own road. Beneath that range of rocks, and between it and another range, there was an awful abyss or chasm of cleft, torn and jagged rocks opening, as it were, from the bowels of the earth, in the shape of a mammoth bowl, in the bottom of which, almost invisible from its great depth, seethed and boiled a mass of dark water of what seemed to be a lost river or a subterranean spring. This terrific phenomenon was called the Devil's Punch Bowl.

Not far from the brink of this awful abyss, and close behind the horseshoe range of rocks, stood a humble log-cabin, occupied by an old free negress, who picked up a scanty living by telling fortunes and showing the way to the Punch Bowl. Her cabin went by the name of the Witch's Hut, or Old Hat's Cabin. A short distance from Hat's cabin the road became impassable, and the travelers got out, and, preceded by the coachman bearing the lantern, struggled along on foot through the drifted snow and against the buffeting wind and sleet to where a faint light guided them to the house.

The pastor knocked. The door was immediately opened by a negro, whose sex from the strange anomalous costume it was difficult to guess. The tall form was rigged out first in a long, red, cloth petticoat, above which was buttoned a blue cloth surtout. A man's old black beaver hat sat upon the strange head and completed this odd attire.

"Well, Hat, how is your patient?" inquired the pastor, as he entered preceding the magistrate.

"You will see, sir," replied the old woman.

The two visitors looked around the dimly-lighted, miserable room, in one corner of which stood a low bed, upon which lay extended the form of an old, feeble and gray-haired woman.

"How are you, my poor soul, and what can I do for you now I am here?" inquired Old Hurricane, who in the actual presence of suffering was not utterly without pity.

"You are a magistrate?" inquired the dying woman.

"Yes, my poor soul."

"And qualified to administer an oath and take your deposition," said the minister.

"Will it be legal—will it be evidence in a court of law?" asked the woman, lifting her dim eyes to the major.

"Certainly, my poor soul—certainly," said the latter, who, by the way, would have said anything to soothe her.

"Send every one but yourself from the room."

"What, my good soul, send the parson out in the storm? That will never do! Won't it be just as well to let him go up in the corner yonder?"

"No! You will repent it unless this communication is strictly private."

"But, my good soul, if it is to be used in a court of law?"

"That will be according to your own discretion!"

"My dear parson," said Old Hurricane, going to the minister, "would you be so good as to retire?"

"There is a fire in the woodshed, master," said Hat, leading the way.

"Now, my good soul, now! You want first to be put upon your oath?"

"Yes, sir."

The old man drew from his great-coat pocket a miniature copy of the Scriptures, and with the usual formalities administered the oath.

"Now, then, my good soul, begin—'the truth, the whole truth, and nothing but the truth,' you know. But first, your name?"

"Is it possible you don't know me, master?"

"Not I, in faith."

"For the love of heaven, look at me, and try to recollect me, sir! It is necessary some one in authority should be able to know me," said the woman, raising her haggard eyes to the face of her visitor.

The old man adjusted his spectacles and gave her a scrutinizing look, exclaiming at intervals:

"Lord bless my soul, it is! it ain't! it must! it can't be! Granny Grewell, the—the—the—midwife that disappeared from here some twelve or thirteen years ago!"

"Yes, master, I am Nancy Grewell, the ladies' nurse, who vanished from sight so mysteriously some thirteen years ago," replied the woman.

"Heaven help our hearts! And for what crime was it you ran away? Come—make a clean breast of it, woman! You have nothing to fear in doing so, for you are past the arm of earthly law now!"

"I know it, master."

"And the best way to prepare to meet the Divine Judge is to make all the reparation that you can by a full confession!"

"I know it, sir—if I had committed a crime; but I have committed no crime; neither did I run away."

"What? what? what? What was it, then? Remember, witness, you are on your oath."

"I know that, sir, and I will tell the truth; but it must be in my own way."

At this moment a violent blast of wind and hail roared down the mountain side and rattled against the walls, shaking the witch's hut, as if it would have shaken it about their ears.

It was a proper overture to the tale that was about to be told. Conversation was impossible until the storm raved past and was heard dying in deep, reverberating echoes from the depths of the Devil's Punch Bowl.

"It is some thirteen years ago," began Granny Grewell, "upon just such a night of storm as this, that I was mounted on my old mule Molly, with my saddlebags full of dried yarbs and 'stilled waters and sich, as I allus carried when I was out 'tendin' on the sick. I was on my way a-going to see a lady as I was sent for to 'tend.

"Well, master, I'm not 'shamed to say, as I never was afraid of man, beast, nor sperrit, and never stopped at going out all hours of the night, through the most lonesome roads, if so be I was called upon to do so. Still I must say that jest as me and Molly, my mule, got into that deep, thick, lonesome woods as stands round the old Hidden House in the hollow I did feel queerish; 'case it was the dead hour of the night, and it was said how strange things were seen and hearn, yes, and done, too, in that dark, deep, lonesome place! I seen how even my mule Molly felt queer, too, by the way she stuck up her ears, stiff as quills. So, partly to keep up my own spirits, and partly to 'courage her, says I, 'Molly,' says I, 'what are ye afeared on? Be a man, Molly!' But Molly stepped out cautious and pricked up her long ears all the same.

"Well, master, it was so dark I couldn't see a yard past Molly's ears, and the path was so narrow and the bushes so thick we could hardly get along; and just as we came to the little creek, as they calls the Spout, 'cause the water jumps and jets along it till it empties into the Punch Bowl, and just as Molly was cautiously putting her fore foot into the water, out starts two men from the bushes and seized poor Molly's bridle!"

"Good Heaven!" exclaimed Major Warfield.

"Well, master, before I could cry out, one of them willains seized me by the scruff of my neck, and, with his other hand upon my mouth, he says:

"'Be silent, you old fool, or I'll blow your brains out!'

"And then, master, I saw for the first time that their faces were covered over with black crape. I couldn't a-screamed if they'd let me! for my breath was gone and my senses were going along with it from the fear that was on me.

"'Don't struggle; come along quietly, and you shall not be hurt,' says the man as had spoke before.

"Struggle! I couldn't a-struggled to a-saved my soul! I couldn't speak! I couldn't breathe! I liked to have a-dropped right offen Molly's back. One on 'em says, says he:

"'Give her some brandy!' And t'other takes out a flask and puts it to my lips and says, says he:

"'Here, drink this.'

"Well, master, as he had me still by the scruff o' my neck I couldn't do no other ways but open my mouth and drink it. And as soon as I took a swallow my breath came back and my speech.

"'And oh, gentlemen,' says I, 'ef it's "your money or your life" you mean, I hain't it about me! 'Deed, 'clare to the Lord-a-mighty, I hain't! It's wrapped up in an old cotton glove in a hole in the plastering in the chimney corner at home, and ef you'll spare my life you can go there and get it,' says I.

"'You old blockhead!' says they, 'we want neither one nor t'other! Come along quietly and you shall receive no harm. But at the first cry, or attempt to escape—this shall stop you!" And with that the willain held the mizzle of a pistil so nigh to my nose that I smelt brimstone, while t'other one bound a silk hankercher round my eyes, and then took poor Molly's bridle and led her along. I couldn't see, in course, and I dassint breathe for fear o' the pistil. But I said my prayers to myself all the time.

"Well, master, they led the mule on down the path until we comed to a place wide enough to turn, when they turned us round and led us back outen the wood, and then 'round and round, and up and down, and crossways and lengthways, as ef they didn't want me to find where they were taking me.

"Well, sir, when they'd walked about in this 'fused way, leadin' of the mule about a mile, I knew we was in the woods again—the very same woods and the very same path—I, knowed by the feel of the place and the sound of the bushes as we hit up against them each side, and also by the rumbling of the Spout as it rumbled along toward the Punch Bowl. We went down and down and down, and lower and lower and lower until we got right down in the bottom of that hollow.

"Then we stopped. A gate was opened. I put up my hand to raise the hankerchief and see where I was; but just at that minute I felt the mizzle o' the pistol like a ring of ice right agin my temple, and the willain growling into my ear:

"'If you do——!'

"But I didn't—I dropped my hand down as if I had been shot, and afore I had seen anything, either. So we went through the gate and up a gravelly walk—I knew it by the crackling of the gravel under Molly's feet—and stopped at a horseblock, where one o' them willains lifted me off. I put up my hand agin.

"'Do if you dare!' says t'other one, with the mizzle o' the pistol at my head.

"I dropped my hand like lead. So they led me on a little way, and then up some steps. I counted them to myself as I went along. They were six. You see, master, I took all this pains to know the house agin. Then they opened a door that opened in the middle. Then they went along a passage and up more stairs—there was ten and a turn, and then ten more. Then along another passage, and up another flight of stairs just like the first. Then along another passage and up a third flight of stairs. They was alike.

"Well, sir, here we was at the top o' the house. One o' them willains opened a door on the left side, and t'other said:

"'There—go in and do your duty!' and pushed me through the door and shut and locked it on me. Good gracious, sir, how scared I was! I slipped off the silk handkercher, and, 'feared as I was, I didn't forget to put it in my bosom.

"Then I looked about me. Right afore me on the hearth was a little weeny taper burning, that showed I was in a great big garret with sloping walls. At one end two deep dormer windows and a black walnut bureau standing between them. At t'other end a great tester bedstead with dark curtains. There was a dark carpet on the floor. And with all there were so many dark objects and so many shadows, and the little taper burned so dimly that I could hardly tell t'other from which, or keep from breaking my nose against things as I groped about.

"And what was I in this room for to do? I couldn't even form an idee. But presently my blood ran cold to hear a groan from behind the curtains! then another! and another! then a cry as of some child in mortal agony, saying:

"'For the love of Heaven, save me!'

"I ran to the bed and dropped the curtains and liked to have fainted at what I saw!"

"And what did you see?" asked the magistrate.

"Master, behind those dark curtains I saw a young creature tossing about on the bed, flinging her hair and beautiful arms about and tearing wildly at the fine lace that trimmed her night-dress. But, master, that wasn't what almost made me faint—it was that her right hand was sewed up in black crape, and her whole face and head completely covered with black crape drawn down and fastened securely around her throat, leaving only a small slit at the lips and nose to breathe through!"

"What! Take care, woman! Remember that you are upon your oath!" said the magistrate.

"I know it, master. And as I hope to be forgiven, I am telling you the truth!"

"Go on, then."

"Well, sir, she was a young creature, scarcely past childhood, if one might judge by her small size and soft, rosy skin. I asked her to let me take that black crape from her face and head, but she threw up her hands and exclaimed:

"'Oh, no; no, no! for my life, no!'

"Well, master, I hardly know how to tell you what followed," said the old woman, hesitating in embarrassment.

"Go right straight on like a car of Juggernaut, woman! Remember—the whole truth!"

"Well, master, in the next two hours there were twins born in that room—a boy and a girl; the boy was dead, the girl living. And all the time I heard the measured tramping of one of them willains up and down the passage outside of that room. Presently the steps stopped, and there was a rap at the door. I went and listened, but did not open it.

"'Is it all over?' the voice asked.

"Before I could answer a cry from the bed caused me to look round. There was the poor, masked mother stretching out her white arms toward me in the most imploring way. I hastened back to her.

"'Tell him—no—no,' she said.

"'Have you got through?' asked the man at the door, rapping impatiently.

"'No, no,' said I, as directed.

"He resumed his tramping up and down, and I went back to my patient. She beckoned me to come close, and whispered:

"'Save my child! The living one, I mean! Hide her! oh, hide her from him! When he demands the babe, give him the poor little dead one—he cannot hurt that! And he will not know there was another. Oh! hide and save my child!'

"Master, I was used to queer doings, but this was a little the queerest. But if I was to conceal that second child in order to save it, it was necessary to stop its mouth, for it was squalling like a wild cat. So I took a vial of paregoric from my pocket and give it a drop and it went off to sleep like an angel. I wrapped it up warm and lay it along with my shawl and bonnet in a dark corner. Just then the man rapped again.

"'Come in, master,' said I.

"'No, bring me the babe,' he said.

"I took up the dead infant. Its mother kissed its brow and dropped tears upon its little cold face. And I carried it to the man outside.

"'Is it asleep?' the willain asked me.

"'Yes, master,' said I as I put it, well wrapped up, in his arms; 'very sound aslep.'

"'So much the better,' said the knave, walking away.

"I bolted the door and went back to my patient. With her free hand she seized mine and pressed it to her lips and then, holding up her left hand, pointed to the wedding ring upon her third finger.

"'Draw it off and keep it,' she said; 'conceal the child under your shawl and take her with you when you go! Save her and your fortune shall be made.'

"I declare, master, I hadn't time to think, before I heard one of them wretches rap at the door.

"'Come! Get ready to go,' he said.

"She also beckoned me. I hastened to her. With eager whispers and imploring gestures she prayed me to take her ring and save her child.

"'But you,' said I, 'who is to attend to you?'

"'I do not know or care! Save her!'

"The rapping continued. I ran to the corner where I had left my things. I put on my bonnet, made a sort of sling around my neck of the silk handkercher, opened the large part of it like a hammock and laid the little sleeping babe there. Then I folded my big shawl around my breast and nobody any the wiser. The rapping was very impatient.

"'I am coming,' said I.

"'Remember!' whispered the poor girl.

"'I will,' said I, and went out and opened the door. There stood t'other willain with his head covered with black crape. I dreamt of nothing but black-headed demons for six months afterward.

"'Are you ready?' says he.

"'Yes, your worship,' says I.

"'Come along, then.'

"And, binding another silk hankercher round my eyes, he led me along.

"Instead of my mule, a carriage stood near the horse-block.

"'Get in,' says he, holding the pistil to my ears by way of an argument.

"I got in. He jumped up upon the driver's seat and we drove like the wind. In another direction from that in which we come, in course, for there was no carriage road there. The carriage whirled along at such a rate it made me quite giddy. At last it stopped again. The man in the mask got down and opened the door.

"'Where are you taking me?' says I.

"'Be quiet,' says he, 'or'——And with that he put the pistil to my cheek, ordered me to get out, take the bandage from my eyes and walk before him. I did so and saw dimly that we were in a part of the country that I was never at before. We were in a dark road through a thick forest. On the left side of the road in a clearing stood an old house; a dim light was burning in a lower window.

"'Go on in there,' said the willain, putting the pistil to the back of my head. As the door stood ajar I went in, to a narrow, dark passage, the man all the time at my back. He opened a door on the left side and made me go into a dark room. Just then the unfortunate child that had been moving restlessly began to wail. Well it might, poor, starved thing!

"'What's that?' says the miscreant under his breath and stopping short.

"'It ain't nothing, sir,' says I, and 'Hush-h-h' to the baby. But the poor little wretch raised a squall.

"'What is the meaning of this? 'says he. 'Where did that child come from? Why the demon don't you speak?' And with that he seized me again by the scruff of the neck and shook me.

"'Oh, master, for the love of Heaven don't!' says I. 'This is only a poor unfortnet infant as its parents wanted to get outen the way, and hired me to take care on. And I have had it wrapped up under my shawl all the time 'cept when I was in your house, when I put it to sleep in the corner.'

"'Humph—and you had that child concealed under your shawl when I first stopped you in the woods?'

"'In course, master,' says I.

"'Whose is it?'

"'Master,' says I, 'it's—it's a dead secret!' for I hadn't another lie ready.

"He broke out into a rude, scornful laugh, and seemed not half to believe me and yet not to care about questioning me too closely. He made me sit down then in the dark, and went out and turned the key on me. I wet my finger with the paregoric and put it to the baby's lips to quiet its pains of hunger. Then I heard a whispering in the next room. Now my eyesight never was good, but to make up for it I believe I had the sharpest ears that ever was, and I don't think anybody could have heard that whispering but me. I saw a little glimmer of light through the chinks that showed me where the door was, and so I creeped up to it and put my ear to the key-hole. Still they whispered so low that no ears could o' heard them but my sharp ones. The first words I heard good was a grumbling voice asking:

"'How old?'

"'Fifty—more or less, but strong, active, a good nurse and a very light mulatto,' says my willain's voice.

"'Hum—too old,' says the other.

"'But I will throw the child in.'

"A low, crackling laugh the only answer.

"'You mean that would be only a bother. Well, I want to get rid of the pair of them,' said my willain, 'so name the price you are willing to give.'

"'Cap'n, you and me have had too many transactions together to make any flummery about this. You want to get shet o' them pair. I hain't no objections to turning an honest penny. So jest make out the papers—bill o' sale o' the 'oman Kate, or whatsoever her name may be, and the child, with any price you please, so it is only a make-believe price, and I'll engage to take her away and make the most I can of them in the South—that won't be much, seeing it's only an old 'oman and child—scarcely a fair profit on the expense o' takin' of her out. Now, as money's no object to you, Cap'n— —'

"'Very well; have your own way; only don't let that woman escape and return, for if you do— —'

"'I understand, Cap'n; but I reckon you needn't threaten, for if you could blow me—why, I would return you the same favor,' said the other, raising his voice and laughing aloud.

"'Be quiet, fool, or come away farther—here.' And the two willains moved out of even my hearing.

"' I should o' been uneasy, master, if it hadn't been the 'oman they were talking about was named Kate, and that wasn't my name, which were well beknown to be Nancy.'

"Presently I heard the carriage drive away. And almost 'mediately after the door was unlocked, and a great, big, black-bearded and black-headed beast of a ruffian came in, and says he:

"'Well, my woman, have you had any supper?'

"'No,' said I, 'I hain't; and ef I'm to stay here any length of time I'd be obleeged to you to let me have some hot water and milk to make pap for this perishing baby.'

"'Follow me,' says he.

"And he took me into the kitchen at the back of the house, where there was a fire in the fireplace and a cupboard with all that I needed. Well, sir, not to tire you, I made a nursing-bottle for the baby and fed it. And then I got something for my own supper, or, rather, breakfast, for it was now near the dawn of day. Well, sir, I thought I would try to get out and look about myself to see what the neighborhood looked like by daylight, but when I tried the door I found myself locked up a close prisoner. I looked out of the window and saw nothing but a little back yard, closed in by the woods. I tried to raise the sash, but it was nailed down. The black-headed monster came in just about that minute, and seeing what I was a-doing of, says he:

"'Stop that!'

"'What am I stopped here for?' says I; 'a free 'oman,' says I, a-'vented of going about her own business?' says I.

"But he only laughed a loud, crackling, scornful laugh, and went out, turning the key after him.

"A little after sunrise an old, dried-up, spiteful looking hag of a woman came in and began to get breakfast.

"'What am I kept here for?' says I to her.

"But she took no notice at all; nor could I get so much as a single word outen her. In fact, master, the little 'oman was deaf an' dumb.

"Well, sir, to be short, I was kept in that place all day long, and when night come I was druv into a shay at the point of the pistil, and rattled along as fast as the horses could gallop over a road as I knew nothing of. We changed horses wunst or twict, and just about the dawn of day we come to a broad river with a vessel laying to, not far from the shore.

"As soon as the shay druv down on the sands, the willain as had run away with me puts a pipe to his willainous mouth and blows like mad. Somebody else blowed back from the wessel. Then a boat was put off and rowed ashore. I was forced to get into it, and was follered by the willain. We was rowed to the wessel, and I was druv up the ladder on to the decks. And there, master, right afore my own looking eyes, me and the baby was traded off to the captain! It was no use for me to 'splain or 'spostulate. I wasn't b'lieved. The willain as had stole me got back into the boat and went ashore, and I saw him get into the shay and drive away. It was no use for me to howl and cry, though I did both, for I couldn't even hear myself for the swearing of the captain and the noise of the crew, as they was a gettin' of the wessel under way. Well, sir, we sailed down that river and out to sea.

"Now, sir, come a strange providence, which the very thoughts of it might convert a heathen! We had been to sea about five days when a dreadful storm riz. Oh, marster! the inky blackness of the sky, the roaring of the wind, the raging of the sea, the leaping of the waves and the rocking of that wessel—and every once in a while sea and ship all ablaze with the blinding lightning—was a thing to see, not to hear tell of! I tell you, marster, that looked like the wrath of God! And then the cursing and swearing and bawling of the captain and the crew, as they were a-takin' in of sail, was enough to raise one's hair on their head! I hugged the baby to my breast, and went to praying as hard as ever I could pray.

"Presently I felt an awful shock, as if heaven an' earth had come together, and then everybody screaming, 'She's struck! She's struck!' I felt the wessel trembling like a live creetur, and the water a-pouring in everywhere. I hugged the babe and scrambled up the companionway to the deck. It was pitch dark, and I heard every man rushing toward one side of the wessel.

"A flash of lightning that made everything as bright as day again showed me that they were all taking to the boat. I rushed after, calling to them to save me and the baby. But no one seemed to hear me; they were all too busy trying to save themselves and keep others out of the boat, and cursing and swearing and hollering that there was no more room, that the boat would be swamped, and so on. The end was, that all who could crowd into the boat did so. And me and the baby and a poor sailor lad and the black cook were left behind to perish.

"But, marster, as it turned out, we as was left to die were the only ones saved. We watched after that boat with longing eyes, though we could only see it when the lightning flashed. And every time we saw it it was farther off. At last, marster, a flash of lightning showed us the boat as far off as ever we could see her, capsized and beaten hither and thither by the wild waves—its crew had perished.

"Marster, as soon as the sea had swallowed up that wicked captain and crew the wind died away, the waves fell and the storm lulled—just as if it had done what it was sent to do and was satisfied. The wreck—where we poor forlorn ones stood—the wreck that had shivered and trembled with every wave that struck it,—until we had feared it would break up every minute, became still and firm on its sand-bar, as a house on dry land.

"Daylight came at last. And a little after sunrise we saw a sail bearing down upon us. We could not signal the sail, but by the mercy of Providence, she saw us and lay to, and sent off a boat and picked us up and took us on board—me and the baby and the cook and the sailor lad.

"It was a foreign wessel, and we could not understand a word they said, nor they us. All we could do was by signs. But they were very good to us—dried our clothes and gave us breakfast and made us lie down and rest, and then put about and continued their course. The sailor lad—Herbert Greyson—soon found out and told me they were bound for New York. And, in fact, marster, in about ten days we made that port.

"When the ship anchored below the Battery, the officers and passengers made me up a little bundle of clothes and a little purse of money and put me ashore, and there I was in a strange city, so bewildered I didn't know which way to turn. While I was a-standing there, in danger of being run over by the omnibuses, the sailor boy came to my side and told me that he and the cook was gwine to engage on board of another 'Merican wessel, and axed me what I was gwine to do. I told him how I didn't know nothing at all 'bout sea sarvice, and so I didn't know what I should do. Then he said he'd show me where I could go and stay all night, and so he took me into a little by-street, to a poor-looking house, where the people took lodgers, and there he left me to go aboard the ship. As he went away he advised me to take care of my money and try to get a servant's place.

"Well, marster, I ain't a gwine to bother you with telling you of how I toiled and struggled along in that great city—first living out as a servant, and afterward renting a room and taking in washing and ironing—ay! how I toiled and struggled—for—ten—long—years, hoping for the time to come when I should be able to return to this neighborhood, where I was known, and expose the evil deeds of them willains. And for this cause I lived on, toiling and struggling and laying up money penny by penny. Sometimes I was fool enough to tell my story in the hopes of getting pity and help—but telling my story always made it worse for me! some thought me crazy and others thought me deceitful, which is not to be wondered at, for I was a stranger and my adventures were, indeed, beyond belief.

"No one ever helped me but the lad Herbert Greyson. W'enver he came from sea he sought me out and made a little present to me or Cap.

"Cap, marster, was Capitola, the child. The reason I gave her that name was because on that ring I had drawn from the masked mother's hand were the two names—Eugene—Capitola.

"Well, marster, the last time Herbert Greyson came home he gave me five dollars, and that, with what I had saved, was enough to pay my passage to Norfolk.

"I left my little Cap in the care of the people of the house—she was big enough to pay for her keep in work—and I took passage for Norfolk. When I got there I fell ill, spent all my money, and was at last taken to the poor-house. Six months passed away before I was discharged, and then six months more before I had earned and saved money enough to pay my way on here.

"I reached here three days ago and found a wheat field growing where my cottage fire used to burn, and all my old cronies dead, all except Old Hat, who has received and given me shelter. Sir, my story is done—make what you can of it," said the invalid, sinking down in her bed as if utterly exhausted.

Old Hurricane, whose countenance had expressed emotions as powerful as they were various while listening to this tale, now arose, stepped cautiously to the door, drew the bolt, and, coming back, bent his head and asked:

"What more of the child?"

"Cap, sir? I have not heard a word of Cap since I left her to try to find out her friends. But any one interested in her might inquire for her at Mrs. Simmons', laundress, No. 8 Rag Alley."

"You say the names upon that ring were Eugene—Capitola?"

"Yes, sir, they were."

"Have you that ring about you?"

"No, marster. I thought it was best in case of accidents to leave it with the child."

"Have you told her any part of this strange history?"

"No, marster, nor hinted at it; she was too young for such a confidence."

"You were right. Had she any mark about her person by which she could be identified?"

"Yes, marster, a very strange one. In the middle of her left palm was the perfect image of a crimson hand, about half an inch in length. There was also another. Henry Greyson, to please me, marked upon her forearm, in India ink, her name and birthday—'Capitola, Oct. 31st, 1832.'"

"Right! Now tell me, my good soul, do you know, from what you were able to observe, what house that was where Capitola was born?"

"I am on my oath! No, sir; I do not know, but——"

"You suspect?"

The woman nodded.

"It was——" said old Hurricane, stooping and whispering a name that was heard by no one but the sick woman.

She nodded again, with a look of intense meaning.

"Does your old hostess here, Hat, know or suspect anything of this story?" inquired Major Warfield.

"Not a word! No soul but yourself has heard it!"

"That is right! Still be discreet! If you would have the wicked punished and the innocent protected, be silent and wary. Have no anxiety about the girl. What man can do for her will I do and quickly! And now, good creature, day is actually dawning. You must seek repose. And I must call the parson in and return home. I will send Mrs. Condiment over with food, wine, medicine, clothing and every comfort that your condition requires," said Old Hurricane, rising and calling in the clergyman, with whom he soon after left the hut for home.

They reached Hurricane Hall in time for an early breakfast, which the astonished housekeeper had prepared, and for which their night's adventures had certainly given them a good appetite.

Major Warfield kept his word, and as soon as breakfast was over he dispatched Mrs. Condiment with a carriage filled with provisions for the sick woman. But they were not needed. In a couple of hours the housekeeper returned with the intelligence that the old nurse was dead. The false strength of mental excitement that had enabled her to tell so long and dreadful a tale had been the last flaring up of the flame of life that almost immediately went out.

"I am not sorry, upon the whole, for now I shall have the game in my own hands!" muttered Old Hurricane to himself. "Ah! Gabrielle Le Noir, better you had cast yourself down from the highest rock of this range and been dashed to pieces below, than have thus fallen into my power!"

CHAPTER III.

THE QUEST.

Then did Sir Knight abandon dwelling
And out he rode.

—Hudibras.

Pursuant to the orders of Major Warfield, the corpse of the old midwife was the next day after her decease brought over and quietly interred in the family graveyard of Hurricane Hall.

And then Major Warfield astonished his household by giving orders to his housekeeper and his body-servant to prepare his wardrobe and pack his trunks for a long journey to the north.

"What can the major be thinking of, to be setting out for the north at this time of the year?" exclaimed good little Mrs. Condiment, as she picked over her employer's shirts, selecting the newest and warmest to be done up for the occasion.

"Lord A'mighty o'ny knows; but 'pears to me marster's never been right in his headpiece since Hollow-eve night, when he took that ride to the Witch's Hut," replied Wool, who, with brush and sponge, was engaged in rejuvenating his master's outer garments.

But, let his family wonder as they would, Old Hurricane kept his own counsel—only just as he was going away, lest mystery should lead to investigation, and that to discovery, the old man gave out that he was going north to invest capital in bank stock, and so, quite unattended, he departed.

His servant Wool, indeed, accompanied him as far as Tip-Top, the little hamlet on the mountain at which he was to meet the eastern stage; but there having seen his master comfortably deposited in the inside of the coach, and the luggage safely stowed in the boot, Wool was ordered to return with the carriage. And Major Warfield proceeded on his journey alone. This also caused much speculation in the family.

"Who's gwine to make his punch and warm his bed and put his slippers on the hearth and hang his gown to de fire?—that what I want to know!" cried the grieved and indignant Wool.

"Oh, the waiters at the taverns where he stops can do that for him," said Mrs. Condiment.

"No, they can't, nuther; they don't know his ways! they don't know nuffin' 'bout him! I 'clare, I think our ole marse done gone clean crazy! I shouldn't be s'prised he'd gone off to de norf to get married, and was to bring home a young wife to we dem!"

"Tut! tut! tut! such talk! That will never do!" exclaimed the deeply shocked Mrs. Condiment.

"Werry well! All I say is, 'Dem as libs longest will see most!'" said Wool, shaking his white head. After which undeniable apothegm the conversation came to a stand.

Meanwhile, Old Hurricane pursued his journey—a lumbering, old-fashioned stage-coach ride—across the mountains, creeping at a snail's crawl up one side of the precipice and clattering thunderously down the other at a headlong speed that pitched the back-seat passengers into the bosoms of the front ones and threatened even to cast the coach over the heads of the horses. Three days and nights of such rugged riding brought the traveler to Washington City, where he rested one night and then took the cars for New York. He rested another night in Philadelphia, resumed his journey by the first train in the morning and reached New York about noon.

The crowd, the noise, the hurry and confusion at the wharf almost drove this irascible old gentleman mad.

"No, confound you!"

"I'll see your neck stretched first, you villain!"

"Out of my way, or I'll break your head, sirrah!" were some of his responses to the solicitous attentions of cabmen and porters. At length, taking up his heavy carpet-bag in both hands, Old Hurricane began to lay about him, with such effect that he speedily cleared a passage for himself through the crowd. Then addressing a cabman who had not offended by speaking first, he said:

"Here, sir! Here are my checks! Go get my luggage and take it to the Astor House. Hand the clerk this card, and tell him I want a good room, well warmed. I shall take a walk around the city before going. And, hark ye! If one of my trunks is missing I'll have you hanged, you rogue!"

"Breach of trust isn't a hanging matter in New York, your honor," laughed the cabman, as he touched his hat and hurried off toward the crowd collected around the baggage car.

Old Hurricane made a step or two as if he would have pursued and punished the flippancy of the man, but finally thought better of it, picked up his portmanteau and walked up the street slowly, with frequent pauses and bewildered looks, as though he had forgotten his directions or lost his way, and yet hesitated to inquire of any one for the obscure little alley in which he had been told to look for his treasure.

CHAPTER IV.

CAPITOLA.

Her sex a page's dress belied,
Obscured her charms but could not hide.

—Scott.

"Please, sir, do you want your carpet-bag carried?" asked a voice near.

Old Hurricane looked around him with a puzzled air, for he thought that a young girl had made this offer, so soft and clear were the notes of the voice that spoke.

"It was I, sir! Here I am, at yours and everybody's service, sir!" said the same voice.

And turning, Old Hurricane saw sitting astride a pile of boxes at the corner store, a very ragged lad some thirteen years of age.

"Good gracious!" thought Old Hurricane, as he gazed upon the boy, "this must be crown prince and heir apparent to the 'king of shreds and patches!'"

"Well, old gent! you'll know me next time, that's certain," said the lad, returning the look with interest.

It is probable Old Hurricane did not hear this irreverent speech, for he continued to gaze with pity and dismay upon the ragamuffin before him. He was a handsome boy, too, notwithstanding the deplorable state of his wardrobe. Thick, clustering curls of jet-black hair fell in tangled disorder around a forehead broad, white and smooth as that of a girl; slender and quaintly arched black eyebrows played above a pair of mischievous, dark-gray eyes that sparkled beneath the shade of long, thick, black lashes; a little turned-up nose, and red, pouting lips completed the character of a countenance full of fun, frolic, spirit and courage.

"Well, governor, if you've looked long enough, maybe you'll take me into service," said the lad, winking to a group of his fellow-newsboys that had gathered at the corner.

"Dear! dear! dear! he looks as if he had never in his life seen soap and water or a suit of whole clothes!" ejaculated the old gentleman, adding, kindly: "Yes, I reckon I will give you the job, my son!"

"His son! Oh, crikey! do you hear that, fellows? His son? Oh, Lor'! my governor's turned up at last. I'm his son! oh, gemini! But what did I tell you! I always had a sort of impression that I must have had a father in some former period of my life; and, behold, here he is! Who knows but I might have had a mother also? But that isn't likely. Still, I'll ask him. How's the old woman, sir?" said the newsboy, jumping off the boxes and taking the carpet-bag in his hand.

"What are you talking about, you infatuated tatterdemalion? Come along! If it weren't for pity I'd have you put in the pillory!" exclaimed Old Hurricane, shaking his cane at the offender.

"Thanky, sir! I've not had a pillow under my head for a long time."

"Silence, ragamuffin!"

"Just so, sir! 'a dumb devil is better than a talking one!'" answered the lad, demurely following his employer.

They went on some distance, Old Hurricane diligently reading the names of the streets at the corners. Presently he stopped again, bewildered, and after gazing around himself for a few minutes, said:

"Boy!"

"Yes, sir!"

"Do you know such a place as Rag Alley in Manillo Street?"

"Rag Alley, sir?"

"Yes; a sort of narrow, dark, musty place, with a row of old, tumble-down tenements each side, where poor wretches live all huddled up together, fifty in a house, eh? I was told I couldn't drive up it in a carriage, so I had to walk. Do you know such a place?"

"Do I know such a place! Do I know Rag Alley? Oh, my eye! Oh, he! he! he! he!"

"What are you laughing at now, you miscellaneous assortment of variegated pieces?"

"Oh! oh, dear! I was laughing to think how well I knew Rag Alley!"

"Humph! you do look as if you were born and bred there."

"But, sir, I wasn't!"

"Humph! How did you get into life, then?"

"I don't know, governor, unless I was raked up from the gutter by some old woman in the rag-picking line!" said the newsboy, demurely.

"Humph. I think that quite likely! But now, do you say that you know where that alley is?"

"Oh, don't set me off again! Oh, he! he! he! Yes, sir, I know."

"Well, then, show me the way and don't be a fool!"

"I'd scorn to be it, sir. This is the way!" said the lad, taking the lead.

They walked on several squares, and then the boy stopped, and pointing down a cross-street, said:

"There, governor; there you are."

"There! Where? Why that's a handsome street!" said Old Hurricane, gazing up in admiration at the opposite blocks of stately brown-stone mansions.

"That's it, hows'ever! That's Rag Alley. 'Tain't called Rag Alley now, though! It's called Hifalutin Terrace! Them tenements you talk of were pulled down more'n a year ago and these houses put up in their place," said the newsboy.

"Dear! dear! dear! what changes! And what became of the poor tenants?" asked Old Hurricane, gazing in dismay at the inroads of improvement.

"The tenants? poor wretches! how do I know? Carted away, blown away, thrown away, with the other rubbish. What became of the tenants?

"'Ask of the winds that far around
With fragments strewed the sea-ty!'

I heard that spouted at a school exhibition once, governor!" said the lad, demurely.

"Humph! well, well well! the trace is lost! What shall I do?—put advertisements in all the daily papers—apply at the chief police office? Yes, I'll do both," muttered Old Hurricane to himself; then, speaking out, he called:

"Boy!"

"Yes, sir?"

"Call me a cab!"

"Yes, sir!" And the lad was off like an arrow to do his bidding.

In a few moments the cab drove up. The newsboy, who was sitting beside the driver, jumped down and said:

"Here it is, sir!"

"Thank you, my son; here is your fee," said Old Hurricane, putting a silver dollar into the lad's hand.

"What! Lor', it can't be I but it is! He must have made a mistake! What if he did, I don't care! Yes, I do, too! 'Honor bright!'" exclaimed the newsboy, looking in wonder and desire and sore temptation upon the largest piece of money he had ever touched in his life. "Governor!"

"Well, boy?" said the old gentleman, with his feet upon the steps of the cab.

"You've been and done and gone and give me a whole dollar by mistake!"

"And why should you think it a mistake, you impertinent monkey?"

"Your honor didn't mean it?"

"Why not, you young rascal? Of course I did. Take it and be off with you!" said Old Hurricane, beginning to ascend the steps.

"I'm a great mind to," said the newsboy, still gazing on the coin with satisfaction and desire—"I'm a great mind to; but I won't! 'tain't fair! Governor, I say!"

"What now, you troublesome fellow?"

"Do stop a minute! Don't tempt me too hard, 'cause, you see, I ain't sure I could keep honest if I was tempted too hard."

"What do you mean now, you ridiculous little ape?"

"I mean I know you're from the country, and don't know no better, and I mus'n't impose upon your ignorance."

"My ignorance, you impudent villain!" exclaimed the old man, with rising wrath.

"Yes, governor; you hain't cut your eye-teeth yet! you hain't up to snuff! you don't know nothing! Why, this is too much for toting a carpet-bag a half a dozen squares; and it's very well you fell in with a honest lad like me, that wouldn't impose on your innocence. Bless you, the usual price isn't more'n a dime, or, if you're rich and generous, a shillin'; but——"

"What the deuce do I care for the usual price, you—you—you perfect prodigy of patches? There, for the Lord's sake, go get yourself a decent suit of clothes! Drive on, cabman!" roared Old Hurricane, flinging an eagle upon the sidewalk and rolling off in his cab.

"Poor dear, old gentleman! I wonder where his keeper is? How could he have got loose? Maybe I'd better go and tell the police! But then I don't know who he is, or where he's gone! But he is very crazy, and I'm afraid he'll fling away every cent of his money before his friends can catch him. I know what I'll do. I'll go to the stand and watch for the cab to come back and ask the driver what he has done with the poor, dear old fellow!" said the newsboy, picking up the gold coin and putting it into his pocket. And then he started, but with an eye to business, singing out:

"Herald! Triebune! Express! last account of the orful accident—steamer," etc., etc., etc., selling his papers as he went on to the cab-stand. He found the cabman already there. And to his anxious inquiries as to the sanity of the old gentleman, that Jehu replied:

"Oh, bless your soul, crazy? No; no more'n you or I. He's a real nob—a real Virginian, F. F. V., with money like the sands on the seashore! Keep the tin, lad; he knowed what he was a-doin' on."

"Oh, it a'most scares me to have so much money!" exclaimed the boy, half in delight, half in dismay; "but to-night I'll have a warm supper and sleep in a bed once more! And to-morrow a new suit of clothes! So here goes—Herald! Express!—full account—the horrible murder—Bell Street—Ledgee-ee-ee," etc., etc., etc., crying his papers until he was out of hearing.

Never in his life had the newsboy felt so prosperous and happy.

CHAPTER V.

THE DISCOVERY.

"And at the magistrate's command,
And next undid the leathern band
That bound her tresses there,
And raised her felt hat from her head,
And down her slender form there spread
Black ringlets rich and rare."

Old Hurricane meanwhile dined at the public table at the Astor, and afterward went to his room to rest, smoke and ruminate. And he finished the evening by supping and retiring to bed.

In the morning, after an early breakfast, he wrote a dozen advertisements and called a cab and rode around to leave them with the various daily papers for immediate publication. Then, to lose no time, he rode up to the Recorder's office to set the police upon the search.

As he was about to enter the front portal he observed the doorway and passage blocked up with even a larger crowd than usual.

And seeing the cabman who had waited upon him the preceding day, he inquired of him:

"What is the matter here?"

"Nothing, your honor, 'cept a boy tuk up for wearing girl's clothes, or a girl tuk up for wearing boy's, I dunno which," said the man, touching his hat.

"Let me pass, then; I must speak to the chief of police," said Old Hurricane, shoving his way into the Recorder's room.

"This is not the office of the chief, sir; you will find him on the other side of the hall," said a bystander.

But before Old Hurricane had gathered the sense of these words, a sight within the office drew his steps thither. Up before the Recorder stood a lad of about thirteen years, who, despite his smart, new suit of gray casinet, his long, rolling, black ringlets and his downcast and blushing face, Old Hurricane immediately recognized as his acquaintance, of the preceding day, the saucy young tatterdemalion.

Feeling sorry for the friendless boy, the old man impulsively went up to him and patted him on the shoulder, saying:

"What! In trouble, my lad? Never mind; never look down! I'll warrant ye an honest lad from what I've seen myself. Come! come! pluck up a spirit! I'll see you through, my lad."

"'Lad!' Lord bless your soul, sir, he's no more a lad than you or I! The young rascal is a girl in boy's clothes, sir!" said the officer who had the culprit in custody.

"What—what—what!" exclaimed Old Hurricane, gazing in consternation from the young prisoner to the accuser; "what—what! my newsboy, my saucy little prince of patches, a girl in boy's clothes?"

"Yes, sir—a young scoundrel! I actually twigged him selling papers at the Fulton Ferry this morning! A little rascal!"

"A girl in boy's clothes! A girl!" exclaimed Old Hurricane, with his eyes nearly starting out of his head.

Just then the young culprit looked up in his face with an expression half melancholy, half mischievous, that appealed to the rugged heart of the old man. Turning around to the policeman, he startled the whole office by roaring out:

"Girl, is she, sir? Then, demmy, sir, whether a girl in boy's clothes, or men's clothes, or soldier's clothes, or sailor's clothes, or any clothes, or no clothes, sir, treat her with the delicacy due to womanhood, sir! ay, and the tenderness owed to childhood! for she is but a bit of a poor, friendless, motherless, fatherless child, lost and wandering in your great Babylon! No more hard words to her, sir—or by the ever-lasting——"

"Order!" put in the calm and dignified Recorder.

Old Hurricane, though his face was still purple, his veins swollen and his eyeballs glaring with anger, immediately recovered himself, turned and bowed to the Recorder and said:

"Yes, sir, I will keep order, if you'll make that brute of a policeman reform his language!"

And so saying Old Hurricane subsided into a seat immediately behind the child, to watch the examination.

"What'll they do with her, do you think?" he inquired of a bystander.

"Send her down, in course."

"Down! Where?"

"To Blackwell's Island—to the work'us, in course."

"To the workhouse—her, that child?—the wretches! Um-m-m-me! Oh-h-h!" groaned Old Hurricane, stooping and burying his shaggy gray head in his great hands.

He felt his shoulder touched, and, looking up, saw that the little prisoner had turned around, and was about to speak to him.

"Governor," said the same clear voice that he had even at first supposed to belong to a girl—"Governor, don't you keep on letting out that way! You don't know nothing! You're in the Recorder's Court! If you don't mind your eye they'll commit you for contempt!"

"Will they? Then they'll do well, my lad! Lass, I mean. I plead guilty to contempt. Send a child like you to the— —! They shan't do it! Simply, they shan't do it! I, Major Warfield of Virginia, tell you so, my boy—girl, I mean!"

"But, you innocent old lion, instead of freeing me, you'll find yourself shut up between four walls! and very narrow ones at that, I tell you! You'll think yourself in your coffin! Governor, they call it The Tombs!" whispered the child.

"Attention!" said the clerk.

The little prisoner turned and faced the court. And the "old lion" buried his shaggy, gray head and beard in his hands and groaned aloud.

"Now, then, what is your name, my lad—my girl, I should say?" inquired the clerk.

"Capitola, sir."

Old Hurricane pricked up his ears and raised his head, muttering to himself: "Cap-it-o-la! That's a very odd name! Can't surely be two in the world of the same! Cap-it-ola!—if it should be my Capitola, after all! I shouldn't wonder at all! I'll listen and say nothing." And with this wise resolution, Old Hurricane again dropped his head upon his hands.

"You say your name is Capitola—Capitola what?" inquired the clerk, continuing the examination.

"Nothing sir."

"Nothing! What do you mean?"

"I have no name but Capitola, sir."

"Who is your father?"

"Never had any that I know, sir."

"Your mother?"

"Never had a mother either, sir, as ever I heard."

"Where do you live?"

"About in spots in the city, sir."

"Oh—oh—oh!" groaned old Hurricane within his hands.

"What is your calling?" inquired the clerk.

"Selling newspapers, carrying portmanteaus and packages sweeping before doors, clearing off snow, blacking boots and so on."

"Little odd jobs in general, eh?"

"Yes, sir, anything that I can turn my hand to and get to do."

"Boy—girl, I should say—what tempted you to put yourself into male attire?"

"Sir?"

"In boy's clothes, then?"

"Oh, yes; want, sir—and—and—danger, sir!" cried the little prisoner, putting her hands to a face crimson with blushes and for the first time since her arrest upon the eve of sobbing.

"Oh—oh—oh!" groaned Old Hurricane from his chair.

"Want? Danger? How is that?" continued the clerk.

"Your honor mightn't like to know."

"By all means! It is, in fact, necessary that you should give an account of yourself," said the clerk.

Old Hurricane once more raised his head, opened his ears and gave close attention.

One circumstance he had particularly remarked—the language used by the poor child during her examination was much superior to the slang she had previously affected, to support her assumed character of newsboy.

"Well, well—why do you pause? Go on—go on, my good boy—girl, I mean I" said the Recorder, in a tone of kind encouragement.

CHAPTER VI.

A SHORT, SAD STORY.

"Ah! poverty is a weary thing!
It burdeneth the brain,
It maketh even the little child
To murmur and complain."

"It is not much I have to tell," began Capitola. "I was brought up in Rag Alley and its neighborhood by an old woman named Nancy Grewell."

"Ah!" ejaculated Old Hurricane.

"She was a washwoman, and rented one scantily furnished room from a poor family named Simmons."

"Oh!" cried Old Hurricane.

"Granny, as I called her, was very good to me, and I never suffered cold nor hunger until about eighteen months ago, when Granny took it into her head to go down to Virginia."

"Umph!" exclaimed Old Hurricane.

"When Granny went away she left me a little money and some good clothes and told me to be sure to stay with the people where she left me, for that she would be back in about a month. But, your honor, that was the last I ever saw or heard of poor Granny! She never came back again. And by that I know she must have died."

"Ah-h-h!" breathed the old man, puffing fast.

"The first month or two after Granny left I did well enough. And then, when the little money was all gone, I eat with the Simmonses and did little odd jobs for my food. But by and by Mr. Simmons got out of work, and the family fell into want, and they wished me to go out and beg for them. I just couldn't do that, and so they told me I should look out for myself."

"Were there no customers of your grandmother that you could have applied to for employment?" asked the Recorder.

"No, sir. My Granny's customers were mostly boarders at the small taverns, and they were always changing. I did apply to two or three houses where the land-ladies knew Granny; but they didn't want me."

"Oh-h-h!" groaned Major Warfield, in the tone of one in great pain.

"I wouldn't have that old fellow's conscience for a good deal," whispered a spectator, "for, as sure as shooting, that gal's his unlawful child!"

"Well, go on! What next?" asked the clerk.

"Well, sir, though the Simmonses had nothing to give me except a crust now and then, they still let me sleep in the house, for the little jobs I could do for them. But at last Simmons he got work on the railroad away off somewhere, and they all moved away from the city."

"And you were left alone?"

"Yes, sir; I was left alone in the empty, unfurnished house. Still it was a shelter, and I was glad of it, and I dreaded the time when it would be rented by another tenant, and I should be turned into the street."

"Oh! oh! oh, Lord!" groaned the major.

"But it was never rented again, for the word went around that the whole row was to be pulled down, and so I thought I had leave to stay at least as long as the rats did!" continued Capitola, with somewhat of her natural roguish humor twinkling in her dark-gray eyes.

"But how did you get your bread?" inquired the Recorder.

"Did not get it at all, sir. Bread was too dear! I sold my clothes, piece by piece, to the old Jew over the way and bought corn-meal and picked up trash to make a fire and cooked a little mush every day in an old tin can that had been left behind. And so I lived on for two or three weeks. And then when my clothes were all gone except the suit I had upon my back, and my meal was almost out, instead of making mush every day I economized and made gruel."

"But, my boy—my good girl, I mean—before you became so destitute you should have found something or other to do," said the Recorder.

"Sir, I was trying to get jobs every hour in the day. I'd have done anything honest. I went around to all the houses Granny knew, but they didn't want a girl. Some of the good-natured landlords said if I was a boy, now, they could keep me opening oysters; but as I was a girl they had no work for me. I even went to the offices to get papers to sell; but they told me that crying papers was not proper work for a girl. I even went down to the ferry-boats and watched for the passengers coming ashore, and ran and offered to carry their carpet-bags or portmanteaus; but some growled at me, and others laughed at me, and one old gentleman asked me if I thought he was a North American Indian to strut up Broadway with a female behind him carrying his pack. And so, sir, while all the ragged boys I knew could get little jobs to earn bread, I, because I was a girl, was not allowed to carry a gentleman's parcel or black his boots, or shovel the snow off a shopkeeper's pavement, or put in coal, or do anything that I could do just as well as they. And so because I was a girl there seemed to be nothing but starvation or beggary before me!"

"Oh, Lord! oh, Lord! that such things should be!" cried Old Hurricane.

"That was bad, sir; but there was worse behind! There came a day when my meal, even the last dust of it, was gone. Then I kept life in me by drinking water and by sleeping all I could. At first I could not sleep for the gnawing—gnawing—in my stomach; but afterwards I slept deeply, from exhaustion, and then I'd dream of feasts and the richest sort of food, and of eating such quantities; and, really, sir, I seemed to taste it and enjoy it and get the good of it, almost as much as if it was all true! One morning after such a dream I was waked up by a great noise outside. I staggered upon my feet and crept to the window, and there, sir, were the workmen all outside a-pulling down the house over my head!"

"Good Heaven!" ejaculated Old Hurricane, who seemed to constitute himself the chorus of this drama.

"Sir, they didn't know that I or any one was in the empty house! Fright gave me strength to run down-stairs and run out. Then I stopped. Oh! I stopped and looked up and down the street. What should I do? The last shelter was gone away from me—the house where I had lived so many years, and that seemed like a friend to me, was falling before my eyes! I thought I'd just go and pitch myself into the river and end it all!"

"That was a very wicked thought," said the Recorder.

"Yes, sir, I know it was, and, besides, I was dreadfully afraid of being suffocated in the dirty water around the wharf!" said Capitola, with a sparkle of that irrepressible humor that effervesced even through all her trouble. "Well, sir, the hand that feeds young ravens kept me from dying that day. I found a five-cent piece in the street and resolved not to smother myself in the river mud as long as it lasted. So I bought a muffin, ate it, and went down to the wharf to look for a job. I looked all day but found none, and when night came I went into a lumber yard and hid myself behind a pile of planks that kept the wind off me, and I went to sleep and dreamed a beautiful dream of living in a handsome house, with friends all around me and everything good to eat and drink and wear!"

"Poor, poor child; but your dream may come true yet!" muttered Old Hurricane to himself.

"Well, your honor, next day I spent another penny out of my half-dime and looked in vain for work all day and slept at night in a broken-down omnibus that had happened to be left on the stand. And so, not to tire your patience, a whole week passed away. I lived on my half-dime, spending a penny a day for a muffin, until the last penny was gone, and sleeping at night wherever I could—sometimes under the front stoop of a house, sometimes in an old broken carriage and sometimes behind a pile of boxes on the sidewalk."

"That was a dreadful exposure for a young girl," said the Recorder.

A burning blush flamed up over the young creature's cheek as she answered:

"Yes, sir, that was the worst of all; that finally drove me to putting on boy's clothes."

"Let us hear all about it."

"Oh, sir, I can't—I—How can I? Well, being always exposed, sleeping out-doors, I was often in danger from bad boys and bad men," said Capitola, and, dropping her head upon her breast and covering her crimson cheeks with her hands, for the first time she burst into tears and sobbed aloud.

"Come, come, my little man—my good little woman, I mean! don't take it so to heart. You couldn't help it!" said Old Hurricane, with raindrops glittering even in his own stormy eyes.

Capitola looked up, with her whole countenance flashing with spirit, and exclaimed: "Oh! but I took care of myself, sir! I did, indeed, your honor! You mustn't, either you or the old gentleman, dare to think but what I did!"

"Oh, of course! of course!" said a bystander, laughing.

Old Hurricane sprang up, bringing his feet down upon the floor with a resound that made the great hall ring again, exclaiming:

"What do you mean by 'of course! of course!' you villain? Demmy! I'll swear she took care of herself, you varlet; and if any man dares to hint otherwise, I'll ram his falsehood down his throat with the point of my walking stick and make him swallow both!"

"Order! order!" said the clerk.

Old Hurricane immediately wheeled to the right about faced and saluted the bench in military fashion, and then said:

"Yes, sir! I'll regard order! but in the meanwhile, if the court does not protect this child from insult I must, order or no order!" and with that the old gentleman once more subsided into his seat.

"Governor, don't you be so noisy! You'll get yourself stopped up into a jug next! Why, you remind me of an uproarious old fellow poor Granny used to talk about, that they called Old Hurricane, because he was so stormy!" whispered Capitola, turning toward him.

"Humph! she's heard of me, then!" muttered the old gentleman to himself.

"Well, sir—I mean, miss—go on!" said the clerk, addressing Capitola.

"Yes, sir. Well, your honor, at the end of five days, being a certain Thursday morning, when I couldn't get a job of work for love nor money, when my last penny was spent for my last roll, and my last roll was eaten up, and I was dreading the gnawing hunger by day and the horrid perils of the night, I thought to myself if I were only a boy I might carry packages and shovel in coal, and do lots of jobs by day, and sleep without terror by night. And then I felt bitter against Fate for not making me a boy. And so, thinking and thinking and thinking I wandered on until I found myself in Rag Alley, where I used to live, standing right between the pile of broken bricks, plaster and lumber that used to be my home, and the old Jew's shop where I sold my clothes for meal. And then all of a sudden a bright thought struck me? and I made up my mind to be a boy!"

"Made up your mind to be a boy?"

"Yes, sir, for it was so easy! I wondered how I came to be so stupid as not to have thought of it before. I just ran across to the old Jew's shop and offered to swap my suit of girl's clothes, that was good, though dirty, for any, even the raggedest suit of boy's clothes he had, whether they'd fit me or not, so they would only stay on me. The old fellow put his finger to his nose as if he thought I'd been stealing and wanted to dodge the police. So he took down an old, not very ragged, suit that he said would fit me, and opened a door and told me to go in his daughter's room and put 'em on.

"Well, not to tire your honors, I went into that little back parlor a girl and I came out a boy, with a suit of pants and jacket, with my hair cut short and a cap on my head! The Jew gave me a penny roll and a sixpence for my black ringlets."

"All seemed grist that came to his mill!" said Old Hurricane.

"Yes, Governor, he was a dealer in general. Well, the first thing I did was to hire myself to the Jew, at a sixpence a day and find myself, to shovel in his coal. That didn't take me but a day. So at night the Jew paid me, and I slept in peace behind a stack of boxes. Next morning I was up before the sun and down to the office of the little penny paper, the 'Morning Star.' I bought two dozen of 'em and ran as fast as I could to the ferry-boats to sell to the early passengers. Well, sir, in an hour's time I had sold out and pocketed just two shillings, and felt myself on the highroad to fortune!"

"And so that was the way by which you came to put yourself in male attire?"

"Yes, sir, and the only thing that made me feel sorry was to see what a fool I had been not to turn to a boy before, when it was so easy! And from that day forth I was happy and prosperous! I found plenty to do! I carried carpet-bags, held horses, put in coal, cleaned sidewalks, blacked gentlemen's boots and did everything an honest lad could turn his hand to. And so for more'n a year I was as happy as a king, and should have kept on so, only I forgot and let my hair grow; and instead of cutting it off, just tucked it up under my cap; and so this morning on the ferry-boat, in a high breeze, the wind blowed off my cap and the policeman blowed on me!"

"'Twasn't altogether her long hair, your honor, for I had seen her before, having known her when she lived with old Mrs. Grewell in Rag Alley," interrupted the officer.

"You may sit down, my child," said the Recorder, in a tone of encouragement.

CHAPTER VII.

METAMORPHOSIS OF THE NEWSBOY.

With caution judge of probability,
Things deemed unlikely, e'en impossible,
Experience oft hath proven to be true.

—SHAKESPEARE.

"What shall we do with her?" inquired the Recorder, sotto voce, of a brother magistrate who appeared to be associated with him on the bench.

"Send her to the Refuge," replied the other, in the same tone.

"What are they consulting about?" asked Old Hurricane, whose ears were not of the best.

"They are talking of sending her to the Refuge," answered a bystander.

"Refuge? Is there a refuge for destitute children in New York? Then Babylon is not so bad as I thought it. What is this Refuge?"

"It is a prison where juvenile delinquents are trained to habits of — —"

"A prison! Send her to a prison? Never!" burst forth Old Hurricane, rising and marching up to the Recorder; he stood, hat in hand, before him and said:

"Your honor, if a proper legal guardian appears to claim this young person and holds himself in all respects responsible for her, may she not be at once delivered into his hands?"

"Assuredly," answered the magistrate, with the manner of one glad to be rid of the charge.

"Then, sir, I, Ira Warfield, of Hurricane Hall, in Virginia, present myself as the guardian of this girl, Capitola Black, whom I claim as my ward. And I will enter into a recognizance for any sum to appear and prove my right if it should be disputed. For my personal responsibility, sir, I refer you to the proprietors of the Astor, who have known me many years."

"It is not necessary, Major Warfield; we assume the fact of your responsibility and deliver up the young girl to your charge."

"I thank you, sir," said Old Hurricane, bowing low. Then hurrying across the room where sat the reporters for the press he said:

"Gentlemen, I have a favor to ask of you; it is that you will altogether drop this case of the boy in girl's clothes—I mean the girl in girl's clothes—I declare I don't know what I mean; nor I shan't, neither, until I see the creature in its proper dress, but this I wish to request of you, gentlemen, that you will drop that item from your report, or if you must mention it, treat it with delicacy, as the good name of a young lady is involved."

The reporters, with sidelong glances, winks and smiles, gave him the required promise, and Old Hurricane returned to the side of his protégée.

"Capitola, are you willing to go with me?"

"Jolly willing, governor."

"Then come along; my cab is waiting," said Old Hurricane, and, bowing to the court, he took the hand of his charge and led her forth, amid the ill-suppressed jibes of the crowd.

"There's a hoary-headed old sinner!" said one.

"She's as like him as two peas," quoth another.

"Wonder if there's any more belonging to him of the same sort?" inquired a third.

Leaving all the sarcasm behind him, Old Hurricane handed his protégée into the cab, took the seat beside her and gave orders to be driven out toward Harlem.

As soon as they were seated in the cab the old man turned to his charge and said:

"Capitola, I shall have to trust to your girl's wit to get yourself into your proper clothes again without exciting further notice."

"Yes, governor."

"My boy—girl, I mean—I am not the governor of Virginia, though if every one had his rights I don't know but I should be. However, I am only Major Warfield," said the old man, naively, for he had not the most distant idea that the title bestowed on him by Capitola was a mere remnant of her newsboys "slang."

"Now, my lad—pshaw! my lass, I mean—how shall we get you metamorphosed again?"

"I know, gov—major, I mean. There is a shop of ready-made clothing at the Needle Woman's Aid, corner of the next square. I can get out there and buy a full suit."

"Very well. Stop at the next corner, driver," called Old Hurricane.

The next minute the cab drew up before a warehouse of ready-made garments.

Old Hurricane jumped out, and, leading his charge, entered the shop.

Luckily, there was behind the counter only one person—a staid, elderly, kind-looking woman.

"Here, madam," said Old Hurricane, stooping confidentially to her ear, "I am in a little embarrassment that I hope you will be willing to help me out of for a consideration. I came to New York in pursuit of my ward—this young girl here—whom I found in boy's clothes. I now wish to restore her to her proper dress, before presenting her to my friends, of course. Therefore, I wish you to furnish her with a half dozen complete suits of female attire, of the very best you have that will fit her. And also to give her the use of a room and of your own aid in changing her dress. I will pay you liberally."

Half suspicious and half scandalized, the worthy woman gazed with scrutiny first into the face of the guardian and then into that of the ward; but finding in the extreme youth of the one and the advanced age of the other, and in the honest expression of both, something to allay her fears, if not to inspire her confidence, she said:

"Very well, sir. Come after me, young gentleman—young lady, I should say." And, calling a boy to mind the shop, she conducted Capitola to an inner apartment.

Old Hurricane went out and dismissed his cab. When it was entirely out of sight he hailed another that was passing by empty, and engaged it to take himself and a young lady to the Washington House.

When he re-entered the shop he found the shop woman and Capitola returned and waiting for him.

Capitola was indeed transfigured. Her bright black hair, parted in the middle, fell in ringlets each side her blushing cheeks; her dark-gray eyes were cast down in modesty at the very same instant that her ripe red lips were puckered up with mischief. She was well and properly attired in a gray silk dress, crimson merino shawl and a black velvet bonnet.

The other clothing that had been purchased was done up in packages and put into the cab.

And after paying the shop woman handsomely, Old Hurricane took the hand of his ward, handed her into the cab and gave the order:

"To the Washington House."

The ride was performed in silence.

Capitola sat deeply blushing at the recollection of her male attire, and profoundly cogitating as to what could be the relationship between herself and the gray old man whose claim the Recorder had so promptly admitted. There seemed but one way of accounting for the great interest he took in her fate. Capitola came to the conclusion that the grim old lion before her was no more nor less than—her own father! for alas! poor Cap had been too long tossed about New York not to know more of life than at her age she should have known. She had indeed the innocence of youth, but not its simplicity.

Old Hurricane, on his part, sat with his thick cane grasped in his two knobby hands, standing between his knees, his grizzled chin resting upon it and his eyes cast down as in deep thought.

And so in silence they reached the Washington House.

Major Warfield then conducted his ward into the ladies' parlor, and went and entered his own and her name upon the books as "Major Warfield and his ward, Miss Black," for whom he engaged two bedrooms and a private parlor.

Then, leaving Capitola to be shown to her apartment by a chambermaid, he went out and ordered her luggage up to her room and dismissed the cab.

Next he walked to the Astor House, paid his bill, collected his baggage, took another carriage and drove back to the Washington Hotel.

All this trouble Old Hurricane took to break the links of his action and prevent scandal. This filled up a long forenoon.

He dined alone with his ward in their private parlor.

Such a dinner poor Cap had never even smelled before. How immensely she enjoyed it, with all its surroundings—the comfortable room, the glowing fire, the clean table, the rich food, the obsequious attendance, her own genteel and becoming dress, the company of a highly respectable guardian—all, all so different from anything she had ever been accustomed to, and so highly appreciated.

How happy she felt! How much happier from the contrast of her previous wretchedness, to be suddenly freed from want, toil, fear and all the evils of destitute orphanage, and to find herself blessed with wealth, leisure and safety, under the care of a rich, good and kind father (or as such Capitola continued to believe her guardian to be). It was an incredible thing! It was like a fairy tale!

Something of what was passing in her mind was perceived by Old Hurricane, who frequently burst into uproarious fits of laughter as he watched her.

At last, when the dinner and the dessert were removed, and the nuts, raisins and wine placed upon the table, and the waiters had retired from the room and left them alone, sitting one on each side of the fire, with the table and its luxuries between them, Major Warfield suddenly looked up and asked:

"Capitola, whom do you think that I am?"

"Old Hurricane, to be sure. I knew you from Granny's description, the moment you broke out so in the police office," answered Cap.

"Humph! Yes, you're right; and it was your Granny that bequeathed you to me, Capitola."

"Then she is really dead?"

"Yes. There—don't cry about her. She was very old, and she died happy. Now, Capitola, if you please me I mean to adopt you as my own daughter."

"Yes, father."

"No, no; you needn't call me father, you know, because it isn't true. Call me uncle, uncle, uncle."

"Is that true, sir?" asked Cap, demurely.

"No, no, no; but it will do, it will do. Now, Cap, how much do you know? Anything? Ignorant as a horse, I am afraid."

"Yes, sir; even as a colt."

"Can you read at all?"

"Yes, sir; I learned to read at Sunday-school."

"Cast accounts and write?"

"I can keep your books at a pinch, sir."

"Humph! Who taught you these accomplishments?"

"Herbert Greyson, sir."

"Herbert Greyson! I've heard that name before; here it is again. Who is that Herbert Greyson?"

"He's second mate on the Susan, sir, that is expected in every day."

"Umph! umph! Take a glass of wine, Capitola."

"No, sir; I never touch a single drop."

"Why? Why? Good wine after dinner, my child, is a good thing, let me tell you."

"Ah, sir, my life has shown me too much misery that has come of drinking wine."

"Well, well, as you please. Why, where has the girl run off to!" exclaimed the old man, breaking off, and looking with amazement at Capitola, who had suddenly started up and rushed out of the room.

In an instant she rushed in again, exclaiming:

"Oh, he's come! he's come! I heard his voice!"

"Whose come, you madcap?" inquired the old man.

"Oh, Herbert Greyson! Herbert Greyson! His ship is in, and he has come here! He always comes here—most of the sea officers do," exclaimed Cap, dancing around until all her black ringlets flew up and down. Then suddenly pausing, she came quietly to his side and said, solemnly:

"Uncle, Herbert has been at sea three years; he knows nothing of my past misery and destitution, nor of my ever wearing boy's clothes. Uncle, please don't tell him, especially of the boy's clothes." And in the earnestness of her appeal Capitola clasped her hands and raised her eyes to the old man's face. How soft those gray eyes looked when praying! But for all that, the very spirit of mischief still lurked about the corners of the plump, arched lips.

"Of course I shall tell no one! I am not so proud of your masquerading as to publish it. And as for this young fellow, I shall probably never see him!" exclaimed Old Hurricane.

CHAPTER VIII.

HERBERT GREYSON.

A kind, true heart, a spirit high,
That cannot fear and will not bow,
Is flashing in his manly eye
And stamped upon his brow.

—HALLECK.

In a few minutes Capitola came bounding up the stairs again, exclaiming joyously:

"Here he is, uncle! Here is Herbert Greyson! Come along, Herbert; you must come in and see my new uncle!" And she broke into the room, dragging before her astonished guardian a handsome, dark-eyed young sailor, who bowed and then stood blushing at his enforced intrusion.

"I beg your pardon, sir," he said, "for bursting in upon you in this way; but——"

"I dragged him here willy-nilly," said Capitola.

"Still, if I had had time to think I should not have intruded."

"Oh, say no more, sir. You are heartily welcome," exclaimed the old man, thrusting out his rugged hand and seizing the bronzed one of the youth. "Sit down, sir, sit down. Good Lord, how like!" he added, mentally.

Then, seeing the young sailor still standing, blushing and hesitating, he struck his cane upon the floor and roared out:

"Demmy, sit down, sir! When Ira Warfield says sit down, he means sit down!"

"Ira Warfield!" exclaimed the young man, starting back in astonishment—one might almost say in consternation.

"Ay, sir; Ira Warfield! That's my name. Never heard any ill of it, did you?"

The young man did not answer, but continued gazing in amazement upon the speaker.

"Nor any good of it either, perhaps—eh, uncle?" archly put in Capitola.

"Silence, you monkey! Well, young man, well, what is the meaning of all this?" exclaimed old Hurricane, impatiently.

"Oh, your pardon, sir; this was sudden. But you must know I had once a relative of that name—an uncle."

"And have still, Herbert; and have still, lad. Come, come, boy; I am not sentimental, nor romantic, nor melodramatic, nor nothing of that sort. I don't know how to strike an attitude and exclaim, 'Come to my bosom, sole remaining offspring of a dear departed sister' or any of the like stage playing. But I tell you, lad, that I like your looks; and I like what I have heard of you from this girl, and another old woman, now dead; and so—But sit down, sit down! demmy, sir, sit down, and we'll talk over the walnuts and the wine. Capitola, take your seat, too," ordered the old man, throwing himself into his chair. Herbert also drew his chair up.

Capitola resumed her seat, saying to herself:

"Well, well, I am determined not to be surprised at anything that happens, being perfectly clear in my own mind that this is all nothing but a dream. But how pleasant it is to dream that I have found a rich uncle and he has found a nephew, and that nephew is Herbert Greyson! I do believe that I had rather die in my sleep than wake from this dream!"

"Herbert," said old Hurricane, as soon as they were gathered around the table—"Herbert, this is my ward, Miss Black, the daughter of a deceased friend. Capitola, this is the only son of my departed sister."

"Hem-m-m! We have had the pleasure of being acquainted with each other before," said Cap, pinching up her lip and looking demure.

"But not of really knowing who 'each other' was, you monkey. Herbert, fill your glass. Here's to our better acquaintance."

"I thank you, sir. I never touch wine," said the young man.

"Never touch wine! Here's another; here's a young prig! I don't believe you—yes, I do, too! Demmy, sir, if you never touch wine it's because you prefer brandy! Waiter!"

"I thank you, sir. Order no brandy for me. If I never use intoxicating liquors it is because I gave a promise to that effect to my dying mother."

"Say no more—say no more, lad. Drink water, if you like. It won't hurt you!" exclaimed the old man, filling and quaffing a glass of champagne. Then he said:

"I quarreled with your mother, Herbert, for marrying a man that I hated—yes, hated, Herbert, for he differed with me about the tariff and—the Trinity! Oh, how I hated him, boy, until he died! And then I wondered in my soul, as I wonder even now, how I ever could have been so infuriated against a poor fellow now cold in his grave, as I shall be in time. I wrote to my sister and expressed my feelings; but, somehow or other, Herbert, we never came to a right understanding again. She answered my letter affectionately enough, but she refused to accept a home for herself and child under my roof, saying that she thanked me for my offer, but that the house which had been closed against her husband ought never to become the refuge of his widow. After that we never corresponded, and I have no doubt, Herbert, that she, naturally enough, taught you to dislike me."

"Not so, sir; indeed, you wrong her. She might have been loyal to my father's memory without being resentful toward you. She said that you had a noble nature, but it was often obscured by violent passions. On her dead-bed she bade me, should I ever meet you, to say that she repented her refusal of your offered kindness."

"And consented that it should be transferred to her orphan boy?" added Old Hurricane, with the tears like raindrops in his stormy eyes.

"No, sir, she said not so."

"But yet she would not have disapproved a service offered to her son."

"Uncle—since you permit me to call you so—I want nothing. I have a good berth in the Susan and a kind friend in her captain."

"You have all your dear mother's pride, Herbert."

"And all his uncle's!" put in Cap.

"Hush, Magpie! But is the merchant service agreeable to you, Herbert?"

"Not perfectly, sir; but one must be content."

"Demmy, sir, my sister's son need not be content unless he has a mind to! And if you prefer the navy——"

"No, sir. I like the navy even less than the merchant service."

"Then what would suit you, lad? Come, you have betrayed the fact that you are not altogether satisfied."

"On the contrary, sir, I told you distinctly that I really wanted nothing, and that I must be satisfied."

"And I say, demmy, sir! you sha'n't be satisfied unless you like to! Come, if you don't like the navy, what do you say to the army, eh?"

"It is a proud, aspiring profession, sir," said the young man, as his face lighted up with enthusiasm.

"Then, demmy, if you like the army, sir, you shall enter it! Yes, sir! Demmy, the administration, confound them, has not done me justice, but they'll scarcely dare to refuse to send my nephew to West Point when I demand it."

"To West Point!" exclaimed Herbert, in delight.

"Ay, youngster, to West Point. I shall see to it when I pass through Washington on my way to Virginia. We start in the early train to-morrow morning. In the meantime, young man, you take leave of your captain, pack up your traps and join us. You must go with me and make Hurricane Hall your home until you go to West Point."

"Oh, what a capital old governor our uncle is!" exclaimed Cap, jumping up and clapping her hands.

"Sir, indeed you overwhelm me with this most unexpected kindness! I do not know as yet how much of it I ought to accept. But accident will make me, whether or no, your traveling companion for a great part of the way, as I also start for Virginia to-morrow, to visit dear friends there, whose house was always my mother's home and mine, and who, since my bereavement, have been to me like a dear mother and brother. I have not seen them for years, and before I go anywhere else, even to your kind roof, I must go there," said Herbert, gravely.

"And who are those dear friends of yours, Hebert, and where do they live? If I can serve them they shall be rewarded for their kindness unto you, my boy."

"Oh, sir, yes; you can indeed serve them. They are a poor widow and her only son. She has seen better days, but now takes in sewing to support herself and boy. When my mother was living, during the last years of her life, when she also was a poor widow with an only son, they joined their slender means and took a house and lived together. When my mother died, leaving me a boy of ten years old, this poor woman still sheltered and worked for me as for her own son until, ashamed of being a burden to her, I ran away and went to sea."

"Noble, woman! I will make her fortune!" exclaimed Old Hurricane, jumping up and walking up and down the floor.

"Oh, do, sir! Oh, do, dear uncle! I don't wish you to expend either money or influence upon my fortunes; but, oh, do educate Traverse! He is such a gifted lad — so intellectual! Even his Sunday-school teacher says that he is sure to work his way to distinction, although now he is altogether dependent on his Sunday-school for his learning. Oh, sir, if you would only educate the son he'd make a fortune for his mother."

"Generous boy, to plead for your friends rather than for yourself. But I am strong enough, thank God, to help you all. You shall go to West Point. Your friend shall go to school and then to college," said Old Hurricane, with a burst of honest enthusiasm.

"And where shall I go, sir?" inquired Cap.

"To the insane asylum, you imp!" exclaimed the old man; then, turning to Herbert, he continued: "Yes, lad; I will do as I say; and as for the poor but noble-hearted widow — —"

"You'll marry her yourself, as a reward; won't you, uncle?" asked the incorrigible Cap.

"Perhaps I will, you monkey, if it is only to bring somebody home to keep you in order," said Old Hurricane; then, turning again to Herbert, he resumed: "As to the widow, Herbert, I will place her above want."

"Over my head," cried Cap.

"And now, Herbert, I will trouble you to ring for coffee, and after we have had that I think we had better separate and prepare for our journey to-morrow."

Herbert obeyed, and, after the required refreshment had been served and partaken of, the little circle broke up for the evening and soon after retired to rest.

Early the next morning, after a hasty breakfast, the three took their seats in the express train for Washington, where they arrived upon the evening of the same day. They put up for the night at Brown's, and the next day Major Warfield, leaving his party at their hotel, called upon the President, the Secretary of the Navy and other high official dignitaries, and put affairs in such a train that he had little doubt of the ultimate appointment of his nephew to a cadetship at West Point.

The same evening, wishing to avoid the stage route over the mountains, he took, with his party, the night boat for Richmond, where, in due time, they arrived, and whence they took the valley line of coaches that passed through Tip-Top, which they reached upon the morning of the fourth day of their long journey. Here they found Major Warfield's carriage waiting for him, and here they were to separate—Major Warfield and Capitola to turn off to Hurricane Hall and Herbert Greyson to keep on the route to the town of Staunton.

It was as the three sat in the parlor of the little hotel where the stage stopped to change horses that their adieus were made.

"Remember, Herbert, that I am willing to go to the utmost extent of my power to benefit the good widow and her son who were so kind to my nephew in his need. Remember that! I hold it a sacred debt that I owe them. Tell them so. And mind, Herbert, I shall expect you back in a week at furthest."

"I shall be punctual, sir. God bless you, my dear uncle. You have made me very happy in being the bearer of such glad tidings to the widow and the fatherless. And now I hear the horn blowing—good-by, uncle; good-by, Capitola. I am going to carry them great joy—such great joy, uncle, as you, who have everything you want, can scarcely imagine." And, shaking hands heartily with his companions, Herbert ran through the door and jumped aboard the coach just as the impatient driver was about to leave him behind.

As soon as the coach had rolled out of sight Major Warfield handed Capitola into his carriage that had long been waiting, and took the seat by her side, much to the scandalization of Wool, who muttered to his horses:

"There, I told you so! I said how he'd go and bring home a young wife, and behold he's gone and done it!"

"Uncle," said Capitola as the carriage rolled lazily along—"uncle, do you know you never once asked Herbert the name of the widow you are going to befriend, and that he never told you?"

"By George, that is true! How strange! Yet I did not seem to miss the name. How did it ever happen, Capitola? Did he omit it on purpose, do you think?"

"Why, no, uncle. He, boylike, always spoke of them as 'Traverse' and 'Traverse's mother'; and you, like yourself, called her nothing but the 'poor widow' and the 'struggling mother' and the 'noble woman,' and so on, and her son as the 'boy,' the 'youth,' 'young Traverse,' Herbert's 'friend,' etc. I, for my part, had some curiosity to see whether you and Herbert would go on talking of them forever without having to use their surnames. And, behold, he even went away without naming them!"

"By George! and so he did. It was the strangest over-sight. But I'll write as soon as I get home and ask him."

"No, uncle; just for the fun of the thing, wait until he comes back, and see how long it will be and how much he will talk of them without mentioning their names."

"Ha, ha, ha! So I will, Cap, so I will! Besides whatever their names are, it's nothing to me. 'A rose by any other name would smell as sweet,' you know. And if she is 'Mrs. Tagfoot Waddle' I shall still think so good a woman exalted as a Montmorencie. Mind there, Wool; this road is getting rough."

"Over it now, marster," said Wool, after a few heavy jolts. "Over it now, missus; and de rest of de way is perfectly delightful."

Cap looked out of the window and saw before her a beautiful piece of scenery—first, just below them, the wild mountain stream of the Demon's Run, and beyond it the wild dell dented into the side of the mountain, like the deep print of an enormous horse's hoof, in the midst of which, gleaming redly among its richly-tinted autumn woods, stood Hurricane Hall.

CHAPTER IX.

MARAH ROCKE.

"There sits upon her matron face
A tender and a thoughtful grace,
Though very still,—for great distress
Hath left this patient mournfulness."

Beside an old rocky road leading from the town of Staunton out to the forest-crowned hills beyond, stood alone a little, gray stone cottage, in the midst of a garden inclosed by a low, moldering stone wall. A few gnarled and twisted fruit trees, long past bearing, stood around the house that their leafless branches could not be said to shade. A little wooden gate led up an old paved walk to the front door, on each side of which were large windows.

In this poor cottage, remote from other neighbors, dwelt the friends of Herbert Greyson—the widow Rocke and her son Traverse.

No one knew who she was, or whence or why she came. Some fifteen years before she had appeared in town, clothed in rusty mourning and accompanied by a boy of about two years of age. She had rented that cottage, furnished it poorly and had settled there, supporting herself and child by needlework.

At the time that Doctor Greyson died and his widow and son were left perfectly destitute, and it became necessary for Mrs. Greyson to look out for a humble lodging where she could find the united advantages of cheapness, cleanliness and pure air, she was providentially led to inquire at the cottage of the widow Rocke, whom she found only too glad to increase her meager income by letting half her little house to such unexceptionable tenants as the widow Greyson and her son.

And thus commenced between the two poor young women and the two boys an acquaintance that ripened into friendship, and thence into that devoted love so seldom seen in this world.

Their households became united. One fire, one candle and one table served the little family, and thus considerable expense was saved as well as much social comfort gained. And when the lads grew too old to sleep with their mothers, one bed held the two boys and the other accommodated the two women. And, despite toil, want, care—the sorrow for the dead and the neglect of the living—this was a loving, contented and cheerful little household. How much of their private history these women might have confided to each other was not known, but it was certain that they continued fast friends up to the time of the death of Mrs. Greyson, after which the widow Rocke assumed a double burden, and became a second mother to the orphan boy, until Herbert himself, ashamed of taxing her small means, ran away, as he had said, and went to sea.

Every year had Herbert written to his kind foster mother and his dear brother, as he called Traverse. And at the end of every prosperous voyage, when he had a little money, he had sent them funds; but not always did these letters or remittances reach the widow's cottage, and long seasons of intense anxiety would be suffered by her for the fate of her sailor boy, as she always called Herbert. Only three times in all these years had Herbert found time and means to come down and see them, and that was long ago. It was many months over two years since they had even received a letter from him. And now the poor widow and her son were almost tempted to think that their sailor boy had quite forsaken them.

It is near the close of a late autumnal evening that I shall introduce you, reader, into the interior of the widow's cottage.

You enter by the little wooden gate, pass up the moldering paved walk, between the old, leafless lilac bushes, and pass through the front door right into a large, clean but poor-looking sitting-room and kitchen.

Everything was old, though neatly and comfortably arranged about this room. A faded home-made carpet covered the floor, a threadbare crimson curtain hung before the window, a rickety walnut table, dark with age, sat under the window against the wall; old walnut chairs were placed each side of it; old plated candlesticks, with the silver all worn off, graced the mantelpiece; a good fire—a cheap comfort in that well-wooded country—blazed upon the hearth; on the right side of the fireplace a few shelves contained some well-worn books, a flute, a few minerals and other little treasures belonging to Traverse; on the left hand there was a dresser containing the little delfware, tea service and plates and dishes of the small family.

Before the fire, with her knitting in her hand, sat Marah Rocke, watching the kettle as it hung singing over the blaze and the oven of biscuits that sat baking upon the hearth.

Marah Rocke was at this time about thirty-five years of age, and of a singularly refined and delicate aspect for one of her supposed rank; her little form, slight and flexible as that of a young girl, was clothed in a poor but neat black dress, relieved by a pure-white collar around her throat; her jet-black hair was parted plainly over her "low, sweet brow," brought down each side her thin cheeks and gathered into a bunch at the back of her shapely little head; her face was oval, with regular features and pale olive complexion; serious lips, closed in pensive thought, and soft, dark-brown eyes, full of tender affection and sorrowful memories, and too often cast down in meditation beneath the heavy shadows of their long, thick eyelashes, completed the melancholy beauty of a countenance not often seen among the hard-working children of toil.

Marah Rocke was a very hard-working woman, sewing all day long and knitting through the twilight, and then again resuming her needle by candle-light and sewing until midnight—and yet Marah Rocke made but a poor and precarious living for herself and son. Needlework, so ill-paid in large cities, is even worse paid in the country towns, and, though the cottage hearth was never cold, the widow's meals were often scant. Lately her son, Traverse, who occasionally earned a trifle of money by doing "with all his might whatever his hand could find to do," had been engaged by a grocer in the town to deliver his goods to his customers during the illness of the regular porter; for which, as he was only a substitute, he received the very moderate sum of twenty-five cents a day.

This occupation took Traverse from home at daybreak in the morning, and kept him absent until eight o'clock at night. Nevertheless, the widow always gave him a hot breakfast before he went out in the morning and kept a comfortable supper waiting for him at night.

It was during this last social meal that the youth would tell his mother all that had occurred in his world outside the home that day, and all that he expected to come to pass the next, for Traverse was wonderfully hopeful and sanguine.

And after supper the evening was generally spent by Traverse in hard study beside his mother's sewing-stand.

Upon this evening, when the widow sat waiting for her son, he seemed to be detained longer than usual. She almost feared that the biscuits would be burned, or, if taken from the oven, be cold before he would come to enjoy them; but, just as she had looked for the twentieth time at the little black walnut clock that stood between those old plated candlesticks on the mantelpiece, the sound of quick, light, joyous footsteps was heard resounding along the stony street, the gate was opened, a hand laid upon the door-latch, and the next instant entered a youth some seventeen years of age, clad in a home-spun suit, whose coarse material and clumsy make could not disguise his noble form or graceful air.

He was like his mother, with the same oval face, regular features and pale olive complexion, with the same full, serious lips, the same dark, tender brown eyes, shaded by long, black lashes, and the same wavy, jet-black hair—but there was a difference in the character of their faces; where hers showed refinement and melancholy, his exhibited strength and cheerfulness—his loving brown eyes, instead of drooping sadly under the shadow of their lashes, looked you brightly and confidently full in the face; and, lastly, his black hair curled crisply around a broad, high forehead, royal with intellect. Such was the boy that entered the room and came joyously forward to his mother, clasping his arm around her neck, saluting her on both cheeks, and then laughingly claiming his childish privilege of kissing "the pretty little black mole on her throat."

"Will you never have outgrown your babyhood, Traverse?" asked his mother, smiling at his affectionate ardor.

"Yes, dear little mother; in everything but the privilege of fondling you; that feature of babyhood I never shall outgrow," exclaimed the youth, kissing her again with all the ardor of his true and affectionate heart, and starting up to help her set the table.

He dragged the table out from under the window, spread the cloth and placed the cups and saucers upon it, while his mother took the biscuits from the oven and made the tea; so that in ten minutes from the moment in which he entered the room, mother and son were seated at their frugal supper.

"I suppose, to-morrow being Saturday, you will have to get up earlier than usual to go to the store?" said his mother.

"No, ma'am," replied the boy, looking up brightly, as if he were telling a piece of good news; "I am not wanted any longer. Mr. Spicer's own man has got well again and returned to work."

"So you are discharged?" said Mrs. Rocke, sadly.

"Yes, ma'am; but just think how fortunate that is, for I shall have a chance to-morrow of mending the fence and nailing up the gate and sawing wood enough to last you a week, besides doing all the other little odd jobs that have been waiting for me so long; and then on Monday I shall get more work."

"I wish I were sure of it," said the widow, whose hopes had long since been too deeply crushed to permit her ever to be sanguine.

When their supper was over and the humble service cleared away, the youth took his books and applied himself to study on the opposite side of the table at which his mother sat busied with her needlework. And there fell a perfect silence between them.

The widow's mind was anxious and her heart heavy; many cares never communicated to cloud the bright sunshine of her boy's soul oppressed hers. The rent had fallen fearfully behindhand, and the landlord threatened, unless the money could be raised to pay him, to seize their furniture and eject them from the premises. And how this money was to be raised she could not see at all. True, this meek Christian had often in her sad experience proved God's special providence at her utmost need, and now she believed in His ultimate interference, but in what manner He would now interpose she could not imagine, and her faith grew dim and her hope dark and her love cold.

While she was revolving these sad thoughts in her mind, Traverse suddenly thrust aside his books, and, with a deep sigh, turned to his mother and said:

"Mother, what do you think has ever become of Herbert?"

"I do not know; I dread to conjecture. It has now been nearly three years since we heard from him," exclaimed the widow, with the tears welling up in her brown eyes.

"You think he has been lost at sea, mother, but I don't. I simply think his letters have been lost. And, somehow, to-night I can't fix my mind on my lesson or keep it off Herbert. He is running in my head all the time. If I were fanciful, now, I should believe that Herbert was dead and his spirit was about me. Good heavens, mother, whose step is that?" suddenly exclaimed the youth, starting up and assuming an attitude of intense listening, as a firm and ringing step, attended by a peculiar whistling, approached up the street and entered the gate.

"It is Herbert! it is Herbert!" cried Traverse, starting across the room and tearing open the door with a suddenness that threw the entering guest forward upon his own bosom; but his arms were soon around the newcomer, clasping him closely there, while he breathlessly exclaimed:

"Oh, Herbert, I am so glad to see you! Oh, Herbert, why didn't you come or write all this long time? Oh, Herbert, how long have you been ashore? I was just talking about you."

"Dear fellow! dear fellow! I have come to make you glad at last, and to repay all your great kindness; but now let me speak to my second mother," said Herbert, returning Traverse's embrace and then gently extricating himself and going to where Mrs. Rocke stood up, pale, trembling and incredulous; she had not yet recovered from the great shock of his unexpected appearance.

"Dear mother, won't you welcome me?" asked Herbert, going up to her. His words dissolved the spell that bound her. Throwing her arms around his neck and bursting into tears, she exclaimed:

"Oh, my son! my son! my sailor boy! my other child! how glad I am to have you back once more! Welcome! To be sure you are welcome! Is my own circulating blood welcome back to my heart? But sit you down and rest by the fire; I will get your supper directly."

"Sweet mother, do not take the trouble. I supped twenty miles back, where the stage stopped."

"And will you take nothing at all?"

"Nothing, dear mother, but your kind hand to kiss again and again!" said the youth, pressing that hand to his lips and then allowing the widow to put him into a chair right in front of the fire.

Traverse sat on one side of him and his mother on the other, each holding a hand of his and gazing on him with mingled incredulity, surprise and delight, as if, indeed, they could not realize his presence except by devouring him with their eyes.

And for the next half hour all their talk was as wild and incoherent as the conversation of long-parted friends suddenly brought together is apt to be.

It was all made up of hasty questions, hurried one upon another, so as to leave but little chance to have any of them answered, and wild exclamations and disjointed sketches of travel, interrupted by frequent ejaculations; yet through all the widow and her son, perhaps through the quickness of their love as well as of their intellect, managed to get some knowledge of the past three years of their "sailor boy's" life and adventures, and they entirely vindicated his constancy when they learned how frequently and regularly he had written, though they had never received his letters.

"And now," said Herbert, looking from side to side from mother to son, "I have told you all my adventures, I am dying to tell you something that concerns yourselves."

"That concerns us?" exclaimed mother and son in a breath.

"Yes, ma'am; yes, sir; that concerns you both eminently. But, first of all, let me ask how you are getting on at the present time."

"Oh, as usual," said the widow, smiling, for she did not wish to dampen the spirits of her sailor boy; "as usual, of course. Traverse has not been able to accomplish his darling purpose of entering the Seminary yet; but— —"

"But I'm getting on quite well with my education, for all that," interrupted Traverse; "for I belong to Dr. Day's Bible class in the Sabbath school, which is a class of young men, you know, and the doctor is so good as to think that I have some mental gifts worth cultivating, so he does not confine his instructions to me to the Bible class alone, but permits me to come to him in his library at Willow Heights for an hour twice a week, when he examines me in Latin and algebra, and sets me new exercises, which I study and write out at night; so that you see I am doing very well."

"Indeed, the doctor, who is a great scholar, and one of the trustees and examiners of the Seminary, says that he does not know any young man there, with all the advantages of the institution around him, who is getting along so fast as Traverse is, with all the difficulties he has to encounter. The doctor says it is all because Traverse is profoundly in earnest, and that one of these days he will be— —"

"There, mother, don't repeat all the doctor's kind speeches. He only says such things to encourage a poor boy in the pursuit of knowledge under difficulties," said Traverse, blushing and laughing.

"'—Will be an honor to his kindred, country and race!'" said Herbert, finishing the widow's incomplete quotation.

"It was something like that, indeed," she said, nodding and smiling.

"You do me proud!" said Traverse, touching his forelock with comic gravity. "But," inquired he, suddenly changing his tone and becoming serious, "was it not—is it not—noble in the doctor to give up an hour of his precious time twice a week for no other cause than to help a poor, struggling fellow like me up the ladder of learning?"

"I should think it was! But he is not the first noble heart I ever heard of!" said Herbert, with an affectionate glance that directed the compliment. "Nor is his the last that you will meet with. I must tell you the good news now."

"Oh, tell it, tell it! Have you got a ship of your own, Herbert?"

"No; nor is it about myself that I am anxious to tell you. Mrs. Rocke, you may have heard that I had a rich uncle whom I had never seen, because, from the time of my dear mother's marriage to that of her death, she and her brother—this very uncle—had been estranged?"

"Yes," said the widow, speaking in a very low tone and bending her head over her work; "yes, I have heard so; but your mother and myself seldom alluded to the subject."

"Exactly; mother never was fond of talking of him. Well, when I came ashore and went, as usual, up to the old Washington House, who should I meet with, all of a sudden, but this rich uncle. He had come to New York to claim a little girl whom I happened to know, and who happened to recognize me and name me to him. Well, I knew him only by his name; but he knew me both by my name and by my likeness to his sister, and received me with wonderful kindness, offered me a home under his roof, and promised to get for me an appointment to West Point. Are you not glad?—say, are you not glad?" he exclaimed, jocosely clapping his hand upon Traverse's knee, and then turning around and looking at his mother.

"Oh, yes, indeed, I am very glad, Herbert," exclaimed Traverse, heartily grasping and squeezing his friend's hand.

"Yes, yes; I am indeed sincerely glad of your good fortune, dear boy," said the widow; but her voice was very faint and her head bent still lower over her work.

"Ha! ha! ha! I knew you'd be glad for me; but now I require you to be glad for yourselves. Now listen! When I told my honest old uncle—for he is honest, with all his eccentricities—when I told him of what friends you had been to me——"

"Oh, no; you did not—you did not mention us to him?" cried the widow, suddenly starting up and clasping her hands together, while she gazed in an agony of entreaty into the face of the speaker.

"Why not? Why in the world not? Was there anything improper in doing so?" inquired Herbert in astonishment, while Traverse himself gazed in amazement at the excessive and unaccountable agitation of his mother.

"Why, mother? Why shouldn't he have mentioned us? Was there anything strange or wrong in that?" inquired Traverse.

"No; oh no; certainly not; I forgot, it was so sudden," said the widow, sinking back in her chair and struggling for self-control.

"Why, mother, what in the world is the meaning of this?" asked her son.

"Nothing, nothing, boy; only we are poor folks, and should not be forced upon the attention of a wealthy gentleman," she said with a cold, unnatural smile, putting her hand to her brow and striving to gain composure. Then, as Herbert continued silent and amazed, she said to him:

"Go on, go on—you were saying something about my—about Major Warfield's kindness to you—go on." And she took up her work and tried to sew, but she was as pale as death and trembling all over at the same time that every nerve was acute with attention to catch every word that might fall from the lips of Herbert.

"Well," recommenced the young sailor, "I was just saying that when I mentioned you and Traverse to my uncle, and told him how kind and disinterested you had been to me—you being like a mother and Traverse like a brother—he was really moved almost to tears. Yes, I declare I saw the raindrops glittering in his tempestuous old orbs as he walked the floor muttering to himself, 'Poor women—good, excellent woman.'"

While Herbert spoke the widow dropped her work without seeming to know that she had done so; her fingers twitched so nervously that she had to hold both hands clasped together, and her eyes were fixed in intense anxiety upon the face of the youth as she repeated:

"Go on—oh, go on. What more did he say when you talked of us?"

"He said everything that was kind and good. He said that he could not do too much to compensate you for the past."

"Oh, did he say that?" exclaimed the widow, breathlessly.

"Yes, and a great deal more—that all that he could do for you or your son was but a sacred debt he owed you."

"Oh, he acknowledged it—he acknowledged it! Thank Heaven! oh, thank Heaven! Go on, Herbert; go on."

"He said that he would in future take the whole charge of the boy's advancement in life, and that he would place you above want forever: that he would, in fact, compensate for the past by doing you and yours full justice."

"Thank Heaven! oh, thank Heaven!" exclaimed the widow, no longer concealing her agitation, but throwing down her work, and starting up and pacing the floor in excess of joy.

"Mother," said Traverse, uneasily, going to her and taking her hand, "mother, what is the meaning of all this? Do come and sit down."

She immediately turned and walked back to the fire, and, resting her hands upon the back of the chair, bent upon them a face radiant with youthful beauty. Her cheeks were brightly flushed, her eyes were sparkling with light, her whole countenance resplendent with joy—she scarcely seemed twenty years of age.

"Mother, tell us what it is," pleaded Traverse, who feared for her sanity.

"Oh, boys, I am so happy! At last! at last! after eighteen years of patient 'hoping against hope!' I shall go mad with joy!"

"Mother," said Herbert, softly.

"Children, I am not crazy! I know what I am saying, though I did not intend to say it! And you shall know, too! But first I must ask Herbert another question: Herbert, are you very sure that he—Major Warfield—knew who we were?"

"Yes, indeed; didn't I tell him all about you—your troubles, your struggles, your disinterestedness and all your history since ever I knew you?" answered Herbert, who was totally unconscious that he had left Major Warfield in ignorance of one very important fact—her surname.

"Then you are sure he knew who he was talking about?"

"Of course he did."

"He could not have failed to do so, indeed. But, Herbert, did he mention any other important fact that you have not yet communicated to us?"

"No, ma'am."

"Did he allude to any previous acquaintance with us?"

"No, ma'am, unless it might have been in the words I repeated to you—there was nothing else—except that he bade me hurry to you and make you glad with his message, and return as soon as possible to let him know whether you accept his offers."

"Accept them! accept them! Of course I do. I have waited for them for years. Oh, children, you gaze on me as if you thought me mad. I am not so; nor can I now explain myself, for, since he has not chosen to be confidential with Herbert, I cannot be so prematurely; but you will know all when Herbert shall have borne back my message to Major Warfield."

It was indeed a mad evening in the cottage. And even when the little family had separated and retired to bed, the two youths, lying together as formerly, could not sleep for talking, while the widow on her lonely couch lay awake for joy.

CHAPTER X.

THE ROOM OF THE TRAP-DOOR.

If you have hitherto concealed this sight,
Let it be tenable, in your silence still;
And whatsoever else doth hap to-night,
Give it an understanding, but no tongue.

—SHAKESPEARE.

Capitola, meanwhile, in the care of the major, arrived at Hurricane Hall, much to the discomfiture of good Mrs. Condiment, who was quite unprepared to expect the new inmate; and when Major Warfield said:

"Mrs. Condiment, this is your young lady; take her up to the best bedroom, where she can take off her bonnet and shawl," the worthy dame, thinking secretly, "The old fool has gone and married a young wife, sure enough; a mere chit of a child," made a very deep curtsy and a very queer cough and said:

"I am mortified, madam, at the fire not being made in the best bedroom; but, then, I was not warned of your coming, madam."

"Madam? Is the old woman crazed? This child is no 'madam.' She is Miss Black, my ward, the daughter of a deceased friend," sharply exclaimed Old Hurricane.

"Excuse me, miss; I did not know; I was unprepared to receive a young lady. Shall I attend you, Miss Black?" said the old lady, in a mollified tone.

"If you please," said Capitola, who arose to follow her.

"Not expecting you, miss, I have no proper room prepared; most of them are not furnished, and in some the chimneys are foul; indeed, the only tolerable room I can put you in is the room with the trap-door—if you would not object to it," said Mrs. Condiment, as with a candle in her hand she preceded Capitola along the gloomy hall and then opened a door that led into a narrow passage.

"A room with a trap-door? That's a curious thing; but why should I object to it? I don't at all. I think I should rather like it," said Capitola.

"I will show it to you and tell you about it, and then if you like it, well and good. If not, I shall have to put you in a room that leaks and has swallows' nests in the chimney," answered Mrs. Condiment, as she led the way along the narrow passages and up and down dark back stairs and through bare and deserted rooms and along other passages until she reached a remote chamber, opened the door and invited her guest to enter.

It was a large, shadowy room, through which the single candle shed such a faint, uncertain light that at first Capitola could see nothing but black masses looming through the darkness.

But when Mrs. Condiment advanced and set the candle upon the chimney-piece, and Capitola's sight accommodated itself to the scene, she saw that upon the right of the chimney-piece stood a tall tester bedstead, curtained with very dark crimson serge; on the left hand, thick curtains of the same color draped the two windows. Between the windows, directly opposite the bed, stood a dark mahogany dressing bureau with a large looking-glass; a washstand in the left-hand corner of the chimney-piece, and a rocking-chair and two plain chairs completed the furniture of this room that I am particular in describing, as upon the simple accident of its arrangement depended, upon two occasions, the life and honor of its occupant. There was no carpet on the floor, with the exception of a large, old Turkey rug that was laid before the fireplace.

"Here, my dear, this room is perfectly dry and comfortable, and we always keep kindlings built up in the fireplace ready to light in case a guest should come," said Mrs. Condiment, applying a match to the waste paper under the pine knots and logs that filled the chimney. Soon there arose a cheerful blaze that lighted up all the room, glowing on the crimson serge bed curtains and window curtains and flashing upon the large looking-glass between them.

"There, my dear, sit down and make yourself comfortable," said Mrs. Condiment, drawing up the rocking-chair.

Capitola threw herself into it, and looked around and around the room, and then into the face of the old lady saying:

"But what about the trap-door? I see no trap-door."

"Ah, yes—look!" said Mrs. Condiment, lifting up the rug and revealing a large drop, some four feet square, that was kept up in its place by a short iron bolt.

"Now, my dear, take care of yourself, for this bolt slides very easily, and if, while you happened to be walking across this place, you were to push the bolt back, the trap-door would drop and you fall down—heaven knows where!"

"Is there a cellar under there?" inquired Capitola, gazing with interest upon the door.

"Lord knows, child; I don't. I did once make one of the nigger men let it down so I could look in it; but, Lord, child, I saw nothing but a great, black, deep vacuity, without bottom or sides. It put such a horror over me that I have never looked down there since, and never want to, I'm sure."

"Ugh! for goodness' sake what was the horrid thing made for?" ejaculated Capitola, gazing as if fascinated by the trap.

"The Lord only knows, my dear; for it was made long before ever the house came into the major's family. But they do say——" whispered Mrs. Condiment, mysteriously.

"Ah! what do they say?" asked Capitola, eagerly, throwing off her bonnet and shawl and settling herself to hear some thrilling explanation.

Mrs. Condiment slowly replaced the rug, drew another chair to the side of the young girl and said:

"They do say it was—a trap for Indians!"

"A trap for Indians?"

"Yes, my dear. You must know that this room belongs to the oldest part of the house. It was all built as far back as the old French and Indian war; but this room belonged to the part that dates back to the first settlement of the country."

"Then I shall like it better than any room in the house, for I dote on old places with stories to them. Go on, please."

"Yes, my dear. Well, first of all, this place was a part of the grant of land given to the Le Noirs. And the first owner, old Henri Le Noir, was said to be one of the grandest villains that ever was heard of. Well, you see, he lived out here in his hunting lodge, which is this part of the house."

"Oh, my! then this very room was a part of the old pioneer hunter's lodge?"

"Yes, my dear; and they do say that he had this place made as a trap for the Indians! You see, they say he was on terms of friendship with the Succapoos, a little tribe of Indians that was nearly wasted away, though among the few that was left there were several braves. Well, he wanted to buy a certain large tract of land from this tribe, and they were all willing to sell it except those half a dozen warriors, who wanted it for camping ground. So what does this awful villain do but lay a snare for them. He makes a great feast in his lodge and invites his red brothers to come to it; and they come. Then he proposes that they stand upon his blanket and all swear eternal brotherhood, which he made the poor souls believe was the right way to do it. Then when they all six stood close together as they could stand, with hands held up touching above their heads, all of a sudden the black villain sprung the bolt, the trap fell and the six men went down—down, the Lord knows where!"

"Oh! that is horrible! horrible!" cried Capitola; "but where do you think they fell to?"

"I tell you the Lord only knows! They say that it is a bottomless abyss, with no outlet but one crooked one, miles long, that reaches to the Demon's Punch Bowl. But if there is a bottom to that abyss, that bottom is strewn with human bones!"

"Oh! horrible! most horrible!" exclaimed Capitola.

"Perhaps you are afraid to sleep here by yourself? If so, there's the damp room— —"

"Oh, no! oh, no! I am not afraid. I have been in too much deadly peril from the living ever to fear the dead! No, I like the room, with its strange legend; but tell me, did that human devil escape without punishment from the tribe of the murdered victims?"

"Lord, child, how were they to know of what was done? There wasn't a man left to tell the tale. Besides, the tribe was now brought down to a few old men, women and children. So, when he showed a bill of sale for the land he wanted, signed by the six braves—'their marks,' in six blood-red arrows, there was none to contradict him."

"How was his villainy found out?"

"Well, it was said he married, had a family and prospered for a long while; but that the poor Succapoos always suspected him, and bore a long grudge, and that when the sons of the murdered warriors grew up to be powerful braves, one night they set upon the house and massacred the whole family except the eldest son, a lad of ten, who escaped and ran away and gave the alarm to the block-house, where there were soldiers stationed. It is said that after killing and scalping father, mother and children, the savages threw the dead bodies down that trap-door. And they had just set fire to the house and were dancing their wild dance around it, when the soldiers arrived and dispersed the party and put out the fire."

"Oh, what bloody, bloody days!"

"Yes, my dear, and as I told you before, if that horrible pit has any bottom, that bottom is strewn with human skeletons!"

"It is an awful thought——"

"As I said, my dear, if you feel at all afraid you can have another room."

"Afraid! What of? Those skeletons, supposing them to be there, cannot hurt me! I am not afraid of the dead! I only dread the living, and not them much, either!" said Capitola.

"Well, my dear, you will want a waiting-woman, anyhow; and I think I will send Pitapat to wait on you; she can sleep on a pallet in your room, and be some company."

"And who is Pitapat, Mrs. Condiment?"

"Pitapat? Lord, child, she is the youngest of the housemaids. I've called her Pitapat ever since she was a little one beginning to walk, when she used to steal away from her mother, Dorcas, the cook, and I would hear her little feet coming pit-a-pat, pit-a-pat, up the dark stairs up to my room. As it was often the only sound to be heard in the still house, I grew to call my little visitor Pitapat."

"Then let me have Pitapat by all means. I like company, especially company that I can send away when I choose."

"Very well, my dear; and now I think you'd better smooth your hair and come down with me to tea, for it is full time, and the major, as you may know, is not the most patient of men."

Capitola took a brush from her traveling-bag, hastily arranged her black ringlets and announced herself ready.

They left the room and traversed the same labyrinth of passages, stairs, empty rooms and halls back to the dining-room, where a comfortable fire burned and a substantial supper was spread.

Old Hurricane took Capitola's hand with a hearty grasp, and placed her in a chair at the side, and then took his own seat at the foot of the table.

Mrs. Condiment sat at the head and poured out the tea.

"Uncle," said Capitola, suddenly, "what is under the trap-door in my room?"

"What! Have they put you in that room?" exclaimed the old man, hastily looking up.

"There was no other one prepared, sir," said the housekeeper.

"Besides, I like it very well, uncle," said Capitola.

"Humph! humph! humph!" grunted the old man, only half satisfied.

"But, uncle, what is under the trap-door?" persisted Capitola; "what's under it?"

"Oh, I don't know—an old cave that was once used as a dry cellar until an underground stream broke through and made it too damp, so it is said. I never explored it."

"But, uncle, what about the——"

Here Mrs. Condiment stretched out her foot and trod upon the toes of Capitola so sharply that it made her stop short, while she dexterously changed the conversation by asking the major if he would not send Wool to Tip-Top in the morning for another bag of coffee.

Soon after supper was over Capitola, saying that she was tired, bade her uncle good night, and, attended by her little black maid Pitapat, whom Mrs. Condiment had called up for the purpose, retired to her distant chamber. There were already collected here three trunks, which the liberality of her uncle had filled.

As soon as she had got in and locked the door she detached one of the strongest straps from her largest trunk and then turned up the rug and secured the end of the strap to the ring in the trap-door. Then she withdrew the bolt, and, holding on to one end of the strap, gently lowered the trap, and, kneeling, gazed down into an awful black void—without boundaries, without sight, without sounds, except a deep, faint, subterranean roaring as of water.

"Bring the light, Pitapat, and hold it over this place, and take care you don't fall in," said Capitola. "Come, as I've got a 'pit' in my name and you've got a 'pit' in yours, we'll see if we can't make something of this third 'pit.'"

"Deed, I'se 'fraid, Miss," said the poor little darkey.

"Afraid! What of?"

"Ghoses."

"Nonsense. I'll agree to lay every ghost you see!"

The little maid approached, candle in hand, but in such a gingerly sort of way, that Capitola seized the light from her hand, and, stooping, held it down as far as she could reach and gazed once more into the abyss. But this only made the horrible darkness "visible;" no object caught or reflected a single ray of light; all was black, hollow, void and silent except the faint, deep, distant, roaring as of subterraneous water!

Capitola pushed the light as far down as she could possibly reach, and then, yielding to a strange fascination, dropped it into the abyss! It went down, down, down, down into the darkness, until far below it glimmered out of sight. Then with an awful shudder Capitola pulled up and fastened the trap-door, laid down the rug and said her prayers and went to bed by the firelight, with little Pitapat sleeping on a pallet. The last thought of Cap, before falling to sleep, was:

"It is awful to go to bed over such a horrible mystery; but I will be a hero!"

CHAPTER XI.

A MYSTERY AND A STORM AT HURRICANE HALL.

Bid her address her prayers to Heaven!
Learn if she there may be forgiven;
Its mercy may absolve her yet!
But here upon this earth beneath
There is no spot where she and I
Together for an hour could breathe!

—BYRON.

Early the next morning Capitola arose, made her toilet and went out to explore the outer walls of her part of the old house, to discover, if possible, some external entrance into the unknown cavity under her room. It was a bright, cheerful, healthy autumnal morning, well adapted to dispel all clouds of mystery and superstition. Heaps of crimson and golden-hued leaves, glimmering with hoar frost, lay drifted against the old walls, and when these were brushed away by the busy hands of the young girl they revealed nothing but the old moldering foundation; not a vestige of a cellar-door or window was visible.

Capitola abandoned the fruitless search, and turned to go into the house. And saying to herself—

"I'll think no more of it! I dare say, after all, it is nothing but a very dark cellar without window and with a well, and the story of the murders and of the skeletons is all moonshine," she ran into the dining-room and took her seat at the breakfast table.

Old Hurricane was just then storming away at his factotum Wool for some misdemeanor, the nature of which Capitola did not hear, for upon her appearance he suffered his wrath to subside in a few reverberating, low thunders, gave his ward a grumphy "Good morning" and sat down to his breakfast.

After breakfast Old Hurricane took his great-coat and old cocked hat and stormed forth upon the plantation to blow up his lazy overseer, Mr. Will Ezy, and his idle negroes, who had loitered or frolicked away all the days of their master's absence.

Mrs. Condiment went away to mix a plum pudding for dinner, and Cap was left alone.

After wandering through the lower rooms of the house the stately, old-fashioned drawing-room, the family parlor, the dining-room, etc., Cap found her way through all the narrow back passages and steep little staircases back to her own chamber.

The chamber looked quite different by daylight—the cheerful wood fire burning in the chimney right before her, opposite the door by which she entered; the crimson draped windows, with the rich, old mahogany bureau and dressing-glass standing between them on her left; the polished, dark oak floor; the comfortable rocking chair; the new work-stand placed there for her use that morning and her own well-filled trunks standing in the corners, looked altogether too cheerful to associate with dark thoughts.

Besides, Capitola had not the least particle of gloom, superstition or marvelousness in her disposition. She loved old houses and old legends well enough to enjoy them; but was not sufficiently credulous to believe, or cowardly to fear, them.

She had, besides, a pleasant morning's occupation before her, in unpacking her three trunks and arranging her wardrobe and her possessions, which were all upon the most liberal scale, for Major Warfield at every city where they had stopped had given his poor little protégée a virtual *carte blanche* for purchases, having said to her:

"Capitola, I'm an old bachelor; I've not the least idea what a young girl requires; all I know is, that you have nothing but your clothes, and must want sewing and knitting needles and brushes and scissors and combs and boxes and smelling bottles and tooth powder and such. So come along with me to one of those Vanity Fairs they call fancy stores and get what you want; I'll foot the bill."

And Capitola, who firmly believed that she had the most sacred of claims upon Major Warfield, whose resources she also supposed to be unlimited, did not fail to indulge her taste for rich and costly toys and supplied herself with a large ivory dressing-case, lined with velvet and furnished with ivory-handled combs and brushes, silver boxes and crystal bottles, a papier-mâché work-box, with gold thimble, needle-case and perforator and gold-mounted scissors and winders; and an ebony writing-desk, with silver-mounted crystal standishes; each of these— boxes and desk—was filled with all things requisite in the several departments. And now as Capitola unpacked them and arranged them upon the top of her bureau, it was with no small degree of appreciation. The rest of the forenoon was spent in arranging the best articles of her wardrobe in her bureau drawers.

Having locked the remainder in her trunks and carefully smoothed her hair, and dressed herself in a brown merino, she went down-stairs and sought out Mrs. Condiment, whom she found in the housekeeper's little room, and to whom she said:

"Now, Mrs. Condiment, if uncle has any needlework wanted to be done, any buttons to be sewed on, or anything of that kind, just let me have it; I've got a beautiful work-box, and I'm just dying to use it."

"My dear Miss Black——"

"Please to call me Capitola, or even Cap. I never was called Miss Black in my life until I came here, and I don't like it at all!"

"Well, then, my dear Miss Cap, I wish you would wait till to-morrow, for I just came in here in a great hurry to get a glass of brandy out of the cupboard to put in the sauce for the plum-pudding, as dinner will be on the table in ten minutes."

With a shrug of her little shoulders, Capitola left the housekeeper's room and hurried through the central front hall and out at the front door, to look about and breathe the fresh air for a while.

As she stepped upon the front piazza she saw Major Warfield walking up the steep lawn, followed by Wool, leading a pretty mottled iron-gray pony, with a side-saddle on his back.

"Ah, I'm glad you're down, Cap! Come! look at this pretty pony! he is good for nothing as a working horse, and is too light to carry my weight, and so I intend to give him to you! You must learn to ride," said the old man, coming up the steps.

"Give him to me! I learn to ride! Oh, uncle! Oh, uncle! I shall go perfectly crazy with joy!" exclaimed Cap, dancing and clapping her hands with delight.

"Oh, well, a tumble or two in learning will bring you back to your senses, I reckon!"

"Oh, uncle! oh, uncle! When shall I begin?"

"You shall take your first tumble immediately after dinner, when, being well filled, you will not be so brittle and apt to break in falling!"

"Oh, uncle! I shall not fall! I feel I shan't! I feel I've a natural gift for holding on!"

"Come, come; get in! get in! I want my dinner!" said Old Hurricane, driving his ward in before him to the dining-room, where the dinner was smoking upon the table.

After dinner Cap, with Wool for a riding-master, took her first lesson in equestrianism. She had the four great requisites for forming a good rider—a well-adapted figure, a fondness for the exercise, perfect fearlessness and presence of mind. She was not once in danger of losing her seat, and during that single afternoon's exercise she made considerable progress in learning to manage her steed.

Old Hurricane, whom the genial autumn afternoon had tempted out to smoke his pipe in his armchair on the porch, was a pleased spectator of her performances, and expressed his opinion that in time she would become the best rider in the neighborhood, and that she should have the best riding-dress and cap that could be made at Tip Top.

Just now, in lack of an equestrian dress, poor Cap was parading around the lawn with her head bare and her hair flying and her merino skirt exhibiting more ankles than grace.

It was while Old Hurricane still sat smoking his pipe and making his comments and Capitola still ambled around and around the lawn that a horseman suddenly appeared galloping as fast as the steep nature of the ground would admit up toward the house, and before they could form an idea who he was the horse was at the block, and the rider dismounted and standing before Major Warfield.

"Why, Herbert, my boy, back so soon? We didn't expect you for a week to come. This is sudden, indeed! So much the better! so much the better! Glad to see you, lad!" exclaimed Old Hurricane, getting up and heartily shaking the hand of his nephew.

Capitola came ambling up, and in the effort to spring nimbly from her saddle tumbled off, much to the delight of Wool, who grinned from ear to ear, and of Old Hurricane, who, with an "I said so," burst into a roar of laughter.

Herbert Greyson sprang to assist her; but before he reached the spot Cap had picked herself up, straightened her disordered dress, and now she ran to meet and shake hands with him.

There was such a sparkle of joy and glow of affection in the meeting between these two that Old Hurricane, who saw it, suddenly hushed his laugh and grunted to himself:

"Humph! humph! humph! I like that; that's better than I could have planned myself; let that go on, and then, Gabe Le Noir, we'll see under what name and head the old divided manor will be held!"

Before his mental soliloquy was concluded, Herbert and Capitola came up to him. He welcomed Herbert again with great cordiality, and then called to his man to put up the horses, and bade the young people to follow him into the house, as the air was getting chilly.

"And how did you find your good friends, lad?" inquired Old Hurricane, when they had reached the sitting parlor.

"Oh, very well, sir! and very grateful for your offered kindness; and, indeed, so anxious to express their gratitude—that—that I shortened my visit and came away immediately to tell you."

"Right, lad, right! You come by the down coach?"

"Yes, sir, and got off at Tip Top, where I hired a horse to bring me here. I must ask you to let one of your men take him back to Mr. Merry at the Antler's Inn to-morrow."

"Surely, surely, lad! Wool shall do it!"

"And so, Herbert, the poor woman was delighted at the prospect of better times?" said Old Hurricane, with a little glow of benevolent self-satisfaction.

"Oh, yes, sir; delighted beyond all measure!"

"Poor thing! poor thing! See, young folks, how easy it is for the wealthy, by sparing a little of their superfluous means, to make the poor and virtuous happy! And the boy, Herbert, the boy?"

"Oh, sir! delighted for himself, but still more delighted for his mother; for her joy was such as to astonish and even alarm me! Before that I had thought Marah Rocke a proud woman, but— —"

"What!—say that again!" exclaimed Major Warfield. "I say that I thought she was a proud woman, but——"

"Thought who was a proud woman, sir?" roared Old Hurricane.

"Marah Rocke!" replied the young man, with wonder.

Major Warfield started up, seized the chair upon which he had sat and struck it upon the ground with such force as to shatter it to pieces; then turning, he strode up and down the floor with such violence that the two young people gazed after him in consternation and fearful expectancy. Presently he turned suddenly, strode up to Herbert Greyson and stood before him.

His face was purple, his veins swollen and they stood out upon his forehead like cords, his eyes were protruded and glaring, his mouth clenched until the grizzly gray mustache and beard were drawn in, his whole huge frame was quivering from head to foot. It was impossible to tell what passion—whether rage, grief or shame—the most possessed him, for all three seemed tearing his giant frame to pieces.

For an instant he stood speechless, and Herbert feared that he would fall into a fit; but the old giant was too strong for that! For one short moment he stood thus, and in a terrible voice he asked:

"Young man, did you—did you know—the shame that you dashed into my face with the name of that woman?"

"Sir, I know nothing but that she is the best and dearest of her sex!" exclaimed Herbert, beyond all measure amazed at what he heard and saw.

"Best and dearest!" thundered the old man. "Oh, idiot; is she still a siren, and are you a dupe? But that cannot be! No, sir! it is I whom you both would dupe! Ah, I see it all now! This is why you artfully concealed her name from me until you had won my promise! It shall not serve either you or her, sir! I break my promise thus!" bending and snapping his own cane and flinging the fragments behind his back. "There, sir! when you can make those ends of dry cedar grow together again and bear green leaves, you may hope to reconcile Ira Warfield and Marah Rocke! I break my promise, sir, as she broke——"

The old man suddenly sank back into the nearest chair, dropped his shaggy head and face into his hands and remained trembling from head to foot, while the convulsive heaving of his chest and the rising and falling of his huge shoulders betrayed that his heart was nearly bursting with such suppressed sobs as only can be forced from manhood by the fiercest anguish.

The young people looked on in wonder, awe and pity; and then their eyes met—those of Herbert silently inquired:

"What can all this mean?" Those of Capitola mutely answered:

"Heaven only knows!"

In his deep pity for the old man's terrible anguish, Herbert could feel no shame or resentment for the false accusation made upon himself. Indeed, his noble and candid nature easily explained all as the ravings of some heartrending remembrance. Waiting, therefore, until the violent convulsions of the old man's frame had somewhat subsided, Herbert went to him, and with a low and respectful inflection of voice, said:

"Uncle, if you think that there was any collusion between myself and Mrs. Rocke you wrong us both. You will remember that when I met you in New York I had not seen or heard from her for years, nor had I then any expectation of ever seeing you. The subject of the poor widow came up between us accidentally, and if it is true that I omitted to call her by name it must have been because we both then felt too tenderly by her to call her anything else but 'the poor widow, the poor mother, the good woman,' and so on—and all this she is still."

The old man, without raising his head, held out one hand to his nephew, saying in a voice still trembling with emotion:

"Herbert, I wronged you; forgive me."

Herbert took and pressed that rugged and hairy old hand to his lips, and said:

"Uncle, I do not in the least know what is the cause of your present emotion, but——"

"Emotion! Demmy, sir, what do you mean by emotion? Am I a man to give way to emotion? Demmy, sir, mind what you say!" roared the old lion, getting up and shaking himself free of all weaknesses.

"I merely meant to say, sir, that if I could possibly be of any service to you I am entirely at your orders."

"Then go back to that woman and tell her never to dare to utter, or even to think of, my name again, if she values her life!"

"Sir, you do not mean it! and as for Mrs. Rocke, she is a good woman I feel it my duty to uphold!"

"Good! ugh! ugh! ugh! I'll command myself! I'll not give way again! Good! ah, lad, it is quite plain to me now that you are an innocent dupe. Tell me now, for instance, do you know anything of that woman's life before she came to reside at Staunton?"

"Nothing; but from what I've seen of her since I'm sure she always was good."

"Did she never mention her former life at all?"

"Never; but, mind, I hold to my faith in her, and would stake my salvation on her integrity," said Herbert, warmly.

"Then you'd lose it, lad, that's all; but I have an explanation to make to you, Herbert. You must give me a minute or two of your company alone, in the library, before tea."

And so saying, Major Warfield arose and led the way across the hall to the library, that was immediately back of the back drawing-room.

Throwing himself into a leathern chair beside the writing-table, he motioned for his companion to take the one on the opposite side. A low fire smoldering on the hearth before them so dimly lighted the room that the young man arose again to pull the bell rope; but the other interrupted with:

"No, you need not ring for lights, Herbert! my story is one that should be told in the dark. Listen, lad; but drop your eyes the while."

"I am all attention, sir!"

"Herbert, the poet says that—

"'At thirty man suspects himself a fool,
Knows it at forty and reforms his rule.'

"But, boy, at the ripe age of forty-five, I succeeded in achieving the most sublime folly of my life. I should have taken a degree in madness and been raised to a professor's chair in some college of lunacy! Herbert, at the age of forty-five I fell in love with and married a girl of sixteen out of a log cabin! merely, forsooth, because she had a pearly skin like the leaf of the white japonica, soft gray eyes like a timid fawn's and a voice like a cooing turtle dove's! because those delicate cheeks flushed and those soft eyes fell when I spoke to her, and the cooing voice trembled when she replied! because the delicate face brightened when I came and faded when I turned away! because—

"'She wept with delight when I gave her a smile,
And trembled with fear at my frown,' etc.;

because she adored me as a sort of god, I loved her as an angel and married her—married her secretly, for fear of the ridicule of my brother officers, put her in a pastoral log cabin in the woods below the block-house and visited her there by stealth, like Numa did his nymph in the cave. But I was watched; my hidden treasure was discovered and coveted by a younger and prettier follow than myself. Perdition! I cannot tell this story in detail! One night I came home very late and quite unexpectedly and found—this man in my wife's cabin! I broke the man's head and ribs and left him for dead. I tore the woman out of my heart and cauterized its bleeding wounds. This man was Gabriel Le Noir! Satan burn him forever! This woman was Marah Rocke, God forgive her! I could have divorced the woman, but as I did not dream of ever marrying again, I did not care to drag my shame before a public tribunal. There! You know all! Let the subject sink forever!" said Old Hurricane, wiping great drops of sweat from his laboring brows.

"Uncle, I have heard your story and believe you, of course. But I am bound to tell you that without even having heard your poor wife's defense, I believe and uphold her to be innocent! I think you have been as grossly deceived as she has been fearfully wronged and that time and Providence will prove this!" exclaimed Herbert, fervently.

A horrible laugh of scorn was his only answer as Old Hurricane arose, shook himself and led the way back to the parlor.

CHAPTER XII.

MARAH'S DREAM.

And now her narrow kitchen walls
Stretched away into stately halls;
The weary wheel to a spinnet turned,
The tallow candle an astral burned;
A manly form at her side she saw,
And joy was duty and love was law.

—WHITTIER.

On the same Saturday morning that Herbert Greyson hurried away from his friend's cottage, to travel post to Hurricane Hall, for the sole purpose of accelerating the coming of her good fortune, Marah Rocke walked about the house with a step so light, with eyes so bright and cheeks so blooming, that one might have thought that years had rolled backward in their course and made her a young girl again.

Traverse gazed upon her in delight. Reversing the words of the text, he said:

"We must call you no longer Marah (which is bitter), but we must call you Naomi (which is beautiful), mother!"

"Young flatterer!" she answered, smiling and slightly flushing. "But tell me truly, Traverse, am I very much faded? Have care and toil and grief made me look old?"

"You old?" exclaimed the boy, running his eyes over her beaming face and graceful form with a look of non-comprehension that might have satisfied her, but did not, for she immediately repeated:

"Yes; do I look old? Indeed I do not ask from vanity, child? Ah, it little becomes me to be vain; but I do wish to look well in some one's eyes."

"I wish there was a looking-glass in the house, mother, that it might tell you; you should be called Naomi instead of Marah."

"Ah! that is just what he used to say to me in the old, happy time—the time in Paradise, before the serpent entered!"

"What 'he,' mother?"

"Your father, boy, of course."

That was the first time she had ever mentioned his father to her son, and now she spoke of him with such a flush of joy and hope that even while her words referred darkly to the past, her eyes looked brightly to the future. All this, taken with the events of the preceding evening, greatly bewildered the mind of Traverse and agitated him with the wildest conjectures.

"Mother, will you tell me about my father, and also what it is beyond this promised kindness of Major Warfield that has made you so happy?" he asked.

"Not now, my boy; dear boy, not now. I must not—I cannot—I dare not yet! Wait a few days and you shall know all. Oh, it is hard to keep a secret from my boy! but then it is not only my secret, but another's! You do not think hard of me for withholding it now, do you, Traverse?" she asked, affectionately.

"No, dear mother, of course I don't. I know you must be right, and I am glad to see you happy."

"Happy! Oh, boy, you don't know how happy I am! I did not think any human being could ever feel so joyful in this erring world, much less me! One cause of this excess of joyful feeling must be from the contrast; else it were dreadful to be so happy."

"Mother, I don't know what you mean," said Traverse uneasily, for he was too young to understand these paradoxes of feeling and thought, and there were moments when he feared for his mother's reason.

"Oh, Traverse, think of it! eighteen long, long years of estrangement, sorrow and dreadful suspense! eighteen long, long, weary years of patience against anger and loving against hatred and hoping against despair! your young mind cannot grasp it! your very life is not so long! I was seventeen then; I am thirty-five now. And after wasting all my young years of womanhood in loving, hoping, longing— lo! the light of life has dawned at last!"

"God save you, mother!" said the boy, fervently, for her wild, unnatural joy continued to augment his anxiety.

"Ah, Traverse, I dare not tell you the secret now, and yet I am always letting it out, because my heart overflows from its fulness. Ah, boy! many, many weary nights have I lain awake from grief; but last night I lay awake from joy! Think of it!"

The boy's only reply to this was a deep sigh. He was becoming seriously alarmed. "I never saw her so excited! I wish she would get calm," was his secret thought. Then, with the design of changing the current of her ideas, he took off his coat and said:

"Mother, my pocket is half torn out, and though there's no danger of my losing a great deal out of it, still I'll get you, please, to sew it in while I mend the fence!"

"Sew the pocket! mend the fence! Well!" smiled Mrs. Rocke; "we'll do so if it will amuse you. The mended fence will be a convenience to the next tenant, and the patched coat will do for some poor boy. Ah, Traverse, we must be very good to the poor, in more ways than in giving them what we do not ourselves need, for we shall know what it is to have been poor," she concluded, in more serious tones than she had yet used.

Traverse was glad of this, and went out to his work feeling somewhat better satisfied.

The delirium of happiness lasted intermittently a whole week, during the last three days of which Mrs. Rocke was constantly going to the door and looking up the road, as if expecting some one. The mail came from Tip-Top to Staunton only once a week—on Saturday mornings. Therefore, when Saturday came again, she sent her son to the post-office, saying:

"If they do not come to-day they will surely write."

Traverse hastened with all his speed, and got there so soon that he had to wait for the mail to be opened.

Meanwhile, at home the widow walked the floor in restless, joyous anticipation, or went to the door and strained her eyes up the road to watch for Traverse, and perhaps for some one else's coming. At last she discerned her son, who came down the road walking rapidly, smiling triumphantly and holding a letter up to view.

She ran out of the gate to meet him, seized and kissed the letter, and then, with her face burning, her heart palpitating and her fingers trembling, she hastened into the house, threw herself into the little low chair by the fire and opened the letter. It was from Herbert, and read thus:

"HURRICANE HALL, Nov. 30th, 1843.

"MY DEAREST AND BEST MRS. ROCKE—May God strengthen you to read the few bitter lines I have to write. Most unhappily, Major Warfield did not know exactly who you were when he promised so much. Upon learning your name he withdrew all his promises. At night, in his library, he told me all your early history. Having heard all, the very worst, I believe you as pure as an angel. So I told him! So I would uphold with my life and seal with my death! Trust yet in God, and believe in the earnest respect and affection of your grateful and attached son,

"HERBERT GREYSON.

"P.S.—For henceforth I shall call you mother."

Quietly she finished reading, pressed the letter again to her lips, reached it to the fire, saw it like her hopes shrivel up to ashes, and then she arose, and with her trembling fingers clinging together, walked up and down the floor.

There were no tears in her eyes, but, oh! such a look of unutterable woe on her pale, blank, despairing face!

Traverse watched her and saw that something had gone frightfully wrong; that some awful revolution of fate or revulsion of feeling had passed over her in this dread hour!

Cautiously he approached her, gently he laid his hand upon her shoulder, tenderly he whispered:

"Mother!"

She turned and looked strangely at him, then exclaiming:

"Oh, Traverse, how happy I was this day week!" She burst into a flood of tears.

Traverse threw his arm around his mother's waist and half coaxed and half bore her to her low chair and sat her in it and knelt by her side and, embracing her fondly, whispered:

"Mother, don't weep so bitterly! You have me; am I nothing? Mother, I love you more than son ever loved his mother, or suitor his sweetheart, or husband his wife! Oh! is my love nothing, mother?"

Only sobs answered him.

"Mother," he pleaded, "you are all the world to me; let me be all the world to you! I can be it, mother; I can be it; try me! I will make every effort for my mother, and the Lord will bless us!"

Still no answer but convulsive sobs.

"Oh, mother, mother! I will try to do for you more than ever son did for mother or man for woman before! Dear mother, if you will not break my heart by weeping so!"

The sobbing abated a little, partly from exhaustion and partly from the soothing influences of the boy's loving words.

"Listen, dear mother, what I will do! In the olden times of chivalry, young knights bound themselves by sacred vows to the service of some lady, and labored long and perilously in her honor. For her, blood was spilled; for her, fields were won; but, mother, never yet toiled knight in the battlefield for his lady-love as I will in the battle of life for my dearest lady—my own mother!"

She reached out her hand and silently pressed his.

"Come, come," said Traverse; "lift up your head and smile! We are young yet—both you and I! for, after all, you are not much older than your son; and we two will journey up and down the hills of life together—all in all to each other; and when at last we are old, as we shall be when you are seventy-seven and I am sixty, we will leave all our fortune that we shall have made to found a home for widows and orphans, as we were, and we will pass out and go to heaven together."

Now, indeed, this poor, modern Hagar looked up and smiled at the oddity of her Ishmael's far-reaching thought.

In that poor household grief might not be indulged. Marah Rocke took down her work-basket and sat down to finish a lot of shirts, and Traverse went out with his horse and saw to look for a job at cutting wood for twenty-five cents a cord. Small beginnings of the fortune that was to found and endow asylums! but many a fortune has been commenced upon less!

Marah Rocke had managed to dismiss her boy with a smile, but that was the last effort of nature; as soon as he was gone and she found herself alone, tear after tear welled up in her eyes and rolled down her pale cheeks; sigh after sigh heaved her bosom.

Ah! the transitory joy of the past week had been but the lightning's arrowy course scathing where it illumined!

She felt as if this last blow that had struck her down from the height of hope to the depth of despair had broken her heart, as if the power of reaction was gone, and she mourned as one who would not be comforted.

While she sat thus the door opened, and before she was aware of his presence, Herbert Greyson entered the room and came softly to her side. Ere she could speak to him he dropped upon one knee at her feet and bowed his young head lowly over the hand that he took and pressed to his lips. Then he arose and stood before her. This was not unnatural or exaggerated; it was his way of expressing the reverential sympathy and compassion he felt for her strange, life-long martyrdom.

"Herbert, you here? Why, we only got your letter this morning," she said, in tones of gentle inquiry, as she arose and placed a chair for him.

"Yes, I could not bear to stay away from you at such a time; I came up in the same mail-coach that brought my letter; but I kept myself out of Traverse's sight, for I could not bear to intrude upon you in the first hour of your disappointment," said Herbert, in a broken voice.

"Oh, that need not have kept you away, dear boy! I did not cry much; I am used to trouble, you know; I shall get over this also—after a little while—and things will go on in the old way," said Marah Rocke, struggling to repress the rising emotion that, however, overcame her, for, dropping her head upon her "sailor boy's" shoulder, she burst into a flood of tears and wept plenteously.

"Dear mother, be comforted!" he said; "dear mother, be comforted!"

CHAPTER XIII.

MARAH'S MEMORIES.

In the shade of the apple-tree again
She saw a rider draw his rein,
And gazing down with a timid grace,
She felt his pleased eyes read her face.

—WHITTIER.

"Dear Marah, I cannot understand your strong attachment to that bronzed and grizzled old man, who has, besides, treated you so barbarously," said Herbert.

"Is he bronzed and gray?" asked Marah, looking up with gentle pity in her eyes and tone.

"Why, of course he is. He is sixty-two."

"He was forty-five when I first knew him, and he was very handsome then. At least, I thought him the very perfection of manly strength and beauty and goodness. True, it was the mature, warm beauty of the Indian summer, for he was more than middle-aged; but it was very genial to the chilly, loveless morning of my own early life," said Marah, dropping her head upon her hand and sliding into reminiscences of the past.

"Dear Marah, I wish you would tell me all about your marriage and misfortunes," said Herbert, in a tone of the deepest sympathy and respect.

"Yes, he was very handsome," continued Mrs. Rocke, speaking more to herself than to her companion; "his form was tall, full and stately; his complexion warm, rich and glowing; his fine face was lighted up by a pair of strong, dark-gray eyes, full of fire and tenderness, and was surrounded by waving masses of jet-black hair and whiskers; they are gray now, you say, Herbert?"

"Gray and grizzled, and bristling up around his hard face like thorn-bushes around a rock in winter!" said Herbert, bluntly, for it enraged his honest but inexperienced boyish heart to hear this wronged woman speak so enthusiastically.

"Ah! it is winter with him now; but then it was glorious Indian summer! He was a handsome, strong and ardent man. I was a young, slight, pale girl, with no beauty but the cold and colorless beauty of a statue; with no learning but such as I had picked up from a country school; with no love to bless my lonely life—for I was a friendless orphan, without either parents or relatives, and living by sufferance in a cold and loveless home."

"Poor girl!" murmured Herbert, in almost inaudible tones.

"Our log cabin stood beside the military road leading through the wilderness to the fort where he was stationed. And, oh! when he came riding by each day upon his noble, coal-black steed and in his martial uniform, looking so vigorous, handsome and kingly, he seemed to me almost a god to worship! Sometimes he drew rein in front of the old oak tree that stood in front of our cabin to breathe his horse or to ask for a draught of water. I used to bring it to him. Oh! then, when he looked at me, his eyes seemed to send new warmth to my chilled heart; when he spoke, too, his tones seemed to strengthen me; while he stayed his presence seemed to protect me!"

"Aye, such protection as vultures give to doves—covering and devouring them," muttered Herbert to himself. Mrs. Rocke, too absorbed in her reminiscences to heed his interruptions, continued:

"One day he asked me to be his wife. I do not know what I answered. I only know that when I understood what he meant, my heart trembled with instinctive terror at its own excessive joy! We were privately married by the chaplain at the fort. There were no accommodations for the wives of officers there. And, besides, my husband did not wish to announce our marriage until he was ready to take me to his princely mansion in Virginia."

"Humph!" grunted Herbert inwardly, for comment.

"But he built for me a pretty cabin in the woods below the fort, furnished it simply and hired a half-breed Indian woman to wait on me. Oh, I was too happy! To my wintry spring of life summer had come, warm, rich and beautiful! There is a clause in the marriage service which enjoins the husband to cherish his wife. I do not believe many people ever stop to think how much is in that word. He did; he cherished my little, thin, chill, feeble life until I became strong, warm and healthful. Oh! even as the blessed sun warms and animates and glorifies the earth, causing it to brighten with life and blossom with flowers and bloom with fruit, so did my husband enrich and cherish and bless my life! Such happiness could not and it did not last!"

"Of course not!" muttered Herbert to himself.

"At first the fault was in myself. Yes, Herbert it was! you need not look incredulous or hope to cast all the blame on him! Listen: Happy, grateful, adoring as I was, I was also shy, timid and bashful—never proving the deep love I bore my husband except by the most perfect self-abandonment to his will. All this deep, though quiet, devotion he understood as mere passive obedience void of love. As this continued he grew uneasy, and often asked me if I cared for him at all, or if it were possible for a young girl like me to love an old man like himself."

"A very natural question," thought Herbert.

"Well, I used to whisper in answer, 'Yes,' and still 'Yes.' But this never satisfied Major Warfield. One day, when he asked me if I cared for him the least in the world, I suddenly answered that if he were to die I should throw myself across his grave and lie there until death should release me! whereupon he broke into a loud laugh, saying, 'Methinks the lady doth protest too much.' I was already blushing deeply at the unwonted vehemence of my own words, although I had spoken only as I felt—the very, very truth. But his laugh and his test so increased my confusion that, in fine, that was the first and last time I ever did protest! Like Lear's Cordelia, I was tongue-tied—I had no words to assure him. Sometimes I wept to think how poor I was in resources to make him happy. Then came another annoyance—my name and fame were freely discussed at the fort."

"A natural consequence," sighed Herbert.

"The younger officers discovered my woodland home, and often stole out to reconnoitre my calm. Among them was Captain Le Noir, who, after he had discovered my retreat, picked acquaintance with Lura, my attendant. Making the woodland sports his pretext, he haunted the vicinity of my cabin, often stopping at the door to beg a cup of water, which, of course, was never denied, or else to offer a bunch of partridges or a brace of rabbits or some other game, the sports of his gun, which equally, of course, was never accepted. One beautiful morning in June, finding my cabin door open and myself alone, he ventured unbidden across my threshold, and by his free conversation and bold admiration offended and alarmed me. Some days afterward, in the mess-room at the fort, being elevated by wine, he boasted among his messmates of the intimate terms of friendly acquaintance upon which he falsely asserted that he had the pleasure of standing with 'Warfield's pretty little favorite,' as he insolently called me. When my husband heard of this I learned for the first time the terrific violence of his temper. It was awful! it frightened me almost to death. There was a duel, of course. Le Noir was very dangerously wounded, scarred across the face for life, and was confined many weeks to his bed. Major Warfield was also slightly hurt and laid up at the fort for a few days, during which I was not permitted to see him."

"Is it possible that even then he did not see your danger and acknowledge your marriage and call you to his bedside?" inquired Herbert, impatiently.

"No, no! if he had all after suffering had been spared. No! at the end of four days he came back to me; but we met only for bitter reproaches on his part and sorrowful tears on mine. He charged me with coldness, upon account of the disparity in our years, and of the preference for Captain Le Noir, because he was a pretty fellow, I knew this was not true of me. I knew that I loved my husband's very footprints better than I did the whole human race besides; but I could not tell him so then. Oh, in those days, though my heart was so full, I had so little power of utterance! There he stood before me! he that had been so ruddy and buoyant, now so pale from loss of blood, and so miserable, that I could have fallen and groveled at his feet in sorrow and remorse at not being able to make him happy!"

"There are some persons whom we can never make happy. It is not in them to be so," commented Herbert.

"He made me promise never to see or to speak to Le Noir again—a promise eagerly given but nearly impossible to keep. My husband spent as much time with me as he possibly could spare from his military duties, and looked forward with impatience to the autumn, when it was thought that he would be at liberty to take me home. He often used to tell me that we should spend our Christmas at his house, Hurricane Hall, and that I should play Lady Bountiful and distribute Christmas gifts to the negroes and that they would love me. And, oh! with what joy I anticipated that time of honor and safety and careless ease, as an acknowledged wife, in the home of my husband! There, too, I fondly believed, our child would be born. All his old tenderness returned for me, and I was as happy, if not as wildly joyful, as at first."

"'Twas but a lull in the storm," said Herbert.

"Aye! 'twas but a lull in the storm, or, rather, before the storm! I do think that from the time of that duel Le Noir had resolved upon our ruin. As soon as he was able to go out he haunted the woods around my cabin and continually lay in wait for me. I could not go out even in the company of my maid Lura to pick blackberries or wild plums or gather forest roses, or to get fresh water at the spring, without being intercepted by Le Noir and his offensive admiration. He seemed to be ubiquitous! He met me everywhere—except in the presence of Major Warfield. I did not tell my husband, because I feared that if I did he would have killed Le Noir and died for the deed."

"Humph! it would have been 'good riddance of bad rubbish' in both cases," muttered Herbert, under his teeth.

"But instead of telling him I confined myself strictly to my cabin. One fatal day my husband, on leaving me in the morning, said that I need not wait up for him at night, for that it would be very late when he came, even if he came at all. He kissed me very fondly when he went away. Alas! alas! it was the last—last time! At night I went to bed disappointed, yet still so expectant that I could not sleep. I know not how long I had waited thus, or how late it was when I heard a tap at the outer door, and heard the bolt undrawn and a footstep enter and a low voice asking:

"Is she asleep?" and Lura's reply in the affirmative. Never doubting it was my husband, I lay there in pleased expectation of his entrance. He came in and began to take off his coat in the dark. I spoke, telling him that there were matches on the bureau. He did not reply, at which I was surprised; but before I could repeat my words the outer door was burst violently open, hurried footsteps crossed the entry, a light flashed into my room, my husband stood in the door in full military uniform, with a light in his hand and the aspect of an avenging demon on his brow, and——

"Horror upon horrors! the half-undressed man in my chamber was Captain Le Noir! I saw and swooned away!"

"But you were saved! you were saved!" gasped Herbert, white with emotion.

"Oh, I was saved, but not from sorrow—not from shame! I awoke from that deadly swoon to find myself alone, deserted, cast away! Oh, torn out from the warmth and light and safety of my husband's heart, and hurled forth shivering, faint and helpless upon the bleak world! and all this in twenty-four hours. Ah, I did not lack the power of expression then! happiness had never given it to me! anguish conferred it upon me; that one fell stroke of fate cleft the rock of silence in my soul, and the fountain of utterance gushed freely forth! I wrote to him, but my letters might as well have been dropped into a well. I went to him, but was spurned away. I prayed him with tears to have pity on our unborn babe; but he laughed aloud in scorn and called it by an opprobrious name! Letters, prayers, tears, were all in vain. He never had acknowledged our marriage; he now declared that he never would do so; he discarded me, disowned my child and forbade us ever to take his name!"

"Oh, Marah! and you but seventeen years of age! without a father or a brother or a friend in the world to employ an advocate!" exclaimed Herbert, covering his face with his hands and sinking back.

"Nor would I have used any of these agencies had I possessed them! If my wifehood and motherhood, my affections and my helplessness were not advocates strong enough to win my cause, I could not have borne to employ others!"

"Oh, Marah, with none to pity or to help; it was monstrous to have abandoned you so!"

"No; hush! consider the overwhelming evidence against me; I considered it even in the tempest and whirlwind of my anguish, and never once blamed and never once was angry with my husband; for I knew—not life, but the terrible circumstantial evidence had ruined me!"

"Ay, but did you not explain it to him?"

"How could I, alas! when I did not understand it myself? How Le Noir knew that Major Warfield was not expected home that fatal night—how he got into my house, whether by conspiring with my little maid or by deceiving her—or, lastly, how Major Warfield came to burst in upon him so suddenly, I did not know, and do not to this day."

"But you told Major Warfield all that you have told me?"

"Oh, yes! again and again, calling heaven to witness my truth! In vain! he had seen with his own eyes, he said. Against all I could say or do there was built up a wall of scornful incredulity, on which I might have dashed my brains out to no purpose."

"Oh, Marah, Marah! with none to pity or to save!" again exclaimed Herbert.

"Yes," said the meek creature, bowing her head; "God pitied and helped me! First he sent me a son that grew strong and handsome in body, good and wise in soul. Then He kept alive in my heart faith and hope and charity. He enabled me, through long years of unremitting and ill-requited toil, to live on, loving against anger, waiting against time, and hoping against despair!"

"Why did you leave your western home and come to Staunton, Marah?" asked Herbert.

"To be where I could sometimes hear of my husband without intruding on him. I took your widowed mother in, because she was his sister, though I never told her who I was, lest she should wrong and scorn me, as he had done. When she died I cherished you, Herbert, first because you were his nephew, but now, dear boy, for your own sake also."

"And I, while I live, will be a son to you, madam! I will be your constant friend at Hurricane Hall. He talks of making me his heir. Should he persist in such blind injustice, the day I come into the property I shall turn it all over to his widow and son. But I do not believe that he will persist; I, for my part, still hope for the best."

"I also hope for the best, for whatever God wills is sure to happen, and His will is surely the best! Yes, Herbert, I also hope—beyond the grave!" said Marah Rocke, with a wan smile.

The little clock that stood between the tall, plated candlesticks on the mantel-piece struck twelve, and Marah rose from her seat, saying:

"Traverse, poor fellow, will be home to his dinner. Not a word to him, Herbert, please! I do not wish the poor lad to know how much he has lost, and above all, I do not wish him to be prejudiced against his father."

"You are right, Marah," said Herbert, "for if he were told, the natural indignation that your wrongs would arouse in his heart would totally unfit him to meet his father in a proper spirit in that event for which I still hope—a future and a perfect family union!"

Herbert Greyson remained a week with his friends, during which time he paid the quarter's rent, and relieved his adopted mother of that cause of anxiety. Then he took leave and departed for Hurricane Hall, on his way to Washington City, where he was immediately going to pass his examination and await his appointment.

CHAPTER XIV.

THE WASTING HEART.

Then she took up the burden of life again
Saying only, "It might have been."
Alas for them both, alas for us all,
Who vainly the dreams of youth recall;
For of all sad words of lips, or pen,
The saddest are these—"It might have been."

—Whittier.

By the tacit consent of all parties, the meteor hope that had crossed and vanished from Marah Rocke's path of life was never mentioned again. Mother and son went about their separate tasks. Traverse worked at jobs all day, studied at night and went twice a week to recite his lessons to his patron, Doctor Day, at Willow Hill. Marah sewed as usual all day, and prepared her boy's meals at the proper times. But day by day her cheeks grew paler, her form thinner, her step fainter. Her son saw this decline with great alarm. Sometimes he found her in a deep, troubled reverie, from which she would awaken with heavy sighs. Sometimes he surprised her in tears. At such times he did not trouble her with questions that he instinctively felt she could not or would not answer; but he came gently to her side, put his arms about her neck, stooped and laid her face against his breast and whispered assurances of "his true love" and his boyish hopes of "getting on," of "making a fortune" and bringing "brighter days" for her.

And she would return his caresses, and with a faint smile reply that he "must not mind" her, that she was only "a little low-spirited," that she would "get over it soon."

But as day followed day, she grew visibly thinner and weaker; dark shadows settled under her hollow eyes and in her sunken cheeks. One evening, while standing at the table washing up their little tea service, she suddenly dropped into her chair and fainted. Nothing could exceed the alarm and distress of poor Traverse. He hastened to fix her in an easy position, bathed her face in vinegar and water, the only restoratives in their meager stock, and called upon her by every loving epithet to live and speak to him. The fit yielded to his efforts, and presently, with a few fluttering inspirations, her breath returned and her eyes opened. Her very first words were attempts to reassure her dismayed boy. But Traverse could no more be flattered. He entreated his mother to go at once to bed. And though the next morning, when she arose, she looked not worse than usual, Traverse left home with a heart full of trouble. But instead of turning down the street to go to his work in the town he turned up the street toward the wooded hills beyond, now glowing in their gorgeous autumn foliage and burning in the brilliant morning sun.

A half-hour's walk brought him to a high and thickly wooded hill, up which a private road led through a thicket of trees to a handsome graystone country seat, situated in the midst of beautifully ornamented grounds and known as Willow Heights, the residence of Dr. William Day, a retired physician of great repute, and a man of earnest piety. He was a widower with one fair daughter, Clara, a girl of fourteen, then absent at boarding-school. Traverse had never seen this girl, but his one great admiration was the beautiful Willow Heights and its worthy proprietor. He opened the highly ornate iron gate and entered up an avenue of willows that led up to the house, a two-storied edifice of graystone, with full-length front piazzas above and below.

Arrived at the door he rang the bell, which was answered promptly by a good-humored-looking negro boy, who at once showed Traverse to the library upstairs, where the good doctor sat at his books. Dr. Day was at this time about fifty years of age, tall and stoutly built, with a fine head and face, shaded by soft, bright flaxen hair and beard: thoughtful and kindly dark-blue eyes, and an earnest, penetrating smile that reached like sunshine the heart of any one upon whom it shone. He wore a cheerful-looking flowered chintz dressing-gown corded around his waist; his feet were thrust into embroidered slippers, and he sat in his elbow-chair at his reading-table poring over a huge folio volume. The whole aspect of the man and of his surroundings was kindly cheerfulness. The room opened upon the upper front piazza, and the windows were all up to admit the bright, morning sun and genial air, at the same time that there was a glowing fire in the grate to temper its chilliness. Traverse's soft step across the carpeted floor was not heard by the doctor, who was only made aware of his presence by his stepping between the sunshine and his table. Then the doctor arose, and with his intense smile extended his hand and greeted the boy with:

"Well, Traverse, lad, you are always welcome! I did not expect you until night, as usual, but as you are here, so much the better. Got your exercises all ready, eh? Heaven bless you, lad, what is the matter?" inquired the good man, suddenly, on first observing the boy's deeply troubled looks.

"My mother sir! my mother!" was all that Traverse could at first utter.

"Your mother! My dear lad, what about her? Is she ill?" inquired the doctor, with interest.

"Oh, sir, I am afraid she is going to die?" exclaimed the boy in a choking voice, struggling hard to keep from betraying his manhood by bursting into tears.

"Going to die! Oh, pooh, pooh, pooh! she is not going to die, lad. Tell me all about it," said the doctor in an encouraging tone.

"She has had so much grief and care and anxiety, sir—doctor, is there any such malady as a broken heart?"

"Broken heart? Pooh, pooh! no, my child, no! never heard of such a thing in thirty years' medical experience! Even that story of a porter who broke his heart trying to lift a ton of stone is all a fiction. No such a disease as a broken heart. But tell me about your mother."

"It is of her that I am talking. She has had so much trouble in her life, and now I think she is sinking under it; she has been failing for weeks, and last night while washing the teacups she fainted away from the table!"

"Heaven help us! that looks badly," said the doctor.

"Oh, does it?—does it, sir? She said it was 'nothing much.' Oh, doctor, don't say she will die—don't! If she were to die, if mother were to die, I'd give right up! I never should do a bit of good in the world, for she is all the motive I have in this life! To study hard, to work hard and make her comfortable and happy, so as to make up to her for all she has suffered, is my greatest wish and endeavor! Oh, don't say mother will die! it would ruin me!" cried Traverse.

"My dear boy, I don't say anything of the sort! I say, judging from your account, that her health must be attended to immediately. And—true I have retired from practice, but I will go and see your mother, Traverse."

"Oh, sir, if you only would! I came to ask you to do that very thing. I should not have presumed to ask such a favor for any cause but this of my dear mother's life and health, and—you will go to see her?"

"Willingly and without delay, Traverse," said the good man, rising immediately and hurrying into an adjoining chamber.

"Order the gig while I dress, Traverse, and I will take you back with me," he added, as he closed the chamber door behind him.

By the time Traverse had gone down, given the necessary orders and returned to the library the doctor emerged from his chamber, buttoned up his gray frock-coat and booted, gloved and capped for the ride.

They went down together, entered the gig and drove rapidly down the willow avenue, slowly through the iron gate and through the dark thicket and down the wooded hill to the high road, and then as fast as the sorrel mare could trot toward town. In fifteen minutes the doctor pulled up his gig at the right-hand side of the road before the cottage gate.

They entered the cottage, Traverse going first in order to announce the doctor. They found Mrs. Rocke, as usual, seated in her low chair by the little fire, bending over her needlework. She looked up with surprise as they came in.

"Mother, this is Doctor Day, come to see you," said Traverse.

She arose from her chair and raised those soft and timid dark gray eyes to the stranger's face, where they met that sweet, intense smile that seemed to encourage while it shone upon her.

"We have never met before, Mrs. Rocke, but we both feel too much interest in this good lad here to meet as strangers now," said the doctor, extending his hand.

"Traverse gives me every day fresh cause to be grateful to you, sir, for kindness that we can never, never repay," said Marah Rocke, pressing that bountiful hand and then placing a chair, which the doctor took.

Traverse seated himself at a little distance, and as the doctor conversed with and covertly examined his mother's face he watched the doctor's countenance as if life and death hung upon the character of its expression. But while they talked not one word was said upon the subject of sickness or medicine. They talked of Traverse. The doctor assured his mother that her boy was of such fine talent, character and promise, and that he had already made such rapid progress in his classical and mathematical studies, that he ought immediately to enter upon a course of reading for one of the learned professions.

The mother turned a smile full of love, pride and sorrow upon the fine, intellectual face of her boy, and said:

"You are like the angel in Cole's picture of life! You point the youth to the far-up temple of fame— —"

"And leave him to get there as he can? Not at all, madam! Let us see: Traverse, you are now going on eighteen years of age; if you had your choice which of the learned professions would you prefer for yourself—law, physic or divinity?"

The boy looked up and smiled, then dropped his head and seemed to reflect.

"Perhaps you have never thought upon the subject. Well, you must take time, so as to be firm in your decision when you have once decided," said the doctor.

"Oh, sir, I have thought of it long, and my choice has been long and firmly decided, were I only free to follow it."

"Speak, lad; what is your choice?"

"Why, don't you know, sir? Can't you guess? Why, your own profession, of course, sir! certainly, sir, I could not think of any other!" exclaimed the boy, with sparkling eyes and flushed cheeks.

"That's my own lad!" exclaimed the doctor, enthusiastically, seizing the boy's hand with one of his and clapping the other down upon his palm—for if the doctor had an admiration in the world it was for his own profession. "That's my own lad! My profession! the healing art! Why, it is the only profession worthy the study of an immortal being! Law sets people by the ears together. Divinity should never be considered as a profession—it is a divine mission! Physic—physic, my boy! the healing art! that's the profession for you! And I am very glad to hear you declare for it, too, for now the way is perfectly clear!"

Both mother and son looked up in surprise.

"Yes, the way is perfectly clear! Nothing is easier! Traverse shall come and read medicine in my office! I shall be glad to have the lad there. It will amuse me to give him instruction occasionally. I have a positive mania for teaching!"

"And for doing good! Oh, sir, how have we deserved this kindness at your hands, and how shall we ever, ever repay it?" cried Mrs. Rocke, in a broken voice, while the tears filled her gentle eyes.

"Oh, pooh, pooh! a mere nothing, ma'am! a mere nothing for me to do, whatever it may prove to him. It is very hard, indeed, if I am to be crushed under a cart-load of thanks for doing something for a boy I like, when it does not cost me a cent of money or a breath of effort!"

"Oh, sir, your generous refusal of our thanks does but deepen our obligation!" said Marah, still weeping.

"Now, my dear madam, will you persist in making me confess that it is all selfishness on my part? I like the boy, I tell you! I shall like his bright, cheerful face in my office! I can make him very useful to me; also— —"

"Oh, sir, if you can and will only make him useful to you— —"

"Why, to be sure I can and will! He can act as my clerk, keep my accounts, write my letters, drive out with me and sit in the rig while I go in to visit my patients, for though I have pretty much retired from practice, still— —"

"Still you visit and prescribe for the sick poor, gratis!" added Marah, feelingly.

"Pooh, pooh! habit, madam—habit! 'ruling passion strong as death,' etc. I can't for the life of me keep from giving people bread pills. And now, by the way, I must be off to see some of my patients in Staunton. Traverse, my lad—my young medical assistant, I mean—are you willing to go with me?"

"Oh, sir," said the boy, and here his voice broke down with emotion.

"Come along, then," laughed the doctor; "You shall drive with me into the village as a commencement."

Traverse got his hat, while the doctor held out his hand to Mrs. Rocke, who, with her eyes full of tears and her voice faltering with emotion, began again to thank him, when he good-humoredly interrupted her by saying:

"Now my good little woman, do pray, hush. I'm a selfish fellow, as you'll see. I do nothing but what pleases my own self and makes me happy. Good-by; God bless you, madam," he said, cordially shaking her hand. "Come, Traverse," he added, hurriedly striding out of the door and through the yard to the gate, before which the old green gig and sorrel mare were still waiting.

"Traverse, I brought you out again to-day more especially to speak of your mother and her state of health," said Doctor Day, very seriously, as they both took their seats in the gig and drove on toward the town. "Traverse, your mother is in no immediate danger of death; in fact, she has no disease whatever."

"Oh, sir, you do not think her ill, then! I thought you did not, from the fact that you never felt her pulse or gave her a prescription," exclaimed Traverse, delightedly, for in one thing the lad resembled his mother—he was sensitive and excitable—easily depressed and easily exhilarated.

"Traverse, I said your mother is in no immediate danger of death, for that, in fact, she has no disease; but yet, Traverse, brace yourself up, for I am about to strike you a heavy blow. Traverse, Marah Rocke is starving!"

"Starving! Heaven of heavens! no! that is not so! it cannot be! My mother starving! oh, horrible! horrible! But, doctor, it cannot—cannot be! Why, we have two meals a day at our house!" cried the boy, almost beside himself with agitation.

"Lad, there are other starvations besides the total lack of food. There are slow starvations and divers ones. Marah Rocke is starving slowly and in every way—mind, soul and body. Her body is slowly wasting from the want of proper nutriment, her heart from the want of human sympathy, her mind from the need of social intercourse. Her whole manner of life must be changed if she is to live at all."

"Oh, sir, I understand you now. I feel, I feel that you speak the very truth. Something must be done. I must do something. What shall it be? Oh, advise me, sir."

"I must reflect a little, Traverse," said the doctor, thoughtfully, as he drove along with very slack reins.

"And, oh, how thoughtless of me! I forgot—indeed, I did, sir—when I so gladly accepted your offer for me to read with you. I forgot that if I spent every day reading in your office, my mother would sadly miss the dollar and a half a week I make by doing odd jobs in town."

"But I did not forget it, boy; rest easy upon that score; and now let me reflect how we can best serve your good little mother," said the doctor; and he drove slowly and thoughtfully along for about twenty minutes before he spoke again, when he said:

"Traverse, Monday is the first of the month. You shall set in with me then. Come to me, therefore, on Monday, and I think by that time I shall have thought upon some plan for your mother. In the mean time, you make as much money at jobs as you can, and also you must accept from me for her a bottle or so of port wine and a turkey or two. Tell her, if she demurs, that it is the doctor's prescription, and that, for fear of accident, he always prefers to send his own physic."

"Oh, Doctor Day, if I could only thank you aright!" cried Traverse.

"Pooh, pooh! nonsense! there is no time for it. Here we are at Spicer's grocery store, where I suppose you are again employed. Yes? Well, jump out, then. You can still make half a day. Mind, remember on Monday next, December 1st, you enter my office as my medical student, and by that time I shall have some plan arranged for your mother. Good-by; God bless you, lad," said the good doctor, as he drove off and left Traverse standing in the genial autumn sunshine, with his heart swelling and his eyes overflowing with excess of gratitude and happiness.

CHAPTER XV.

CAP'S COUNTRY CAPERS.

"A willful elf—an uncle's child,
That half a pet and half a pest,
Was still reproved, endured, caressed,
Yet never tamed, though never spoiled."

Capitola at first was delighted and half incredulous at the great change in her fortunes. The spacious and comfortable mansion of which she found herself the little mistress; the high rank of the veteran officer who claimed her as his ward and niece; the abundance, regularity and respectability of her new life; the leisure, the privacy, the attendance of servants, were all so different from anything to which she had previously been accustomed that there were times when she doubted its reality and distrusted her own identity.

Sometimes of a morning, after a very vivid dream of the alleys, cellars and gutters, ragpickers, newsboys, and beggars of New York, she would open her eyes upon her own comfortable chamber, with its glowing fire and crimson curtains, and bright mirror crowning the walnut bureau between them, she would jump up and gaze wildly around, not remembering where she was or how she came thither.

Sometimes, suddenly startled by an intense realization of the contrast between her past and her present life, she would mentally inquire:

"Can this be really I, myself, and not another? I, the little houseless wanderer through the streets and alleys of New York? I, the little newsgirl in boy's clothes? I, the wretched little vagrant that was brought up before the recorder and was about to be sent to the House of Refuge for juvenile delinquents? Can this be I, Capitola, the little outcast of the city, now changed into Miss Black, the young lady, perhaps the heiress of a fine old country seat; calling a fine old military officer uncle; having a handsome income of pocket money settled upon me; having carriages and horses and servants to attend me? No; it can't be! It's just impossible! No; I see how it is. I'm crazy! that's what I am, crazy! For, now I think of it, the last thing I remember of my former life was being brought before the recorder for wearing boy's clothes. Now, I'm sure that it was upon that occasion that I went suddenly mad with trouble, and all the rest is a lunatic's fancy! This fine old country seat of which I vainly think myself the mistress, is just the pauper madhouse to which the magistrates have sent me. This fine old military officer whom I call uncle is the head doctor. The servants who come at my call are the keepers.

"There is no figure out of my past life in my present one except Herbert

Greyson. But, pshaw! he is not 'the nephew of his uncle;' he is only my old comrade, Herbert Greyson, the sailor lad, who comes here to the madhouse to see me, and, out of compassion, humors all my fancies.

"I wonder how long they'll keep me here? Forever, I hope. Until I get cured, I'm sure. I hope they won't cure me; I vow I won't be cured. It's a great deal too pleasant to be mad, and I'll stay so. I'll keep on calling myself Miss Black, and this madhouse my country seat, and the head doctor my uncle, and the keepers servants, until the end of time, so I will. Catch me coming to my senses, when it's so delightful to be mad. I'm too sharp for that. I didn't grow up in Rag Alley, New York, for nothing."

So, half in jest and half in earnest, Capitola soliloquized upon her change of fortune.

Her education was commenced, but progressed rather irregularly. Old Hurricane bought her books and maps, slates and copy-books, set her lessons in grammar, geography and history, and made her write copies, do sums and read and recite lessons to him. Mrs. Condiment taught her the mysteries of cutting and basting, back-stitching and felling, hemming and seaming. A pupil as sharp as Capitola soon mastered her tasks, and found herself each day with many hours of leisure with which she did not know what to do.

These hours were at first occupied with exploring the old house, with all its attics, cuddies, cock-lofts and cellars; then in wandering through the old ornamental grounds, that were, even in winter and in total neglect, beautiful with their wild growth of evergreens; thence she extended her researches into the wild and picturesque country around.

She was never weary of admiring the great forest that climbed the heights of the mountains behind their house; the great bleak precipices of gray rock seen through the leafless branches of the trees; the rugged falling ground that lay before the house and between it and the river; and the river itself, with its rushing stream and raging rapids.

Capitola had become a skilful as she had first been a fearless rider. But her rides were confined to the domain between the mountain range and the river; she was forbidden to ford the one or climb the other. Perhaps if such a prohibition had never been made Capitola would never have thought of doing the one or the other; but we all know the diabolical fascination there is in forbidden pleasures for young human nature. And no sooner had Cap been commanded, if she valued her safety, not to cross the water or climb the precipice than, as a natural consequence, she began to wonder what was in the valley behind the mountain and what might be in the woods across the river. And she longed, above all things, to explore and find out for herself. She would eagerly have done so, notwithstanding the prohibition; but Wool, who always attended her rides, was sadly in the way. If she could only get rid of Wool, she resolved to go upon a limited exploring expedition.

One day a golden opportunity occurred. It was a day of unusual beauty, when autumn seemed to be smiling upon the earth with her brightest smiles before passing away. In a word, it was Indian summer. The beauty of the weather had tempted Old Hurricane to ride to the county seat on particular business connected with his ward herself.

Capitola, left alone, amused herself with her tasks until the afternoon; then, calling a boy, she ordered him to saddle her horse and bring him around.

"My dear, what do you want with your horse? There is no one to attend you; Wool has gone with his master," said Mrs. Condiment, as she met Capitola in the hall, habited for her ride.

"I know that; but I cannot be mewed up here in the old house and deprived of my afternoon ride," exclaimed Capitola decidedly.

"But, my dear, you must never think of riding out alone," exclaimed the dismayed Mrs. Condiment.

"Indeed I shall, though—and glad of the opportunity," added Cap, mentally.

"But, my dear love, it is improper, imprudent, dangerous."

"Why so?" asked Cap.

"Good gracious, upon every account! Suppose you were to meet with ruffians; suppose—oh, heaven!—suppose you were to meet with—Black Donald!"

"Mrs. Condiment, once for all do tell me who this terrible Black Donald is? Is he the Evil One himself, or the Man in the Iron Mask, or the individual that struck Billy Patterson, or—who is he?"

"Who is Black Donald? Good gracious, child, you ask me who is Black Donald!"

"Yes; who is he? where is he? what is he? that every cheek turns pale at the mention of his name?" asked Capitola.

"Black Donald! Oh, my child, may you never know more of Black Donald than I can tell you. Black Donald is the chief of a band of ruthless desperadoes that infest these mountain roads, robbing mail coaches, stealing negroes, breaking into houses and committing every sort of depredation. Their hands are red with murder and their souls black with darker crimes."

"Darker crimes than murder!" ejaculated Capitola.

"Yes, child, yes; there are darker crimes. Only last winter he and three of his gang broke into a solitary house where there was a lone woman and her daughter, and—it is not a story for you to hear; but if the people had caught Black Donald then they would have burned him at the stake! His life is forfeit by a hundred crimes. He is an outlaw, and a heavy price is set upon his head."

"And can no one take him?"

"No, my dear; at least, no one has been able to do so yet. His very haunts are unknown, but are supposed to be in concealed mountain caverns."

"How I would like the glory of capturing Black Donald!" said Capitola.

"You, child! You capture Black Donald! You are crazy!"

"Oh, by stratagem, I mean, not by force. Oh, how I should like to capture Black Donald!—There's my horse; good-by!" and before Mrs. Condiment could raise another objection Capitola ran out, sprang into her saddle and was seen careering down the hill toward the river as fast as her horse could fly.

"My Lord, but the major will be hopping if he finds it out!" was good Mrs. Condiment's dismayed exclamation.

Rejoicing in her freedom, Cap galloped down to the water's edge, and then walked her horse up and down along the course of the stream until she found a good fording place. Then, gathering up her riding skirt and throwing it over the neck of her horse she plunged boldly into the stream, and, with the water splashing and foaming all around her, urged him onward till they crossed the river and climbed up the opposite bank. A bridle-path lay before her, leading from the fording place through a deep wood. That path attracted her; she followed it, charmed alike by the solitude of the wood, the novelty of the scene and her own sense of freedom. But one thought was given to the story of Black Donald, and that was a reassuring one:

"If Black Donald is a mail robber, then this little bridle-path is far enough off his beat."

And, so saying, she gayly galloped along, singing as she went, following the narrow path up hill and down dale through the wintry woods. Drawn on by the attraction of the unknown, and deceiving herself by the continued repetition of one resolve, namely—"When I get to the top of the next hill, and see what lies beyond, then I will turn back"—she galloped on and on, on and on, on and on, until she had put several miles between herself and her home; until her horse began to exhibit signs of weariness, and the level rays of the setting sun were striking redly through the leafless branches of the trees.

Cap drew rein at the top of a high, wooded hill and looked about her. On her left hand the sun was sinking like a ball of fire below the horizon; all around her everywhere were the wintry woods; far away, in the direction whence she had come, she saw the tops of the mountains behind Hurricane Hall, looking like blue clouds against the southern horizon; the Hall itself and the river below were out of sight.

"I wonder how far I am from home?" said Capitola, uneasily; "somewhere between six and seven miles, I reckon. Dear me, I didn't mean to ride so far. I've got over a great deal of ground in these two hours. I shall not get back so soon; my horse is tired to death; it will take me three hours to reach Hurricane Hall. Good gracious! it will be pitch dark before I get there. No, thank heaven, there will be a moon. But won't there be a row though? Whew! Well, I must turn about and lose no time. Come, Gyp, get up, Gyp, good horse; we're going home."

And so saying, Capitola turned her horse's head and urged him into a gallop.

She had gone on for about a mile, and it was growing dark, and her horse was again slackening his pace, when she thought she heard the sound of another horse's hoofs behind her. She drew rein and listened, and was sure of it.

Now, without being the least of a coward, Capitola thought of the loneliness of the woods, the lateness of the hour, her own helplessness, and—Black Donald! And thinking "discretion the better part of valor," she urged her horse once more into a gallop for a few hundred yards; but the jaded beast soon broke into a trot and subsided into a walk that threatened soon to come to a standstill.

The invisible pursuer gained on her.

In vain she urged her steed with whip and voice; the poor beast would obey and trot for a few yards, and then fall into a walk.

The thundering footfalls of the pursuing horse were close in the rear.

"Oh, Gyp, is it possible that, instead of my capturing Black Donald, you are going to let Black Donald or somebody else catch me?" exclaimed Capitola, in mock despair, as she urged her wearied steed.

In vain! The pursuing horseman was beside her; a strong hand was laid upon her bridle; a mocking voice was ringing in her ear:

"Whither away so fast, pretty one?"

CHAPTER XVI.

CAP'S FEARFUL ADVENTURE.

Who passes by this road so late?
Companion of the Majolaine!
Who passes by this road so late?
Say! oh, say?

—OLD FRENCH SONG.

Of a naturally strong constitution and adventurous disposition, and inured from infancy to danger, Capitola possessed a high degree of courage, self-control and presence of mind.

At the touch of that ruthless hand, at the sound of that gibing voice, all her faculties instantly collected and concentrated themselves upon the emergency. As by a flash of lightning she saw every feature of her imminent danger—the loneliness of the woods, the lateness of the hour, the recklessness of her fearful companion and her own weakness. In another instant her resolution was taken and her course determined. So, when the stranger repeated his mocking question:

"Whither away so fast, pretty one?" she answered with animation:

"Oh, I am going home, and so glad to have company; for, indeed, I was dreadfully afraid of riding alone through these woods to-night."

"Afraid, pretty one—of what?"

"Oh, of ghosts and witches, wild beasts, runaway negroes, and—Black Donald."

"Then you are not afraid of me?"

"Lors, no, indeed! I guess I ain't! Why should I be afraid of a respectable-looking gentleman like you, sir?"

"And so you are going home? Where is your home, pretty one?"

"On the other side of the river. But you need not keep on calling me 'pretty one;' it must be as tiresome to you to repeat it as it is to me to hear it."

"What shall I call you, then, my dear?"

"You may call me Miss Black; or, if you are friendly, you may call me Capitola."

"Capitola!" exclaimed the man, in a deep and changed voice, as he dropped her bridle.

"Yes—Capitola; what objection have you got to that? It is a pretty name, isn't it? But if you think it is too long, and if you feel very friendly, you may call me Cap."

"Well, then, my pretty Cap, where do you live across the river?" asked the stranger, recovering his self-possession.

"Oh, at a rum old place they call Hurricane Hall, with a rum old military officer they call Old Hurricane," said Capitola, for the first time stealing a sidelong glance at her fearful companion.

It was not Black Donald; that was the first conclusion to which she rashly jumped. He appeared to be a gentlemanly ruffian about forty years of age, well dressed in a black riding-suit; black beaver hat drawn down close over his eyes: black hair and whiskers; heavy black eyebrows that met across his nose; drooping eyelashes, and eyes that looked out under the corners of the lids; altogether a sly, sinister, cruel face—a cross between a fox and a tiger. It warned Capitola to expect no mercy there. After the girl's last words he seemed to have fallen into thought for a moment, and then again he spoke:

"Well, my pretty Cap, how long have you been living at. Hurricane Hall?"

"Ever since my guardian, Major Warfield, brought me from the City of New York, where I received my education (in the streets)," she mentally added.

"Humph! Why did you ride so fast, my pretty Cap?" he asked, eying her from the corner of his eyes.

"Oh, sir, because I was afraid, as I told you before; afraid of runaway negroes and wild beasts, and so on; but now, with a good gentleman like you, I don't feel afraid at all; and I'm very glad to be able to walk poor Gyp, because he is tired, poor fellow."

"Yes, poor fellow," said the traveler, in a mocking tone, "he is tired; suppose you dismount and let him rest. Come, I'll get off, too, and we will sit down here by the roadside and have a friendly conversation."

Capitola stole a glance at his face. Yes, notwithstanding his light tone, he was grimly in earnest; there was no mercy to be expected from that sly, sinister, cruel face.

"Come, my pretty Cap, what say you?"

"I don't care if I do," she said, riding to the edge of the path, drawing rein and looking down as if to examine the ground.

"Come, little beauty, must I help you off?" asked the stranger.

"N-n-no," answered Capitola, with deliberate hesitation; "no, this is not a good place to sit down and talk; it's all full of brambles."

"Very well; shall we go on a little further?"

"Oh, yes; but I don't want to ride fast, because it will tire my horse."

"You shall go just as you please, my angel," said the traveler.

"I wonder whether this wretch thinks me very simple or very depraved? He must come to one or the other conclusion," thought Capitola.

They rode on very slowly for a mile further, and then, having arrived at an open glade, the stranger drew rein and said:

"Come, pretty lark, hop down; here's a nice place to sit and rest."

"Very well; come help me off," said Capitola, pulling up her horse; then, as by a sudden impulse, she exclaimed: "I don't like this place either; it's right on top of the hill; so windy, and just see how rocky the ground is. No, I'll not sit and rest here, and that I tell you."

"I am afraid you are trifling with me, my pretty bird. Take care; I'll not be trifled with," said the man.

"I don't know what you mean by trifling with you any more than the dead. But I'll not sit down there on those sharp rocks, and so I tell you. If you will be civil and ride along with me until we get to the foot of the hill, I know a nice place where we can sit down and have a good talk, and I will tell you all my travels and you shall tell me all yours."

"Ex-actly; and where is that nice place?"

"Why, in the valley at the foot of the hill."

"Come—come on, then."

"Slowly, slowly," said Capitola; "I won't tire my horse."

They rode over the hill, down the gradual descent and on toward the center of the valley.

They were now within a quarter of a mile of the river, on the opposite side of which was Hurricane Hall and—safety! The stranger drew rein, saying:

"Come, my cuckoo; here we are at the bottom of the valley; now or never."

"Oh, now, of course; you see, I keep my promise," answered Capitola, pulling up her horse.

The man sprang from his saddle and came to her side.

"Please be careful, now; don't let my riding-skirt get hung in the stirrup," said Capitola, cautiously disengaging her drapery, rising in the saddle and giving the stranger her hand. In the act of jumping she suddenly stopped and looked down, exclaiming:

"Good gracious! how very damp the ground is here, in the bottom of the valley!"

"More objections, I suppose, my pretty one; but they won't serve you any longer. I am bent upon having a cozy chat with you upon that very turf," said the stranger, pointing to a little cleared space among the trees beside the path.

"Now, don't be cross; just see how damp it is there; it would spoil my riding-dress and give me my death of cold."

"Humph!" said the stranger, looking at her with a sly, grim, cruel resolve.

"I'll tell you what it is," said Cap, "I'm not witty nor amusing, nor will it pay to sit out in the night air to hear me talk; but, since you wish it, and since you were so good as to guard me through these woods, and since I promised, why, damp as it is, I will even get off and talk with you."

"That's my birdling!"

"But hold on a minute; is there nothing you can get to put there for me to sit on—no stump nor dry stone?"

"No, my dear; I don't see any."

"Could you not turn your hat down and let me sit on that?"

"Ha, ha, ha! Why, your weight would crush it as flat as a flounder!"

"Oh, I know now!" exclaimed Capitola, with sudden delight; "you just spread your saddle-cloth down there, and that will make a beautiful seat, and I'll sit and talk with you so nicely—only you must not want me to stay long, because if I don't get home soon I shall catch a scolding."

"You shall neither catch a scolding nor a cold on my account, pretty one," said the man, going to his horse to get the saddle-cloth.

"Oh, don't take off the saddle—it will detain you too long," said Cap, impatiently.

"My pretty Cap, I cannot get the cloth without taking it off," said the man, beginning to unbuckle the girth.

"Oh, yes, you can; you can draw it from under," persisted Cap.

"Impossible, my angel," said the man, lifting off the saddle from his horse and laying it carefully by the roadside.

Then he took off the gay, crimson saddle-cloth and carried it into the little clearing and began carefully to spread it down.

Now was Cap's time. Her horse had recovered from his fatigue. The stranger's horse was in the path before her. While the man's back was turned she raised her riding whip and, with a shout, gave the front horse a sharp lash that sent him galloping furiously ahead. Then, instantaneously putting whip to her own horse, she started into a run.

Hearing the shout, the lash and the starting of the horses, the baffled villain turned and saw that his game was lost; he had been outwitted by a child! He gnashed his teeth and shook his fist in rage.

Turning as she wheeled out of sight, Capitola—I am sorry to say—put her thumb to the side of her nose and whirled her fingers into a semicircle, in a gesture more expressive than elegant.

CHAPTER XVII.

ANOTHER STORM AT HURRICANE HALL.

At this, Sir Knight grew high in wroth,
And lifting hands and eyes up both,
Three times he smote on stomach stout,
From whence, at length, fierce words broke out

—HUDIBRAS.

The moon was shining full upon the river and the homestead beyond when Capitola dashed into the water and, amid the sparkling and leaping of the foam, made her way to the other bank and rode up the rugged ascent. On the outer side of the lawn wall the moonbeams fell full upon the little figure of Pitapat waiting there.

"Why, Patty, what takes you out so late as this?" asked Capitola, as she rode up to the gate.

"Oh, Miss Catterpillar, I'se waitin' for you. Old marse is dreadful he is! Jest fit to bust the shingles offen the roof with swearing! So I come out to warn you, so you steal in the back way and go to your room so he won't see you, and I'll go and send Wool to put your horse away, and then I'll bring you up some supper and tell old marse how you've been home ever so long, and gone to bed with a werry bad head-ache."

"Thank you, Patty. It is perfectly astonishing how easy lying is to you! You really deserve to have been born in Rag Alley; but I won't trouble the recording angel to make another entry against you on my account."

"Yes, miss," said Pitapat, who thought that her mistress was complimenting her.

"And now, Patty, stand out of my way. I am going to ride straight up to the horse-block, dismount and walk right into the presence of Major Warfield," said Capitola, passing through the gate.

"Oh, Miss Catterpillar, don't! don't! he'll kill you, so he will!"

"Who's afeard?" muttered Cap to herself, as she put her horse to his mettle and rode gayly through the evergreens up to the horse-block, where she sprang down lightly from her saddle.

Gathering up her train with one hand and tossing back her head, she swept along toward the house with the air of a young princess.

There was a vision calculated to test her firmness. Reader, did you ever see a raging lion tearing to and fro the narrow limits of his cage, and occasionally shaking the amphitheatre with his tremendous roar; or a furious bull tossing his head and tail and plowing up the earth with his hoofs as he careered back and forth between the boundaries of his pen? If you have seen and noted these mad brutes, you may form some idea of the frenzy of Old Hurricane as he stormed up and down the floor of the front piazza.

Cap had just escaped an actual danger of too terrible a character to be frightened now by sound and fury. Composedly she walked up into the porch and said:

"Good evening, uncle."

The old man stopped short in his furious strides and glared upon her with his terrible eyes.

Cap stood fire without blanching, merely remarking:

"Now, I have no doubt that in the days when you went battling that look used to strike terror into the heart of the enemy, but it doesn't into mine, somehow."

"Miss!" roared the old man, bringing down his cane with a resounding thump upon the floor; "miss! how dare you have the impudence to face me, much less the—the—the assurance!—the effrontery!—the audacity!—the brass! to speak to me!"

"Well, I declare," said Cap, calmly untying her hat; "this is the first time I ever heard it was impudent in a little girl to give her uncle good evening!"

The old man trotted up and down the piazza two or three turns, then, stopping short before the delinquent, he struck his cane down upon the floor with a ringing stroke and thundered:

"Young woman, tell me instantly and without prevarication where you've been!"

"Certainly, sir; 'going to and fro in the earth and walking up and down in it,'" said Cap, quietly.

"Flames and furies! that is no answer at all! Where have you been?" roared Old Hurricane, shaking with excitement.

"Look here, uncle; if you go on that way you'll have a fit presently," said Cap, calmly.

"Where have you been?" thundered Old Hurricane.

"Well, since you will know—just across the river and through the woods and back again."

"And didn't I forbid you to do that, minion? and how dare you disobey me? You the creature of my bounty; you, the miserable little vagrant that I picked up in the alleys of New York and tried to make a young lady of; but an old proverb says 'You can't make a silken purse out of a pig's ear.' How dare you, you little beggar, disobey your benefactor?—a man of my age, character and position? I—I—" Old Hurricane turned abruptly and raged up and down the piazza.

All this time Capitola had been standing quietly, holding up her train with one hand and her riding habit in the other. At this last insult she raised her dark-gray eyes to his face with one long indignant, sorrowful gaze; then, turning silently away and entering the house, she left Old Hurricane to storm up and down the piazza until he had raged himself to rest.

Reader, I do not defend, far less approve, poor Cap. I only tell her story and describe her as I have seen her, leaving her to your charitable interpretation.

Next morning Capitola came down into the breakfast-room with one idea prominent in her hard little head, to which she mentally gave expression:

"Well as I like that old man, he must not permit himself to talk to me in that indecent strain, and so he must be made to know."

When she entered the breakfast-room she found Mrs. Condiment already at the head of the table and Old Hurricane at the foot. He had quite got over his rage, and turned around blandly to welcome his ward, saying;

"Good morning, Cap."

Without taking the slightest notice of the salutation, Cap sailed on to her seat.

"Humph. Did you hear me say 'Good morning,' Cap?"

Without paying the least attention, Capitola reached out her hand and took a cup of coffee from Mrs. Condiment.

"Humph! Humph! Good morning, Capitola!" said Old Hurricane, with marked emphasis. Apparently without hearing him. Cap helped herself to a buck-wheat cake and daintily buttered it.

"Humph! humph! humph! Well as you said yourself, 'a dumb devil is better than a speaking one,'" ejaculated Old Hurricane, as he sat down and subsided into silence.

Doubtless the old man would have flown into another passion, had that been possible; but, in truth, he had spent so much vitality in rage number one that he had none left to sustain rage number two. Besides, he knew it would be necessary to blow up Bill Ezy, his lazy overseer, before night, and perhaps saved himself for that performance. He finished his meal in silence and went out.

Cap finished hers, and, 'tempering justice with mercy,' went up-stairs to his room and looked over all his appointments and belongings to find what she would do for his extra comfort, and found a job in newly lining his warm slippers and the sleeves of his dressing-gown.

They met again at the dinner-table.

"How do you do, Cap?" said Old Hurricane, as he took his seat.

Capitola poured out a glass of water and drank it in silence.

"Oh, very well, 'a dumb devil,' etc.," exclaimed Old Hurricane, addressing himself to his dinner. When the meal was over they again separated. The old man went to his study to examine his farm books, and Capitola back to her chamber to finish lining his warm slippers.

Again at tea they met.

"Well, Cap is 'the dumb devil' cast out yet?" he said, sitting down.

Capitola took a cup of tea from Mrs. Condiment and passed it on to him in silence.

"Humph! not gone yet, eh? Poor girl, how it must try you," said Old Hurricane.

After supper the old man found his dressing-gown and slippers before the fire all ready for his use.

"Cap, you monkey, you did this," he said, turning around. But Capitola had already left the room.

Next morning at breakfast there was a repetition of the same scene. Early in the forenoon Major Warfield ordered his horses and, attended by Wool rode up to Tip-Top. He did not return either to dinner or tea, but as that circumstance was not unusual, it gave no uneasiness. Mrs. Condiment kept his supper warm, and Capitola had his dressing-gown and slippers ready.

She was turning them before the fire when the old man arrived. He came in quite gayly, saying:

"Now, Cap, I think I have found a talisman at last to cast out that 'dumb devil.' I heard you wishing for a watch the other day. Now, as devils belong to eternity, and have no business with time, of course the sight of this little time-keeper must put yours to flight," and so saying he laid upon the table, before the eyes of Capitola, a beautiful little gold watch and chain. She glanced at it as it lay glittering and sparkling in the lamplight, and then turned abruptly and walked away.

"Humph! that's always the way the devils do—fly when they can't stand shot."

Capitola deliberately walked back, laid a paper over the little watch and chain, as if to cover its fascinating sparkle and glitter, and said:

"Uncle, your bounty is large and your present is beautiful; but there is something that poor Capitola values more than— —"

She paused, dropped her head upon her bosom, a sudden blush flamed up over her face, and tear-drops glittered in her downcast eyes. She put both hands before her burning face for a moment, and then, dropping them, resumed:

"Uncle, you rescued me from misery and, perhaps—perhaps, early death; you have heaped benefits and bounties upon me without measure; you have placed me in a home of abundance, honor and security. For all this if I were not grateful I should deserve no less than death. But, uncle, there is a sin that is worse, at least, more ungenerous, than ingratitude; it is to put a helpless fellow-creature under heavy obligations and then treat that grateful creature with undeserved contempt and cruel unkindness." Once more her voice was choked with feeling.

For some reason or other Capitola's tears—perhaps because they were so rare—always moved Old Hurricane to his heart's center. Going toward her softly, he said:

"Now, my dear; now, my child; now, my little Cap, you know it was all for your own good. Why, my dear, I never for one instant regretted bringing you to the house, and I wouldn't part with you for a kingdom. Come, now, my child; come to the heart of your old uncle."

Now, the soul of Capitola naturally abhorred sentiment. If ever she gave way to serious emotion, she was sure to avenge herself by being more capricious than before. Consequently, flinging herself out of the caressing arms of Old Hurricane, she exclaimed:

"Uncle, I won't be treated with both kicks and half-pennies by the same person, and so I tell you. I am not a cur to be fed with roast beef and beaten with a stick, nor—nor—nor a Turk's slave to be caressed and oppressed as her master likes. Such abuse as you heaped upon me I never heard—no, not even in Rag Alley!"

"Oh, my dear! my dear! my dear! for heaven's sake forget Rag Alley?"

"I won't! I vow I'll go back to Rag Alley for a very little more. Freedom and peace is even sweeter than wealth and honors."

"Ah, but I won't let you, my little Cap."

"Then I'd have you up before the nearest magistrate, to show by what right you detained me. Ah, ha! I wasn't brought up in New York for nothing."

"Whee-eu! and all this because, for her own good, I gave my own niece and ward a little gentle admonition."

"Gentle admonition! Do you call that gentle admonition? Why, uncle, you are enough to frighten most people to death with your fury. You are a perfect dragon! a griffin! a Russian bear! a Bengal tiger! a Numidian lion! You're all Barnum's beasts in one! I declare, if I don't write and ask him to send a party down here to catch you for his museum! You'd draw, I tell you!"

"Yes, especially with you for a keeper to stir me up once in a while with a long pole."

"And that I'd engage to do—cheap."

The entrance of Mrs. Condiment with the tea-tray put an end to the controversy. It was, as yet, a drawn battle.

"And what about the watch, my little Cap?"

"Take it back, uncle, if you please."

"But they won't have it back; it has got your initials engraved upon it. Look here," said the old man, holding the watch to her eyes. "'C. L. N.'—those are not my initials," said Capitola, looking up with surprise.

"Why, so they are not; the blamed fools have made a mistake. But you'll have to take it, Cap."

"No, uncle; keep it for the present," said Capitola, who was too honest to take a gift that she felt she did not deserve, and yet too proud to confess as much.

Peace was proclaimed—for the present.

Alas! 'twas but of short continuance. During these two days of coolness and enforced quietude Old Hurricane had gathered a store of bad humors that required expenditure.

So the very next day something went wrong upon the farm, and Old Hurricane came storming home, driving his overseer, poor, old, meek Billy Ezy, and his man Wool before him.

Bill Ezy was whimpering; Wool was sobbing aloud; Old Hurricane was roaring at them both as he drove them on before him, swearing that Ezy should go and find himself a new home and Wool should go and seek another master.

And for this cause Old Hurricane was driving them on to his study, that he might pay the overseer his last quarter's salary and give the servant a written order to find a master.

He raged past Capitola in the hall, and, meeting Mrs. Condiment at the study door, ordered her to bring in her account book directly, for that he would not be imposed upon any longer, but meant to drive all the lazy, idle, dishonest eye-servants and time-servers from the house and land!

"What's the matter now?" said Capitola, meeting her.

"Oh, child, he's in his terrible tantrums again! He gets into these ways every once in a while, when a young calf perishes, or a sheep is stolen, or anything goes amiss, and then he abuses us all for a pack of loiterers, sluggards and thieves, and pays us off and orders us off. We don't go, of course, because we know he doesn't mean it; still, it is very trying to be talked to so. Oh, I should go, but Lord, child, he's a bear, but we love him."

Just as she spoke the study door opened and Bill Ezy came out sobbing, and Wool lifting up his voice and fairly roaring.

Mrs. Condiment stepped out of the parlor door.

"What's the matter, you blockhead?" she asked of Wool.

"Oh! boo-hoo-woo! Ole marse been and done and gone and guv me a line to find an—an—another—boo-hoo-woo!" sobbed Wool, ready to break his heart.

"Give you a line to find another boo-hoo-woo! I wouldn't do it, if I were you, Wool," said Capitola.

"Give me the paper, Wool," said Mrs. Condiment, taking the "permit" and tearing it up, and adding:

"There, now, you go home to your quarter, and keep out of your old master's sight until he gets over his anger, and then you know very well that it will be all right. There, go along with you."

Wool quickly got out of the way and made room for the overseer, who was sniveling like a whipped schoolboy, and to whom the housekeeper said:

"I thought you were wiser than to take this so to heart, Mr. Ezy."

"Oh, mum, what could you expect? An old sarvint as has sarved the major faithful these forty years, to be discharged at sixty-five! Oh, hoo-ooo-oo!" whimpered the overseer.

"But then you have been discharged so often you ought to be used to it by this time. You get discharged, just as Wool gets sold, about once a month—but do you ever go?"

"Oh, mum, but he's in airnest this time; 'deed he is, mum; terrible in airnest; and all about that misfortnet bobtail colt getting stole. I know how it wur some of Black Donald's gang as done it—as if I could always be on my guard against them devils; and he means it this time, mum; he's terrible in airnest!"

"Tut! he's always in earnest for as long as it lasts; go home to your family and to-morrow go about your business as usual."

Here the study bell rang violently and Old Hurricane's voice was heard calling, "Mrs. Condiment! Mrs. Condiment!"

"Oh, Lor', he's coming!" cried Bill Ezy, running off as fast as his age and grief would let him.

"Mrs. Condiment! Mrs. Condiment!" called the voice.

"Yes, sir, yes," answered the housekeeper, hurrying to obey the call.

Capitola walked up and down the hall for half an hour, at the end of which Mrs. Condiment came out "with a smile on her lip and a tear in her eye," and saying:

"Well, Miss Capitola, I'm paid off and discharged also."

"What for?"

"For aiding and abetting the rebels; in a word, for trying to comfort poor Ezy and Wool."

"And are you going?"

"Certainly not; I shan't budge; I would not treat the old man so badly as to take him at his word." And, with a strange smile, Mrs. Condiment hurried away just in time to escape Old Hurricane, who came raving out of the study.

"Get out of my way, you beggar!" he cried, pushing past Capitola and hurrying from the house.

"Well, I declare, that was pleasant!" thought Cap, as she entered the parlor.

"Mrs. Condiment, what will he say when he comes back and finds you all here still?" she asked.

"Say? Nothing. After this passion is over he will be so exhausted that he will not be able to get up another rage in two or three days."

"Where has he gone?"

"To Tip-Top, and alone, too; he was so mad with poor Wool that he wouldn't even permit him to attend."

"Alone? Has he gone alone? Oh, won't I give him a dose when he comes back," thought Capitola.

Meanwhile Old Hurricane stormed along toward Tip-Top, lashing off the poor dogs that wished to follow him and cutting at every living thing that crossed his path. His business at the village was to get bills printed and posted offering an additional reward for the apprehension of "the marauding outlaw, Black Donald." That day he dined at the village tavern—"The Antlers," by Mr. Merry—and differed, disputed or quarrelled, as the case might be, with every man with whom he came in contact.

Toward evening he set off for home. It was much later than his usual hour for returning; but he felt weary, exhausted and indisposed to come into his own dwelling where his furious temper had created so much unhappiness. Thus, though it was very late, he did not hurry; he almost hoped that every one might be in bed when he should return. The moon was shining brightly when he passed the gate and rode up the evergreen avenue to the horse-block in front of the house. There he dismounted and walked up into the piazza, where a novel vision met his surprised gaze.

It was Capitola, walking up and down the floor with rapid, almost masculine strides, and apparently in a state of great excitement.

"Oh, is it you, my little Cap? Good evening, my dear," he said, very kindly.

Capitola "pulled up" in her striding walk, wheeled around, faced him, drew up her form, folded her arms, threw back her head, set her teeth and glared at him.

"What the demon do you mean by that?" cried Old Hurricane.

"Sir!" she exclaimed, bringing down one foot with a sharp stamp; "sir! how dare you have the impudence to face me? much less the—the—the—the brass! the bronze! the copper! to speak to me!"

"Why, what in the name of all the lunatics in Bedlam does the girl mean? Is she crazy?" exclaimed the old man, gazing upon her in astonishment.

Capitola turned and strode furiously up and down the piazza, and then, stopping suddenly and facing him, with a sharp stamp of her foot exclaimed:

"Old gentleman! Tell me instantly and without prevarication, where have you been?"

"To the demon with you! What do you mean? Have you taken leave of your senses?" demanded Old Hurricane.

Capitola strode up and down the floor a few times, and, stopping short and shaking her fist, exclaimed:

"Didn't you know, you headstrong, reckless, desperate, frantic veteran—didn't you know the jeopardy in which you placed yourself in riding out alone at this hour? Suppose three or four great runaway negresses had sprung out of the bushes and—and—and——" She broke off apparently for want of breath, and strode up and down the floor; then, pausing suddenly before him, with a stern stamp of her foot and a fierce glare of her eye, she continued:

"You shouldn't have come back here any more! No dishonored old man should have entered the house of which I call myself the mistress!"

"Oh, I take! I take! ha, ha, ha! Good, Cap, good! You are holding up the glass before me; but your mirror is not quite large enough to reflect 'Old Hurricane,' my dear. 'I owe one,'" said the old man, as he passed into the house, followed by his capricious favorite.

CHAPTER XVIII.

THE DOCTOR'S DAUGHTER.

Oh, her smile, it seemed half holy,
As if drawn from thoughts more far,
Than our common jestings are.
And, if any painter drew her,
He would paint her unaware
With a hallow round her hair.

E. B. BROWNING.

On the appointed day Traverse took his way to Willow Heights to keep his tryst and enter upon his medical studies in the good doctor's office. He was anxious also to know if his patron had as yet thought of any plan by which his mother might better her condition. He was met at the door by little Mattie, the parlor-maid, who told him to walk right up-stairs into the study, where her master was expecting him.

Traverse went up quietly and opened the door of that pleasant study-room, to which the reader has already been introduced, and the windows of which opened upon the upper front piazza.

Now, however, as it was quite cold, the windows were down, though the blinds were open, and through them streamed the golden rays of the morning sun that fell glistening upon the fair hair and white raiment of a young girl who sat reading before the fire.

The doctor was not in the room, and Traverse, in his native modesty, was just about to retreat when the young creature looked up from her book and, seeing him, arose with a smile and came forward, saying:

"You are the young man whom my father was expecting, I presume. Sit down; he has stepped out, but will be in again very soon."

Now, Traverse, being unaccustomed to the society of young ladies, felt excessively bashful when suddenly coming into the presence of this refined and lovely girl. With a low bow and a deep blush he took the chair she placed for him.

With natural politeness she closed her book and addressed herself to entertaining him.

"I have heard that your mother is an invalid; I hope she is better."

"I thank you—yes, ma'am—miss," stammered Traverse, in painful embarrassment. Understanding the *mauvaise honte* of the bashful boy, and seeing that her efforts to entertain only troubled him, she placed the newspapers on the table before him, saying:

"Here are the morning journals, if you would like to look over them, Mr. Rocke," and then she resumed her book.

"I thank you, miss," replied the youth, taking up a paper, more for the purpose of covering up his embarrassment than for any other.

Mr. Rocke! Traverse was seventeen years of age, and had never been called Mr. Rocke before. This young girl was the very first to compliment him with the manly title, and he felt a boyish gratitude to her and a harmless wish that his well-brushed Sunday suit of black was not quite so rusty and threadbare, tempered by an innocent exultation in the thought that no gentleman in the land could exhibit fresher linen, brighter shoes or cleaner hands than himself.

But not many seconds were spent in such egotism. He stole a glance at his lovely companion sitting on the opposite side of the fireplace—he was glad to see that she was already deeply engaged in reading, for it enabled him to observe her without embarrassment or offense. He had scarcely dared to look at her before, and had no distinct idea of her beauty.

There has been for him only a vague, dazzling vision of a golden-haired girl in floating white raiment, wafting the fragrance of violets as she moved, and with a voice sweeter than the notes of the cushat dove as she spoke.

Now he saw that the golden hair flowed in ringlets around a fair, roseate face, soft and bright with feeling and intelligence. As her dark-blue eyes followed the page, a smile intense with meaning deepened the expression of her countenance. That intense smile—it was like her father's, only lovelier—more heavenly.

That intense smile—it had, even on the old doctor's face, an inexpressible charm for Traverse—but on the lovely young face of his daughter it exercised an ineffable fascination. So earnest and so unconscious became the gaze of poor Traverse that he was only brought to a sense of propriety by the opening of the door and the entrance of the doctor, who exclaimed:

"Ah, here already, Traverse? That is punctual. This is my daughter Clara, Traverse; Clare, this is Traverse you've heard me speak about. But I daresay you've already become acquainted," concluded the doctor, drawing his chair up to the reading table, sitting down and folding his dressing-gown around his limbs.

"Well, Traverse, how is the little mother?" he presently inquired.

"I was just telling Miss Day that she was much better, sir," said Traverse.

"Ah, ha, ha, ha!" muttered the doctor to himself; "that's kitchen physic—roast turkey and port wine—and moral medicine, hope—and mental medicine, sympathy."

"Well, Traverse," he said aloud, "I have been racking my brain for a plan for your mother, and to no purpose. Traverse, your mother should be in a home of peace, plenty and cheerfulness—I can speak before my little Clare here; I never have any secrets from her. Your mother wants good living, cheerful company and freedom from toil and care. The situation of gentleman's or lady's housekeeper in some home of abundance, where she would be esteemed as a member of the family, would suit her. But where to find such a place? I have been inquiring—without mentioning her name, of course—among all my friends, but not one of them wants a housekeeper or knows a soul who does want one; and so I am 'at sea on the subject.' I'm ashamed of myself for not succeeding better."

"Oh, sir, do not do yourself so great an injustice," said Traverse.

"Well, the fact is, after boasting so confidently that I would find a good situation for Mrs. Rocke, lo and behold! I have proved myself as yet only a boaster."

"Father," said Clara, turning upon him her sweet eyes.

"Well, my love?"

"Perhaps Mrs. Rocke would do us the favor to come here and take charge of our household."

"Eh! What? I never thought of that! I never had a housekeeper in my life!" exclaimed the doctor.

"No, sir; because you never needed one before, but now we really do. Aunt Moggy has been a very faithful and efficient manager, although she is a colored woman; but she is getting very old."

"Yes, and deaf and blind and careless. I know she is. I have no doubt in the world she scours the coppers with the table napkins and washes her face and hands in the soup tureen."

"Oh, father!" said Clara.

"Well, Clare, at least she wants looking after."

"Father, she wants rest in her old age."

"No doubt of it; no doubt of it."

"And, father, I intend, of course, in time, to be your housekeeper; but, having spent all my life in a boarding school, I know very little about domestic affairs, and I require a great deal of instruction; so I really do think that there is no one needs Mrs. Rocke's assistance more than we do, and if she will do us the favor to come we cannot do better than to engage her."

"To be sure; to be sure! Lord bless my soul! to think it should never have entered my stupid old head until it was put there by Clare! Here I was searching blindly all over the country for a situation for Mrs. Rocke, and wanting her all the time more than any one else! That's the way, Traverse; that's the way with us all, my boy! While we are looking away off yonder for the solution of our difficulties, the remedy is all the time lying just under our noses!"

"But so close to our eyes, father, that we cannot see it," said Clara.

"Just so, Clare; just so. You are always ahead of me in ideas. Now, Traverse, when you go home this evening you shall take a note to your mother setting forth our wishes—mine and Clara's; if she accedes to them she will make us very happy."

With a great deal of manly strength of mind, Traverse had all his mother's tenderness of heart. It was with difficulty that he could keep back his tears or control his voice while he answered:

"I remember reading, sir, that the young queen of England, when she came to her throne, wished to provide handsomely for an orphan companion of her childhood; and, seeing that no office in her household suited the young person, she created one for her benefit. Sir, I believe you have made one for my mother."

"Not at all; not at all! If she doesn't come to look after our housekeeping, old Moggy will be greasing our griddles with tallow candle ends next! If you don't believe me; ask Clara, ask Clara!"

Not "believe" him! If the doctor had affirmed that the moon was made of moldy cheese, Traverse would have deemed it his duty to stoutly maintain that astronomical theory. He felt hurt that the doctor should use such a phrase.

"Yes, indeed, we really do need her, Traverse," said the doctor's daughter.

"Traverse!" It had made him proud to hear her call him for the first time in his life, "Mr. Rocke!" but it made him deeply happy to hear her call him "Traverse." It had such a sisterly sound coming from this sweet creature. How he wished that she really were his sister! But, then, the idea of that fair, golden-haired, blue-eyed, white-robed angel being the sister of such a robust, rugged, sunburned boy as himself! The thought was so absurd, extravagant, impossible, that the poor boy heaved an unconscious sigh.

"Why, what's the matter, Traverse? What are you thinking of so intently?"

"Of your great goodness, sir, among other things."

"Tut! let's hear no more of that. I pleased myself," said the doctor; "and now, Traverse, let's go to work decently and in order. But first let me settle this point—if your good little mother determines in our favor, Traverse, then, of course, you will live with us also, so I shall have my young medical assistant always at hand. That will be very convenient; and then we shall have no more long, lonesome evenings, Clara, shall we, dear? And now, Traverse, I will mark out your course of study and set you to work at once."

"Shall I leave the room, father?" inquired Clara.

"No, no, my dear; certainly not. I have not had you home so long as to get tired of the sight of you yet! No, Clare, no; you are not in our way—is she, Traverse?"

"Oh, sir, the idea—" stammered Traverse, blushing deeply to be so appealed to.

In his way! Why, a pang had shot through his bosom at the very mention of her going.

"Very well, then. Here, Traverse, here are your books. You are to begin with this one; keep this medical dictionary at hand for reference. Bless me, it will bring back my student days to go over the ground with you, my boy."

Clara took her work-box and sat down to stitch a pair of dainty wristbands for her father's shirts.

The doctor took up the morning papers.

Traverse opened his book and commenced his readings. It was a quiet but by no means a dull circle. Occasionally Clara and her father exchanged words, and once in a while the doctor looked over his pupil's shoulder or gave him a direction.

Traverse studied *con amore* and with intelligent appreciation. The presence of the doctor's lovely daughter, far from disturbing him, calmed and steadied his soul into a state of infinite content. If the presence of the beautiful girl was ever to become an agitating element, the hour had not yet come.

So passed the time until the dinner bell rang.

By the express stipulation of the doctor himself, it was arranged that Traverse should always dine with his family. After dinner an hour—which the doctor called a digestive hour—was spent in loitering about and then the studies were resumed.

At six o'clock in the evening Traverse took leave of the doctor and his fair daughter and started for home.

"Be sure to persuade your mother to come, Traverse," said Clara.

"She will not need persuasion; she will be only too glad to come, miss," said Traverse, with a deep bow, turning and hurrying away toward home. With "winged feet" he ran down the wooded hill and got into the highway, and hastened on with such speed that in half an hour he reached his mother's little cottage. He was agog with joy and eagerness to tell her the good news.

CHAPTER XIX.

THE RESIGNED SOUL.

This day be bread and peace my lot;
All else beneath the sun
Thou knowest if best bestowed or not,
And let thy will be done.

—POPE.

Poor Marah Rocke had schooled her soul to resignation; had taught herself just to do the duty of each day as it came, and leave the future—where, indeed, it must always remain—in the hands of God. Since the doctor's delicate and judicious kindness had cherished her life, some little health and cheerfulness had returned to her.

Upon this particular evening of the day upon which Traverse entered upon his medical studies she felt very hopeful.

The little cottage fire burned brightly; the hearth was swept clean; the tea kettle was singing over the blaze; the tiny tea table, with its two cups and saucers and two plates and knives was set: everything was neat, comfortable and cheerful for Traverse's return. Marah sat in her little low chair, putting the finishing touches to a set of fine shirts.

She was not anxiously looking for her son, for he had told her that he should stay at the doctor's until six o'clock; therefore she did not expect him until seven.

But so fast had Traverse walked that just as the minute hand pointed to half-past six the latch was raised and Traverse ran in—his face flushed with joy.

The first thing he did was to run to his mother, fling his arms around her neck and kiss her. Then he threw himself into his chair to take breath.

"Now, then, what's the matter, Traverse? You look as if somebody had left you a fortune!"

"And so they have, or, as good as done so!" exclaimed Traverse, panting for breath.

"What in the world do you mean?" exclaimed Marah, her thoughts naturally flying to Old Hurricane, and suggesting his possible repentance or relenting.

"Read that, mother! read that!" said Traverse, eagerly putting a note into her hand.

She opened it and read:

WILLOW HEIGHTS—Monday.

DEAR MADAM—My little daughter Clara, fourteen years of age, has just returned from boarding-school to pursue her studies at home. Among other things,
she must learn domestic affairs, of which she knows nothing. If you will accept the
position of housekeeper and matronly companion of my daughter, I will make the
terms such as shall reconcile you to the change. We shall also do all that we can
to make you happy. Traverse will explain to you the details. Take time to think of
it, but if possible let us have your answer by Traverse when he comes to-morrow.
If you accede to this proposition you will give my daughter and myself sincere
satisfaction.

Yours truly,
WILLIAM DAY.

Marah finished reading, and raised her eyes, full of amazement, to the face of
her son.

"Mother!" said Traverse, speaking fast and eagerly, "they say they really cannot do without you! They have troops of servants; but the old cook is in her dotage
and does all sorts of strange things, such as frying buckwheat cakes in lamp oil
and the like!"

"Oh, hush! what exaggeration!"

"Well, I don't say she does that exactly, but she isn't equal to her situation
without a housekeeper to look after her, and they want you very much, indeed!"

"And what is to become of your home, if I break up?" suggested the mother.

"Oh, that is the very best of it! The doctor says if you consent to come that
I must also live there, and that then he can have his medical assistant always at
hand, which will be very convenient!"

Marah smiled dubiously.

"I do not understand it, but one thing I do know, Traverse! There is not such
a man as the doctor appears in this world more than once in a hundred years."

"Not in a thousand years, mother, and as for his daughter—oh, you should
see Miss Clara, mother! Her father calls her Clare—Clare Day! how the name suits
her! She is so fair and bright! with such a warm, thoughtful, sunny smile that goes
right to your heart! Her face is, indeed, like a clear day, and her beautiful smile is
the sunshine that lights it up!" said the enthusiastic youth, whose admiration was
as yet too simple and single-hearted and unselfish to tie his tongue.

The mother smiled at his earnestness—smiled without the least misgiving; for,
to her apprehension, the youth was still a boy, to wonder at and admire beauty,
without being in the least danger of having his peace of mind disturbed by love.
And as yet her idea of him was just.

"And mother, of course, you will go," said Traverse.

"Oh, I do not know! The proposition was so sudden and unexpected, and is so serious and important, that I must take time to reflect," said Mrs. Rocke, thoughtfully.

"How much time, mother? Will until to-morrow morning do? It must, little mother, because I promised to carry your consent back with me! Indeed, I did, mother!" exclaimed the impatient boy.

Mrs. Rocke dropped her head upon her hand, as was her custom when in deep thought. Presently she said:

"Travy, I'm afraid this is not a genuine offer of a situation of housekeeper! I'm afraid that it is only a ruse to cover a scheme of benevolence! and that they don't really want me, and I should only be in their way."

"Now, mother, I do assure you, they do want you! Think of that young girl and elderly gentleman! Can either of them take charge of a large establishment like that of Willow Heights?"

"Well argued, Traverse; but granting that they need a housekeeper, how do I know I would suit them?"

"Why, you may take their own words for that, mother!"

"But how can they know? I am afraid they would be disappointed!"

"Wait until they complain, mother!"

"I don't believe they ever would!"

"I don't believe they ever would have cause!"

"Well, granting also that I should suit them"—the mother paused and sighed. Traverse filled up the blank by saying:

"I suppose you mean—if you should suit them they might not suit you!"

"No, I do not mean that! I am sure they would suit me; but there is one in the world who may one day come to reason and take bitter umbrage at the fact that I should accept a subordinate situation in any household," murmured Mrs. Rocke, almost unconsciously.

"Then that 'one in the world,' whoever he, she, or it may be, had better place you above the necessity, or else hold his, her, or its tongue! Mother, I think that goods thrown in our way by Providence had better be accepted, leaving the consequences to Him!"

"Traverse, dear, I shall pray over this matter to-night and sleep on it; and He to whom even the fall of a sparrow is not indifferent will guide me," said Mrs. Rocke; and here the debate ended.

The remainder of the evening was spent in laudation of Clare Day, and in writing a letter to Herbert Greyson, at West Point, in which all these laudations were reiterated, and in the course of which Traverse wrote these innocent words: "I have known Clare Day scarcely twelve hours, and I admire her as much as I love you! and oh, Herbert! If you could only rise to be a major-general and marry Clare Day, I should be the happiest fellow alive!" Would Traverse as willingly dispose of Clare's hand a year or two after this time? I trow not!

The next morning after breakfast Mrs. Rocke gave in her decision.

"Tell the doctor, Traverse," she said, "that I understand and appreciate his kindness; that I will not break up my humble home as yet, but I will lock up my house and come a month, on trial. If I can perform the duties of the situation satisfactorily, well and good! I will remain; if not, why then, having my home still in possession, I can return to it."

"Wise little mother! She will not cut down the bridge behind her!" exclaimed Traverse, joyfully, as he bade his mother good-by for the day, and hastened up to Willow Heights with her answer. This answer was received by the good doctor and his lovely daughter with delight as unfeigned as it was unselfish. They were pleased to have a good housekeeper, but they were far better pleased to offer a poor struggling mother a comfortable and even luxurious home.

On the next Monday morning Mrs. Rocke having completed all her arrangements, and closed up the house, entered upon the duties of her new situation.

Clara gave her a large, airy bed-chamber for her own use, communicating with a smaller one for the use of her son; besides this, as housekeeper, she had of course, the freedom of the whole house.

Traverse watched with anxious vigilance to find out whether the efforts of his mother really improved the condition of the housekeeping, and was delighted to find that the coffee was clearer and finer-flavored; the bread whiter and lighter; the cream richer, the butter fresher, and the beefsteak juicier than he had ever known them to be on the doctor's table; that on the dinner table, from day to day, dishes succeeded each other in a well-ordered variety and well-dressed style—in a word, that, in every particular, the comfort of the family was greatly enhanced by the presence of the housekeeper, and that the doctor and his daughter knew it.

While the doctor and his student were engaged in the library, Clara spent many hours of the morning in Mrs. Rocke's company, learning the arts of domestic economy and considerably assisting her in the preparation of delicate dishes.

In the evening the doctor, Clara, Mrs. Rocke and Traverse gathered around the fire as one family—Mrs. Rocke and Clara engaged in needlework, and the doctor or Traverse in reading aloud, for their amusement, some agreeable book. Sometimes Clara would richly entertain them with music—singing and accompanying herself upon the piano.

An hour before bedtime the servants were always called in, and general family prayer offered up.

Thus passed the quiet, pleasant, profitable days. Traverse was fast falling into a delicious dream, from which, as yet, no rude shock threatened to wake him. Willow Heights seemed to him Paradise, its inmates angels, and his own life—beatitude!

CHAPTER XX.

THE OUTLAW'S RENDEZVOUS.

Our plots fall short like darts which rash hands throw
With an ill aim, and have too far to go;
Nor can we long discoveries prevent;
God is too much about the innocent!

—SIR ROBERT HOWARD.

"The Old Road Inn," described in the dying deposition of poor Nancy Grewell, was situated some miles from Hurricane Hall, by the side of a forsaken turnpike in the midst of a thickly wooded, long and narrow valley, shut in by two lofty ranges of mountains.

Once this turnpike was lively with travel and this inn gay with custom; but for the last twenty-five years, since the highway had been turned off in another direction, both road and tavern had been abandoned, and suffered to fall to ruin. The road was washed and furrowed into deep and dangerous gullies, and obstructed by fallen timber; the house was disfigured by moldering walls, broken chimneys and patched windows.

Had any traveler lost himself and chanced to have passed that way, he might have seen a little, old, dried-up woman, sitting knitting at one of the windows. She was known by those who were old enough to remember her and her home, as Granny Raven, the daughter of the last proprietor of the inn. She was reputed to be dumb, but none could speak with certainty of the fact. In truth, for as far back as the memory of the "oldest inhabitant" could reach, she had been feared, disliked and avoided, as one of malign reputation; indeed, the ignorant and superstitious believed her to possess the "evil eye," and to be gifted with "second sight."

But of late years, as the old road and the old inn were quite forsaken, so the old beldame was quite forgotten.

It was one evening, a few weeks after Capitola's fearful adventure in the forest, that this old woman carefully closed up every door and window in the front of the house, stopping every crevice through which a ray of light might gleam and warn that impossible phenomenon—a chance traveler, on the old road, of life within the habitation.

Having, so to speak, hermetically sealed the front of the house, she betook herself to a large back kitchen.

This kitchen was strangely and rudely furnished, having an extra broad fireplace with the recesses, on each side of the chimney filled with oaken shelves, laden with strong pewter plates, dishes and mugs; all along the walls were arranged rude, oaken benches; down the length of the room was left, always standing, a long deal table, capable of accommodating from fifteen to twenty guests.

On entering this kitchen Granny Raven struck a light, kindled a fire and began to prepare a large supper.

Nor unlike the ill-omened bird whose name she bore did this old beldame look in her close-clinging black gown, and flapping black cape and hood, and with her sharp eyes, hooked nose and protruding chin.

Having put a huge sirloin of beef before the fire, she took down a pile of pewter plates and arranged them along on the sides of the table; then to every plate she placed a pewter mug. A huge wheaten loaf of bread, a great roll of butter and several plates of pickles were next put upon the board, and when all was ready the old woman sat down to the patient turning of the spit.

She had not been thus occupied more than twenty minutes when a hasty, scuffling step was heard at the back of the house, accompanied by a peculiar whistle, immediately under the window.

"That's 'Headlong Hal,' for a penny! He never can learn the cat's tread!" thought the crone, as she arose and withdrew the bolt of the back door.

A little dark-skinned, black-eyed, black-haired, thin and wiry man came hurrying in, exclaiming:

"How now, old girl—supper ready!"

She shook her head, pointed to the roasting beef, lifted up both hands with the ten fingers spread out twice, and then made a rotary motion with one arm.

"Oh, you mean it will be done in twenty turns; but hang me if I understand your dumb show half the time! Have none of the men come yet?"

She put her fingers together, flung her hands widely apart in all directions, brought them slowly together again and pointed to the supper table.

"Um! That is to say they are dispersed about their business, but will all be here to-night?"

She nodded.

"Where's the capt'n?"

She pointed over her left shoulder upwards, placed her two hands out broad from her temples, then made a motion as of lifting and carrying a basket, and displaying goods.

"Humph! humph! gone to Tip-top to sell goods disguised as a peddler!"

She nodded. And before he could put another question a low, soft mew was heard at the door.

"There's 'Stealthy Steve!'—he might walk with hob-nailed high-lows upon a gravelly road, and you would never hear his footfall," said the man, as the door noiselessly opened and shut, a soft-footed, low-voiced, subtle-looking mulatto entered the kitchen, and gave good evening to its occupants.

"Ha! I'm devilish glad you've come, Steve, for hang me if I'm not tired to death trying to talk to this crone, who, to the charms of old age and ugliness, adds that of dumbness. Seen the cap'n?"

"No, he's gone out to hear the people talk, and find out what they think of him."

Hal burst into a loud and scornful laugh, saying: "I should think it would not require much seeking to discover that!"

Here the old woman came forward, and, by signs, managed to inquire whether he had brought her "the tea."

Steve drew a packet from his pocket, saying, softly:

"Yes, mother, when I was in Spicer's store I saw this lying with other things on the counter, and, remembering you, quietly put it into my pocket."

The old crone's eyes danced. She seized the packet, patted the excellent thief on the shoulder, wagged her head deridingly at the delinquent one, and hobbled off to prepare her favorite beverage.

While she was thus occupied the whistle was once more heard at the door, followed by the entrance of a man decidedly the most repulsive looking of the whole party—a man one having a full pocket would scarcely like to meet on a lonely road in a dark night. In form he was of Dutch proportions, short but stout, with a large, round head covered with stiff, sandy hair; broad, flat face; coarse features, pale, half-closed eyes, and an expression of countenance strangely made up of elements as opposite as they were forbidding—a mixture of stupidity and subtlety, cowardice and ferocity, caution and cruelty. His name in the gang was Demon Dick, a sobriquet of which he was eminently deserving and characteristically proud.

He came in sulkily, neither saluting the company nor returning their salutations. He pulled a chair to the fire, threw himself into it, and ordered the old woman to draw him a mug of ale.

"Dick's in a bad humor to-night," murmured Steve, softly.

"When was he ever in a good one?" roughly broke forth Hal.

"H-sh!" said Steve, glancing at Dick, who, with a hideous expression, was listening to the conversation.

"There's the cap'n!" exclaimed Hal, as a ringing footstep sounded outside, followed by the abrupt opening of the door and entrance of the leader.

Setting down a large basket, and throwing off a broad-brimmed Quaker hat and broad-skirted overcoat, Black Donald stood roaring with laughter.

Black Donald, from his great stature, might have been a giant walked out of the age of fable into the middle of the nineteenth century. From his stature alone, he might have been chosen leader of this band of desperadoes. He stood six feet eight inches in his boots, and was stout and muscular in proportion. He had a well-formed, stately head, fine aquiline features, dark complexion, strong, steady, dark eyes, and an abundance of long curling black hair and beard that would have driven to despair a Broadway beau, broken the heart of a Washington belle, or made his own fortune in any city of America as a French count or a German baron! He had decidedly "the air noble and distinguished."

While he threw his broad brim in one direction and his broad coat in another, and gave way to peals of laughter, Headlong Hal said:

"Cap'n, I don't know what you think of it, but I think it just as churlish to laugh alone as to get drunk in solitude."

"Oh, you shall laugh! You shall all laugh! Wait until I tell you! But first, answer me: Does not my broad-skirted gray coat and broad-brimmed gray hat make me look about twelve inches shorter and broader?"

"That's so, cap'n!"

"And when I bury my black beard and chin deep down in this drab neck-cloth, and pull the broad brim low over my black hair and eyes, I look as mild and respectable as William Penn?"

"Yea, verily, friend Donald," said Hal.

"Well, in this meek guise I went peddling to-day!"

"Aye, cap'n, we knew it; and you'll go once too often!"

"I have gone just once too often!"

"I knew it!"

"We said so!"

"D——n!" were some of the ejaculations as the members of the band sprang to their feet and handled secret arms.

"Pshaw! put up your knives and pistols! There is no danger. I was not traced — our rendezvous is still a secret for which the government would pay a thousand dollars!"

"How, then, do you say that you went once too often, cap'n?"

"It was inaccurate! I should have said that I had gone for the last time, for that it would not be safe to venture again. Come—I must tell you the whole story! But in the mean time let us have supper. Mother Raven, dish the beef! Dick, draw the ale! Hal, cut the bread! Steve, carve! Bestir yourselves, burn you, or you shall have no story!" exclaimed the captain, flinging himself into a chair at the head of the table.

When his orders had been obeyed, and the men were gathered around the table, and the first draught of ale had been quaffed by all, Black Donald asked:

"Where do you think I went peddling to-day?"

"Devil knows," said Hal.

"That's a secret between the Demon and Black Donald" said Dick.

"Hush! he's about to tell us," murmured Steve.

"Wooden heads! you'd never guess! I went—I went to—do you give it up? I went right straight into the lion's jaws—not only into the very clutches, but into the very teeth, and down the very throat of the lion, and have come out as safe as Jonah from the whale's belly! In a word, I have been up to the county seat where the court is now in session, and sold cigar cases, snuff boxes and smoking caps to the grand and petit jury, and a pair of gold spectacles to the learned judge himself!"

"No!"

"No!!"

"No!!!" exclaimed Hal, Steve and Dick in a breath.

"Yes! and, moreover, I offered a pair of patent steel spring handcuffs to the sheriff, John Keepe, in person, and pressed him to purchase them, assuring him that he would have occasion for their use if ever he caught that grand rascal, Black Donald!"

"'Ah, the atrocious villain, if I thought I should ever have the satisfaction of springing them upon his wrists, I'd buy them at my own proper cost!' said the sheriff, taking them in his hands and examining them curiously.

"'Ah! he's a man of Belial, that same Black Donald—thee'd better buy the handcuffs, John,' said I.

"'Nay, friend, I don't know; and as for Black Donald, we have some hopes of taking the wretch at last!' said the simple gentleman.

"'Ah, verily, John, that's a good hearing for peaceful travelers like myself,' said I.

"'Excellent! excellent! For when that fell marauder once swings from the gallows——'

"'His neck will be broken, John?'

"'Yes, friend! yes, probably; after which honest men may travel in safety! Ah, never have I adjusted a hempen cravat about the throat of any aspirant for such an honor with less pain than I shall officiate at the last toilet of Black Donald!'

"'If thee catch him!'

"'Exactly, friend, if I catch him; but the additional reward offered by Major Warfield, together with the report that he often frequents our towns and villages in disguise, will stimulate people to renewed efforts to discover and capture him,' said the sheriff.

"'Ah! that will be a great day for Alleghany. And when Black Donald is hanged, I shall make an effort to be present at the solemnity myself!'

"'Do, friend,' said the sheriff, 'and I will see to getting you a good place for witnessing the proceedings.'

"'I have no doubt thee will, John—a very good place! And I assure thee that there will not be one present more interested in those proceedings than myself,' said I.

"'Of course, that is very natural, for there is no one more in danger from these marauders than men of your itinerant calling. Good heavens! It was but three years ago a peddler was robbed and murdered in the woods around the Hidden House.'

"'Just so, John,' said I; 'and it's my opinion that often when I've been traveling along the road at night Black Donald hasn't been far off! But tell me, John, so that I may have a chance of earning that thousand dollars—what disguises does this son of Moloch take?'

"'Why, friend, it is said that he appears as a Methodist missionary, going about selling tracts; and sometimes as a knife grinder, and sometimes simulates your calling, as a peddler!' said the unsuspicious sheriff.

"I thought, however, it was time to be off, so I said 'Thee had better let me sell thee those handcuffs, John. Allow me! I will show thee their beautiful machinery! Hold out thy wrists, if thee pleases, John.'

"The unsuspicious officer, with a face brimful of interest, held out his wrists for experiment.

"I snapped the ornaments on them in a little less than no time, and took up my pack and disappeared before the sheriff had collected his faculties and found out his position!"

"Ha, ha, ha! Haw, haw, haw! Ho, ho, ho!" laughed the outlaws, in every key of laughter. "And so our captain, instead of being pinioned by the sheriff, turned the tables and actually manacled his honor! Hip, hip, hurrah! Three times three for the merry captain, that manacled the sheriff!"

"Hush, burn ye! There's some one coming!" exclaimed the captain, rising and listening. "It is Le Noir, who was to meet me here to-night on important business!"

CHAPTER XXI.

GABRIEL LE NOIR.

Naught's had! all's spent!
When our desires are gained without content.

—SHAKESPEARE.

"The colonel!" exclaimed the three men in a breath, as the door opened and a tall, handsome and distinguished-looking gentleman, wrapped in a black military cloak and having his black beaver pulled low over his brow, strode into the room.

All arose upon their feet to greet him as though he had been a prince.

With a haughty wave of the hand, he bade them resume their seats, and beckoning their leader, said:

"Donald, I would have a word with you!"

"At your command, colonel!" said the outlaw, rising and taking a candle and leading the way into the adjoining room, the same in which fourteen years before old Granny Grewell and the child had been detained.

Setting the candle upon the mantelpiece, Black Donald stood waiting for the visitor to open the conversation, a thing that the latter seemed in no hurry to do, for he began walking up and down the room in stern silence.

"You seem disturbed, colonel," at length said the outlaw.

"I am disturbed—more than disturbed! I am suffering!"

"Suffering, colonel?"

"Aye, suffering! From what think you? The pangs of remorse!"

"Remorse! Ha, ha, ha, ha, ha!" laughed the outlaw till all the rafters rang.

"Aye, man, you may laugh; but I repeat that I am tortured with remorse! And for what do you suppose? For those acts of self-preservation that fanatics and fools would stigmatize as crimes? No, my good fellow, no! but for one 'unacted crime!'"

"I told your honor so!" cried the outlaw, triumphantly.

"Donald, when I go to church, as I do constantly, I hear the preacher prating of repentance; but man, I never knew the meaning of the word until recently."

"And I can almost guess what it is that has enlightened your honor?" said the outlaw.

"Yes, it is that miserable old woman and babe! Donald, in every vein of my soul I repent not having silenced them both forever while they were yet in my power!"

"Just so, colonel; the dead never come back, or if they do, are not recognized as property holders in this world. I wish your honor had taken my advice and sent that woman and child on a longer journey."

"Donald, I was younger then than now. I—shrank from bloodshed," said the man in a husky voice.

"Bah! superstition! Bloodshed—blood is shed every day! 'We kill to live!' say the butchers. So do we. Every creature preys upon some other creature weaker than himself—the big beasts eat up the little ones—artful men live on the simple! So be it! The world was made for the strong and cunning! Let the weak and foolish look to themselves!" said the outlaw, with a loud laugh.

While he spoke the visitor resumed his rapid, restless striding up and down the room. Presently he came again to the side of the robber and whispered:

"Donald, that girl has returned to the neighborhood, brought back by old Warfield. My son met her in the woods a month ago, fell into conversation with her, heard her history, or as much of it as she herself knows. Her name is Capitola! She is the living image of her mother! How she came under the notice of old Warfield—to what extent he is acquainted with her birth and rights—what proofs may be in his possession I know not. All that I have discovered after the strictest inquiry that I was enabled to make, is this—that the old beggar woman that died and was buried at Major Warfield's expense, was no other than Nancy Grewell, returned—that the night before she died she sent for Major Warfield and had a long talk with him, and that shortly afterward the old scoundrel traveled to the north and brought home this girl!"

"Humph! it is an ugly business, your honor, especially with your honor's little prejudice against——"

"Donald, this is no time for weakness! I have gone too far to stop! Capitola must die!"

"That's so, colonel—the pity is that it wasn't found out fourteen years ago. It is so much easier to pinch a baby's nose until it falls asleep than to stifle a young girl's shrieks and cries—then the baby would not have been missed—but the young girl will be sure to be inquired after."

"I know that there will be additional risk, but there shall be the larger compensation, larger than your most sanguine hopes would suggest. Donald, listen!" said the colonel, stooping and whispering low—"the day that you bring me undeniable proofs that Capitola Le Noir is dead, you finger one thousand dollars!"

"Ha, ha, ha!" laughed the outlaw, in angry scorn. "Capitola Le Noir is the sole heiress of a fortune—in land, negroes, coal mines, iron foundries, railway shares and bank stock of half a million of dollars—and you ask me to get her out of your way for a thousand dollars—I'll do it—you know I will! Ha, ha, ha!"

"Why, the government doesn't value your whole carcass at more than I offer you for the temporary use of your hands, you villain!" frowned the colonel.

"No ill names, your honor—between us they are like kicking guns—apt to recoil!"

"You forget that you are in my power!"

"I remember that your honor is in mine! Ha, ha, ha! The day Black Donald stands at the bar—the honorable Colonel Le Noir will probably be beside him!"

"Enough of this! Confound you, do you take me for one of your pals?"

"No, your worship, my pals are too poor to hire their work done, but then they are brave enough to do it themselves."

"Enough of this, I say! Name the price of this new service!"

"Ten thousand dollars—five thousand in advance—the remainder when the deed is accomplished."

"Extortioner! Shameless, ruthless extortioner!"

"Your honor will fall into that vulgar habit of calling ill names. It isn't worth while! It doesn't pay! If your honor doesn't like my terms, you needn't employ me. What is certain is that I cannot work for less!"

"You take advantage of my necessities."

"Not at all; but the truth is, Colonel, that I am tired of this sort of life, and wish to retire from active business. Besides, every man has his ambition, and I have mine. I wish to emigrate to the glorious West, settle, marry, turn my attention to politics, be elected to Congress, then to the Senate, then to the Cabinet, then to the White House—for success in which career, I flatter myself nature and education have especially fitted me. Ten thousand dollars will give me a fair start! Many a successful politician, your honor knows, has started on less character and less capital!"

To this impudent slander the colonel made no answer. With his arms folded and his head bowed upon his chest he walked moodily up and down the length of the apartment. Then muttering, "Why should I hesitate?" he came to the side of the outlaw and said:

"I agree to your terms—accomplish the work and the sum shall be yours. Meet me here on to-morrow evening to receive the earnest money. In the meantime, in order to make sure of the girl's identity, it will be necessary for you to get sight of her beforehand, at her home, if possible—find out her habits and her haunts—where she walks, or rides, when she is most likely to be alone, and so on. Be very careful! A mistake might be fatal."

"Your honor may trust me."

"And now good-by—remember, to-morrow evening," said the colonel, as, wrapping himself closely in his dark cloak, and pulling his hat low over his eyes, he passed out by the back passage door and left the house.

"Ha, ha, ha! Why does that man think it needful to look so villainous? If I were to go about in such a bandit-like dress as that, every child I met would take me for—what I am!" laughed Black Donald, returning to his comrades.

During the next hour other members of the band dropped in until some twenty men were collected together in the large kitchen around the long table, where the remainder of the night was spent in revelry.

CHAPTER XXII.

THE SMUGGLER AND CAPITOLA.

Come buy of me! come buy! come buy!
Buy, lads, or else the lassies cry;
I have lawns as white as snow;
Silk as black as e'er was crow;
Gloves as sweet as damask roses;
Veils for faces; musk for noses;
Pins and needles made of steel;
All you need from head to heel.

—SHAKESPEARE.

"If I am not allowed to walk or ride out alone, I shall 'gang daft!' I know I shall! Was ever such a dull, lonesome, humdrum place as this same Hurricane Hall?" complained Cap, as she sat sewing with Mrs. Condiment in the housekeeper's room.

"You don't like this quiet country life?" inquired Mrs. Condiment.

"No! no better than I do a quiet country graveyard! I don't want to return to dust before my time, I tell you!" said Cap, yawning dismally over her work.

"I hear you, vixen!" roared the voice of Old Hurricane, who presently came storming in and saying:

"If you want a ride go and get ready quickly, and come with me, I am going down to the water mill, please the Lord, to warn Hopkins off the premises, worthless villain! Had my grain there since yesterday morning and hasn't sent it home yet! Shan't stay in my mill another month! Come, Cap, be off with you and get ready!"

The girl did not need a second bidding but flew to prepare herself, while the old man ordered the horses.

In ten minutes more Capitola and Major Warfield cantered away.

They had been gone about two hours, and it was almost time to expect their return, and Mrs. Condiment had just given orders for the tea table to be set, when Wool came into her room and said there was a sailor at the hall door with some beautiful foreign goods which he wished to show to the ladies of the house.

"A sailor, Wool—a sailor with foreign goods for sale? I am very much afraid he's one of these smugglers I've heard tell of, and I'm not sure about the right of buying from smugglers! However, I suppose there's no harm in looking at his goods. You may call him in, Wool," said the old lady, tampering with temptation.

"He do look like a smudgeler, dat's a fact," said Wool whose ideas of the said craft were purely imaginary.

"I don't know him to be a smuggler, and it's wrong to judge, particularly beforehand," said the old lady, nursing ideas of rich silks and satins, imported free of duty and sold at half price, and trying to deceive herself.

While she was thus thinking the door opened and Wool ushered in a stout, jolly-looking tar, dressed in a white pea-jacket, duck trousers and tarpaulin hat, and carrying in his hand a large pack. He took off his hat and scraped his foot behind him, and remained standing before the housekeeper with his head tied up in a red bandana handkerchief and his chin sunken in a red comforter that was wound around his throat.

"Sit down, my good man, and rest while you show me the goods," said Mrs. Condiment, who, whether he were smuggler or not, was inclined to show the traveler all lawful kindness.

The sailor scraped his foot again, sat down on a low chair, put his hat on one side, drew the pack before him, untied it and first displayed a rich golden-hued fabric, saying:

"Now here, ma'am, is a rich China silk I bought in the streets of Shanghai, where the long-legged chickens come from. Come, now, I'll ship it off cheap——"

"Oh, that is a great deal too gay and handsome for an old woman like me," said Mrs. Condiment.

"Well, ma'am, perhaps there's young ladies in the fleet? Now, this would rig out a smart young craft as gay as a clipper! Better take it, ma'am. I'll ship it off cheap!"

"Wool!" said Mrs. Condiment, turning to the servant, "go down to the kitchen and call up the house servants—perhaps they would like to buy something."

As soon as Wool had gone and the good woman was left alone with the sailor, she stooped and said:

"I did not wish to inquire before the servant man, but, my good sir, I do not know whether it is right to buy from you!"

"Why so, ma'am?" asked the sailor, with an injured look.

"Why, I am afraid—I am very much afraid you risk your life and liberty in an unlawful trade!"

"Oh, ma'am, on my soul, these things are honestly come by, and you have no right to accuse me!" said the sailor, with a look of subdued indignation.

"I know I haven't, and I meant no harm, but did these goods pass through the custom house?"

"Oh, ma'am, now, that's not a fair question!"

"It is as I suspected! I cannot buy from you, my good friend. I do not judge you—I don't know whether smuggling is right or wrong, but I know that it is unlawful, and I cannot feel free to encourage any man in a traffic in which he risks his life and liberty, poor fellow!"

"Oh, ma'am," said the sailor, evidently on the brink of bursting into laughter, "if we risk our lives, sure, it's our own business, and if you've no scruples on your own account, you needn't have any on ours!"

While he was speaking the sound of many shuffling feet was heard along the passage, and the room was soon half filled with colored people come in to deal with the sailor.

"You may look at these goods, but you must not buy anything."

"Lor' missus, why?" asked little Pitapat.

"Because I want you to lay out all your money with my friend Mr. Crash at Tip-Top."

"But after de good gemman has had de trouble?" said Pitapat.

"He shall have his supper and a mug of ale and go on his journey," said Mrs. Condiment.

The sailor arose and scraped his foot behind him in acknowledgment of this kindness and began to unpack his wares and display them all over the floor.

And while the servants in wonder and delight examined these treasures and inquired their prices, a fresh young voice was heard carolling along the hall, and the next moment Capitola, in her green riding habit and hat entered the room.

She turned her mischievous gray eyes about, pursed up her lips and asked Mrs. Condiment if she were about to open a fancy bazaar.

"No, my dear Miss Capitola! It is a sailor with foreign goods for sale," answered the old lady.

"A sailor with foreign goods for sale! Umph! yes, I know. Isn't he a smuggler?" whispered Capitola.

"Indeed. I'm afraid so, my dear—in fact, he don't deny it!" whispered back the matron.

"Well, I think it's strange a man that smuggles can't lie!"

"Well, I don't know, my dear—may be he thinks it's no harm to smuggle, and he knows it would be a sin to lie. But where is your uncle, Miss Capitola?"

"Gone around to the stable to blow Jem up for mounting on a lame horse. He swears Jem shall find another master before to-morrow's sun sets. But now I want to talk to that bold buccaneer. Say, you sir, show me your foreign goods—I'm very fond of smugglers myself!"

"You are right, my dear young lady! You would give poor sailors some little chance to turn an honest penny!"

"Certainly! Brave fellows! Show me that splendid fabric that shines like cloth of gold."

"This, my young lady, this is a real, genuine China silk. I bought it myself in my last cruise in the streets of Shanghai, where the long-legged chickens — —"

"And fast young men come from! I know the place! I've been along there!" interrupted Capitola, her gray eyes glittering with mischief.

"This you will perceive, young lady, is an article that cannot be purchased anywhere except — —"

"From the manufactory of foreign goods in the city of New York, or from their traveling agents!"

"Oh, my dear young lady, how you wrong me! This article came from — —"

"The factory of Messrs. Hocus & Pocus, corner of Can't and Come-it Street, City of Gotham!"

"Oh, my dear young lady — —"

"Look here, my brave buccaneer, I know all about it! I told you I'd been along there!" said the girl, and, turning to Mrs. Condiment, she said. "See here, my dear, good soul, if you want to buy that 'India' silk that you are looking at so longingly, you may do it with a safe conscience! True, it never passed through the custom house—because it was made in New York. I know all about it! All these 'foreign goods' are manufactured at the north and sent by agents all over the country. These agents dress and talk like sailors and assume a mysterious manner on purpose to be suspected of smuggling, because they know well enough fine ladies will buy much quicker and pay much more if they only fancy they are cheating Uncle Sam in buying foreign goods from a smuggler at half price."

"So, then, you are not a smuggler, after all!" said Mrs. Condiment, looking almost regretfully at the sailor.

"Why, ma'am, you know I told you you were accusing me wrongfully."

"Well, but really, now, there was something about you that looked sort of suspicious."

"What did I tell you? A look put on on purpose," said Cap.

"Well, he knows that if he wanted to pass for a smuggler, it didn't take here," said Mrs. Condiment.

"No, that it didn't!" muttered the object of these commentaries.

"Well, my good man, since you are, after all, an honest peddler, just hand me that silk and don't ask me an unreasonable price for it, because I'm a judge of silks and I won't pay more than it is worth," said the old lady.

"Madam, I leave it to your own conscience! You shall give me just what you think it's worth."

"Humph! that's too fair by half! I begin to think this fellow is worse than he seems!" said Capitola to herself.

After a little hesitation a price was agreed upon and the dress bought.

Then the servants received permission to invest their little change in ribbons, handkerchiefs, tobacco, snuff, or whatever they thought they needed. When the purchases were all made and the peddler had done up his diminished pack and replaced his hat upon his head and was preparing to leave, Mrs. Condiment said:

"My good man, it is getting very late, and we do not like to see a traveler leave our house at this hour—pray remain until morning, and then, after an early breakfast, you can pursue your way in safety."

"Thank you kindly, ma'am, but I must be far on my road to-night," said the peddler.

"But, my good man, you are a stranger in this part of the country and don't know the danger you run," said the housekeeper.

"Danger, ma'am, in this quiet country?"

"Oh, dear, yes, my good man, particularly with your valuable pack—oh, my good gracious!" cried the old lady, with an appalled look.

"Indeed, ma'am, you—you make me sort of uneasy! What danger can there be for a poor, peaceful peddler pursuing his path?"

"Oh, my good soul, may heaven keep you from—Black Donald!"

"Black Donald—who's he?"

"Oh, my good man, he's the awfullest villain that ever went unhung!"

"Black Donald? Black Donald? Never heard that name before in my life? Why is the fellow called Black Donald?"

"Oh, sir, he's called Black Donald for his black soul, black deeds and—and—also, I believe, for his jet black hair and beard."

"'Oh, my countrymen, what a falling up was there,'" exclaimed Capitola at this anti-climax.

"And how shall I keep from meeting this villain?" asked the peddler.

"Oh, sir, how can I tell you? You never can form an idea where he is or where he isn't! Only think, he may be in our midst any time, and we not know it! Why, only yesterday the desperate villain handcuffed the very sheriff in the very courtyard! Yet I wonder the sheriff did not know him at once! For my own part, I'm sure I should know Black Donald the minute I clapped my two looking eyes on him!"

"Should you, ma'am?"

"Yes, indeed, by his long, black hair and beard! They say it is half a yard long—now a man of such a singular appearance as that must be easily recognized!"

"Of course! Then you never met this wretch face to face?"

"He? Me? Am I standing here alive? Do you suppose I should be standing here if ever I had met that demon? Why, man, I never leave this house, even in the day time, except with two bull dogs and a servant, for fear I should meet Black Donald! I know if ever I should meet that demon, I should drop dead with terror! I feel I should!"

"But maybe, now, ma'am, the man may not be so bad, after all? Even the devil is not so bad as he is painted."

"The devil may not be, but Black Donald is!"

"What do you think of this outlaw, young lady?" asked the peddler, turning to Capitola.

"Why, I like him!" said Cap.

"You do!"

"Yes, I do! I like men whose very names strike terror into the hearts of commonplace people!"

"Oh, Miss Black!" exclaimed Mrs. Condiment.

"Yes, I do, ma'am. And if Black Donald were only as honest as he is brave I should quite adore him. So there! And if there is one person in the world I should like to see it is Black Donald!"

"Do you really wish to see him?" asked the peddler, looking intently into the half earnest, half satirical face of the girl.

"Yes, I do wish to see him above all things!"

"And do you know what happened the rash girl who wished to see the devil!"

"No—what did?"

"She saw him!"

"Oh, if that's all, I dare it! And if wishing will bring me the sight of this notorious outlaw, lo, I wish it! I wish to see Black Donald!" said Capitola.

The peddler deliberately arose and put down his pack and his hat; then he suddenly tore off the scarf from his neck and the handkerchief from his head, lifted his chin and shook loose a great rolling mass of black hair and beard, drew himself up, struck an attitude, called up a look, and exclaimed:

"Behold Black Donald!"

With a piercing shriek, Mrs. Condiment swooned and fell to the floor; the poor negroes, men and maids, were struck dumb and motionless with consternation; Capitola gazed for one lost moment in admiration and curiosity; in the meantime Black Donald quickly resumed his disguises, took up his pack and walked out of the room.

Capitola was the first to recover her presence of mind; the instinct of the huntress possessed her; starting forward, she exclaimed:

"Pursue him! catch him! come with me! Cowards, will you let a robber and murderer escape?" and she ran out and overtook the outlaw in the middle of the hall. With the agile leap of a little terrier she sprang up behind him, seized the thick collar of his pea-jacket with both hands, and, drawing up her feet, hung there with all her weight, crying:

"Help! murder! murder! help! Come to my aid! I've caught Black Donald!"

He could have killed her instantly in any one of a dozen ways. He could have driven in her temples with a blow of his sledge-hammer fist; he could have broken her neck with the grip of his iron fingers; he only wished to shake her off without hurting her—a difficult task, for there she hung, a dead weight, at the collar of his coat at the back of his neck.

"Oh, very well!" he cried, laughing aloud! "Such adhesiveness I never saw! You stick to me like a wife to her husband. So if you won't let go, I shall have to take you along, that's all! So here I go like Christian with his bundle of sin on his back!"

And loosing the upper button of his pea-jacket so as to give him more breath, and, putting down his peddler's pack to relieve himself as much as possible, the outlaw strode through the hall door, down the steps, and down the evergreen avenue leading to the woods.

Capitola still clinging to the back of his coat-collar, with feet drawn up, a dead weight, and still crying:

"Help! Murder! I've caught Black Donald, and I'll die before I'll let him go!"

"You're determined to be an outlaw's bride, that's certain! Well, I've no particular objection!" cried Black Donald, roaring with laughter as he strode on.

It was a "thing to see, not hear"—that brave, rash, resolute imp clinging like a terrier, or a crab, or a briar, on to the back of that gigantic ruffian, whom, if she had no strength to stop, she was determined not to release.

They had nearly reached the foot of the descent, when a great noise and hallooing was heard behind them. It was the negroes, who, having recovered from their panic, and armed themselves with guns, pistols, swords, pokers, tongs and pitchforks, were now in hot pursuit!

And cries of "Black Donald! Black Donald! Black Donald!" filled the air.

"I've got him! I've got him! help! help! quick! quick!" screamed Capitola, clinging closer than ever.

Though still roaring with laughter at the absurdity of his position, Black Donald strode on faster than before, and was in a fair way of escape, when lo! suddenly coming up the path in front of him, he met—Old Hurricane!!!

As the troop of miscellaneously armed negroes running down the hill were still making eve hideous with yells of "Black Donald!" and Capitola still clinging and hanging on at the back of his neck, continued to cry, "I've caught him! help! help!" something like the truth flashed in a blinding way upon Old Hurricane's perceptions.

Roaring forth something between a recognition and a defiance, the old man threw up his fat arms, and as fast as age and obesity would permit, ran up the hill to intercept the outlaw.

There was no time for trifling now! The army of negroes was at his heels; the old veteran in his path; the girl clinging a dead weight to his jacket behind. An idea suddenly struck him which he wondered had not done so before—quickly unbuttoning and throwing off his garment he dropped both jacket and captor behind him on the ground.

And before Capitola had picked herself up, Black Donald, bending his huge head and shoulders forward and making a battering ram of himself, ran with all his force and butted Old Hurricane in the stomach, pitching him into the horse pond, leaped over the park fence and disappeared in the forest.

What a scene! what a row followed the escape and flight of the famous outlaw!

Who could imagine, far less describe it!—a general tempest in which every individual was a particular storm!

There stood the baffled Capitola, extricating her head from the pea-jacket, and with her eyes fairly flashing out sparks of anger, exclaiming, "Oh, wretches! wretches that you are! If you'd been worth salt you could have caught him while I clung to him so!"

There wallowed Old Hurricane, spluttering, floundering, half drowning, in the horse pond, making the most frantic efforts to curse and swear as he struggled to get out.

There stood the crowd of negroes brought to a sudden stand by a panic of horror at seeing the dignity of their master so outraged!

And, most frenzied of all, there ran Wool around and around the margin of the pond, in a state of violent perplexity how to get his master out without half drowning himself!

"Blurr-urr-rr! flitch! flitch! Blurr!-ur!" spluttered and sneezed and strangled, Old Hurricane, as he floundered to the edge of the pond—"Burr-urr-rr! Help me out, you scoundrel! I'll break every bone in your—flitch! body! Do you hear me—ca-snish!—villain you! flitch! flitch! ca-snish! oh-h!"

Wool with his eyes starting from his head and his hair standing up with terrors of all sorts, plunged at last into the water and pulled his old master up upon his feet.

"Ca-snish! ca-snish! blurr-rr! flitch!—what are you gaping there for as if you'd raised the devil, you crowd of born fools!" bawled Old Hurricane as soon as he could get the water out of his mouth and nose—"what are you standing there for! After him! After him, I say! Scour the woods in every direction! His freedom to any man who brings me Black Donald, dead or alive—Wool!"

"Yes, sir," said that functionary, who was busying himself with squeezing the water out of his master's garments.

"Wool, let me alone? Take the fleetest horse in the stable! Ride for your life to the Court House! Tell Keepe to have new bills posted everywhere, offering an additional five hundred dollars for the apprehension of that—that—that"—for the want of a word strong enough to express himself, Old Hurricane suddenly stopped, and for the lack of his stick to make silence emphatic, he seized his gray hair with both hands and groaned aloud!

Wool waited no second bidding, but flew to do his errand.

Capitola came to the old man's side, saying:

"Uncle, hadn't you better hurry home—you'll take cold."

"Cold? Cold! demmy! I never was so hot in my life!" cried the old man; "but, demmy! you're right! Run to the house, Capitola, and tell Mrs. Condiment to have me a full suit of dry clothes before the fire in my chamber. Go, child! every man-jack is off after Black Donald, and there is nobody but you and Condiment and the housemaids to take care of me. Stop! look for my stick first. Where did that black demon throw it? Demmy! I'd as well be without my legs!"

Capitola picked up the old man's cane and hat and put the one on his head and the other in his hand, and then hastened to find Mrs. Condiment and tell her to prepare to receive her half-drowned patron. She found the old lady scarcely recovered from the effects of her recent fright, but ready on the instant to make every effort in behalf of Old Hurricane, who presently after arrived dripping wet at the house.

Leaving the old gentleman to the care of his housekeeper, we must follow Black Donald.

Hatless and coatless, with his long black hair and beard blown by the wind, the outlaw made tracks for his retreat—occasionally stopping to turn and get breath, and send a shout of laughter after his baffled pursuers.

That same night, at the usual hour, the gang met at their rendezvous, the deserted inn, beside the old road through the forest. They were in the midst of their orgies around the supper table, when the well-known ringing step of the leader sounded under the back windows without, the door was burst open, and the captain, hatless, coatless, with his dark elf locks flying, and every sign of haste and disorder, rushed into the room.

He was met by a general rising and outcry: "Hi! hillo! what's up?" exclaimed every man, starting to his feet and laying hands upon secret arms, prepared for instant resistance.

For a moment Black Donald stood with his leonine head turned and looking back over his stalwart shoulders, as if in expectation of pursuit, and then, with a loud laugh, turned to his men, exclaiming:

"Ho! you thought me followed! So I have been; but not as close as hound to heel!"

"In fact, captain, you look as if you'd but escaped with your skin this time!" said Hal.

"Faith! the captain looks well peeled!" said Stephen.

"Worse than that, boys! worse than that! Your chief has not only lost his pack, his hat and his coat, but—his heart! Not only are the outworks battered, but the citadel itself is taken! Not only has he been captured, but captivated! And all by a little minx of a girl! Boys, your chief is in love!" exclaimed Black Donald, throwing himself into his seat at the head of the table, and quaffing off a large draught of ale.

"Hip! hip! hurraw! three times three for the captain's love!" cried Hal, rising to propose the toast, which was honored with enthusiasm.

"Now tell us all about it, captain. Who is she? Where did you see her? Is she fair or dark; tall or short; thin or plump; what's her name, and is she kind?" asked Hal.

"First, guess where I have been to-day?"

"You and your demon only know!"

"I guess they also know at Hurricane Hall, for it is there I have been!"

"Well, then, why didn't you go to perdition at once?" exclaimed Hal, in a consternation that was reflected in every countenance present.

"Why, because when I go there I intend to take you all with me and remain!" answered Black Donald.

"Tell us about the visit to Hurricane Hall," said Hal.

Whereupon Black Donald commenced, and concealing only the motive of his visit, gave his comrades a very graphic, spicy and highly colored narrative of his adventure at Hurricane Hall, and particularly of his "passages at arms" with the little witch, Capitola, whom he described as:

"Such a girl! slender, petite, lithe, with bright, black ringlets dancing around a little face full of fun, frolic, mischief and spirit, and bright eyes quick and vivacious as those of a monkey, darting hither and thither from object to object."

"The captain is in love sure enough," said Steve.

"Bravo! here's success to the captain's love!—she's a brick!" shouted the men.

"Oh, she is!" assented their chief, with enthusiasm.

"Long life to her! three times three for the pretty witch of Hurricane Hall!" roared the men, rising to their feet and waving their full mugs high in the air, before pledging the toast.

"That is all very well, boys; but I want more substantial compliments than words—boys, I must have that girl!"

"Who doubts it, captain? Of course you will take her at once if you want her," said Hal, confidently.

"But, I must have help in taking her."

"Captain, I volunteer for one!" exclaimed Hal.

"And I, for another," added Stephen.

"And you, Dick?" inquired the leader, turning toward the sullen man, whose greater atrocity had gained for him the name of Demon Dick.

"What is the use of volunteering when the captain has only to command," said this individual, sulkily.

"Ay! when the enterprise is simply the robbing of a mail coach, in which you all have equal interest, then, indeed, your captain has only to command, and you to obey; but this is a more delicate matter of entering a lady's chamber and carrying her off for the captain's arms, and so should only be entrusted to those whose feelings of devotion to the captain's person prompt them to volunteer for the service," said Black Donald.

"How elegantly our captain speaks! He ought to be a lawyer," said Steve.

"The captain knows I'm with him for everything," said Dick, sulkily.

"Very well, then, for a personal service like this, a delicate service requiring devotion, I should scorn to give commands! I thank you for your offered assistance, my friends, and shall count on you three Hal, Stephen and Richard for the enterprise!" said the captain.

"Ay, ay, ay!" said the three men, in a breath.

"For the time and place and manner of the seizure of the girl, we must reflect. Let us see! There is to be a fair in the village next week, during the session of the court. Old Hurricane will be at court as usual. And for one day, at least, his servants will have a holiday to go to the fair. They will not get home until the next morning. The house will be ill-guarded. We must find out the particular day and night when this shall be so. Then you three shall watch your opportunity, enter the house by stealth, conceal yourselves in the chamber of the girl, and at midnight when all is quiet, gag her and bring her away."

"Excellent!" said Hal.

"And mind, no liberty, except the simple act of carrying her off, is to be taken with your captain's prize!" said the leader, with a threatening glare of his lion-like eye.

"Oh, no, no, not for the world! She shall be as sacred from insult as though she were an angel and we saints!" said Hal, both the others assenting.

"And now, not a word more. We will arrange the further details of this business hereafter," said the captain, as a peculiar signal was given at the door.

Waving his hand for the men to keep their places, Black Donald went out and opened the back passage door, admitting Colonel Le Noir.

"Well!" said the latter anxiously.

"Well, sir, I have contrived to see her; come into the front room and I will tell you all about it!" said the outlaw, leading the way into the old parlor that had been the scene of so many of their conspiracies.

"Does Capitola Le Noir still live?" hoarsely demanded the colonel, as the two conspirators reached the parlor.

"Still live? Yes; 'twas but yesterday we agreed upon her death! Give a man time! Sit down, colonel! Take this seat. We will talk the matter over again."

With something very like a sigh of relief, Colonel Le Noir threw himself into the offered chair.

Black Donald drew another chair up and sat down beside his patron.

"Well, colonel, I have contrived to see the girl as I told you," he began.

"But you have not done the deed! When will it be done?"

"Colonel, my patron, be patient! Within twelve days I shall claim the last instalment of the ten thousand dollars agreed upon between us for this job!"

"But why so long, since it is to be done, why not have it over at once?" said Colonel Le Noir, starting up and pacing the floor impatiently.

"Patience, my colonel! The cat may play with the mouse most delightfully before devouring it!"

"What do you mean?"

"My colonel, I have seen the girl, under circumstances that has fired my heart with an uncontrollable desire for her."

"Ha, ha ha!" scornfully laughed the colonel. "Black Donald, the mail robber, burglar, outlaw, the subject of the grand passion!"

"Why not, my colonel? Listen, you shall hear! And then you shall judge whether or not you yourself might not have been fired by the fascinations of such a witch!" said the outlaw, who straightway commenced and gave his patron the same account of his visit to Hurricane Hall that he had already related to his comrades.

The colonel heard the story with many a "pish," "tush" and "pshaw," and when the man had concluded the tale he exclaimed:

"Is that all? Then we may continue our negotiations, I care not! Carry her off! marry her! do as you please with her! only at the end of all—kill her!" hoarsely whispered Le Noir.

"That is just what I intend, colonel!"

"That will do if the event be certain: but it must be certain! I cannot breathe freely while my brother's heiress lives," whispered Le Noir.

"Well, colonel, be content; here is my hand upon it! In six days Capitola will be in my power! In twelve days you shall be out of hers!"

"It is a bargain," said each of the conspirators, in a breath, as they shook hands and parted—Le Noir to his home and Black Donald to join his comrades' revelry.

CHAPTER XXIII.

THE BOY'S LOVE

Endearing! endearing!
Why so endearing
Are those soft shining eyes,
Through their silk fringe peering?
They love thee! they love thee!
Deeply, sincerely;
And more than aught else on earth
Thou lovest them dearly!

—MOTHERWELL.

While these dark conspiracies were hatching elsewhere, all was comfort, peace and love in the doctor's quiet dwelling.

Under Marah Rocke's administration the business of the household went on with the regularity of clockwork. Every one felt the advantage of this improved condition.

The doctor often declared that for his part he could not for the life of him think how they had ever been able to get along without Mrs. Rocke and Traverse.

Clara affirmed that however the past might have been, the mother and son were a present and future necessity to the doctor's comfort and happiness.

The little woman herself gained rapidly both health and spirits and good looks. Under favorable circumstances, Marah Rocke, even at thirty-six, would have been esteemed a first-rate beauty; and even now she was pretty, graceful and attractive to a degree that she herself was far from suspecting.

Traverse advanced rapidly in his studies, to the ardent pursuit of which he was urged by every generous motive that could fire a human bosom—affection for his mother, whose condition he was anxious to elevate; gratitude to his patron, whose great kindness he wished to justify, and admiration for Clara, whose esteem he was ambitious to secure.

He attended his patron in all his professional visits; for the doctor said that actual, experimental knowledge formed the most important part of a young medical student's education.

The mornings were usually passed in reading, in the library; the middle of the day in attending the doctor on his professional visits, and the evenings were passed in the drawing-room with the doctor, Clara and Mrs. Rocke. And if the morning's occupation was the most earnest and the day's the most active, the evening's relaxation with Clara and music and poetry was certainly the most delightful! In the midst of all this peace and prosperity a malady was creeping upon the boy's heart and brain that, in his simplicity and inexperience, he could neither understand nor conquer.

Why was it that these evening fireside meetings with the doctor's lovely daughter, once such unalloyed delight, were now only a keenly pleasing pain? Why did his face burn and his heart beat and his voice falter when obliged to speak to her? Why could he no longer talk of her to his mother, or write of her to his friend, Herbert Greyson? Above all, why had his favorite day dream of having his dear friends, Herbert and Clara married together, grown so abhorrent as to sicken his very soul?

Traverse himself could not have answered these questions. In his ignorance of life he did not know that all his strong, ardent, earnest nature was tending toward the maiden by a power of attraction seated in the deepest principles of being and of destiny.

Clara in her simplicity did not suspect the truth; but tried in every innocent way to enliven the silent boy, and said that he worked too hard, and begged her father not to let him study too much.

Whereupon the doctor would laugh and bid her not be uneasy about Traverse—that the boy was all right and would do very well! Evidently the doctor, with all his knowledge of human nature, did not perceive that his protégé was in process of forming an unadvisable attachment to his daughter and heiress.

Mrs. Rocke, with her woman's tact and mother's forethought, saw all! She saw that in the honest heart of her poor boy, unconsciously there was growing up a strong, ardent, earnest passion for the lovely girl with whom he was thrown in such close, intimate, daily association, and who was certainly not indifferent in her feelings toward him; but whom he might never, never hope to possess.

She saw this daily growing, and trembled for the peace of both. She wondered at the blindness of the doctor, who did not perceive what was so plain to her own vision. Daily she looked to see the eyes of the doctor open and some action taken upon the circumstances; but they did not open to the evil ahead, for the girl and boy! for morning after morning their hands would be together tying up the same vines, or clearing out the same flower bed; day after day at the doctor's orders Traverse attended Clara on her rides; night after night their blushing faces would be bent over the same sketch book, chess board, or music sheet.

"Oh! if the doctor cannot and will not see, what shall I do? What ought I to do?" said the conscientious little woman to herself, dreading above all things, and equally for her son and the doctor's daughter, the evils of an unhappy attachment, which she, with her peculiar temperament and experiences, believed to be the worst of sorrows—a misfortune never to be conquered or outlived.

"Yes! It is even better that we should leave the house than that Traverse should become hopelessly attached to Clara; or, worse than all, that he should repay the doctor's great bounty by winning the heart of his only daughter," said Marah Rocke to herself; and so "screwing her courage to the sticking place," she took an opportunity one morning early while Traverse and Clara were out riding, to go into the study to speak to the doctor.

As usual, he looked up with a smile to welcome her as she entered; but her downcast eyes and serious face made him uneasy, and he hastened to inquire if she was not well, or if anything had happened to make her anxious, and at the same time he placed a chair and made her sit in it.

"Yes, I am troubled, doctor, about a subject that I scarcely know how to break to you," she said, in some considerable embarrassment.

"Mrs. Rocke, you know I am your friend, anxious to serve you! Trust in me, and speak out!"

"Well, sir," said Marah, beginning to roll up the corner of her apron, in her embarrassment, "I should not presume to interfere, but you do not see; gentlemen, perhaps, seldom do until it is too late." She paused, and the good doctor turned his head about, listening first with one ear and then with the other, as if he thought by attentive hearing he might come to understand her incomprehensible words.

"Miss Clara has the misfortune to be without a mother, or an aunt, or any lady relative——"

"Oh, yes, I know it, my dear madam; but then I am sure you conscientiously try to fill the place of a matronly friend and adviser to my daughter," said the doctor, striving after light.

"Yes, sir, and it is in view of my duties in this relation that I say—I and Traverse ought to go away."

"You and Traverse go away! My good little woman, you ought to be more cautious how you shock a man at my time of life—fifty is a very apoplectic age to a full-blooded man, Mrs. Rocke! But now that I have got over the shock, tell me why you fancy that you and Traverse ought to go away?"

"Sir, my son is a well-meaning boy——"

"A high-spirited, noble-hearted lad!" put in the doctor. "I have never seen a better!"

"But granting all that to be what I hope and believe it is—true, still, Traverse Rocke is not a proper or desirable daily associate for Miss Day."

"Why?" curtly inquired the doctor.

"If Miss Clara's mother were living, sir, she would probably tell you that young ladies should never associate with any except their equals of the opposite sex," said Marah Rocke.

"Clara's dear mother, were she on earth, would understand and sympathize with me, and esteem your Traverse as I do, Mrs. Rocke," said the doctor, with moist eyes and a tremulous voice.

"But oh, sir, exceeding kind as you are to Traverse, I dare not, in duty, look on and see things going the way in which they are, and not speak and ask your consent to withdraw Traverse!"

"My good little friend," said the doctor, rising and looking kindly and benignantly upon Marah, "My good little woman 'sufficient unto the day is the evil thereof!' Suppose you and I trust a little in Divine Providence, and mind our own business?"

"But, sir, it seems to me a part of our business to watch over the young and inexperienced, that they fall into no snare."

"And also to treat them with 'a little wholesome neglect' that our over-officiousness may plunge them into none!"

"I wish you would comprehend me, sir!"

"I do, and applaud your motives; but give yourself no further trouble! Leave the young people to their own honest hearts and to Providence. Clara, with all her softness, is a sensible girl, and as for Traverse, if he is one to break his heart from an unhappy attachment, I have been mistaken in the lad, that is all!" said the doctor, heartily.

Mrs. Rocke sighed, and, saying, "I deemed it my duty to speak to you, sir, and having done so, I have no more to say," she slightly curtsied and withdrew.

"He does not see! His great benevolence blinds him! In his wish to serve us he exposes Traverse to the most dreadful misfortune—the misfortune of becoming hopelessly attached to one far above him in station, whom he can never expect to possess!" said Marah Rocke to herself, as she retired from the room.

"I must speak to Traverse himself and warn him against this snare," she said, as she afterward ruminated over the subject.

And accordingly that evening, when she had retired to her chamber and heard Traverse enter the little adjoining room where he slept, she called him in, and gave him a seat, saying that she must have some serious conversation with him.

The boy looked uneasy, but took the offered chair and waited for his mother to speak.

"Traverse," she said, "a change has come over you recently that may escape all other eyes but those of your mother; she, Traverse, cannot be blind to anything that seriously affects her boy's happiness."

"Mother, I scarcely know what you mean," said the youth in embarrassment.

"Traverse, you are beginning to think too much of Miss Day."

"Oh, mother!" exclaimed the boy, while a violent blush overspread and empurpled his face! Then in a little while and in faltering tones he inquired. "Have I betrayed, in any way, that I do?"

"To no one but to me, Traverse, to me whose anxiety for your happiness makes me watchful; and now, dear boy, you must listen to me. I know it is very sweet to you, to sit in a dark corner and gaze on Clara, when no one, not even herself, witnesses your joy, and to lie awake and think and dream of her when no eye but that of God looks down upon your heart; and to build castles in the air for her and for you; all this I know is very sweet, but, Traverse, it is a sweet poison—fatal if indulged in—fatal to your peace and integrity."

"Oh, my mother! Oh, my mother! What are you telling me!" exclaimed Traverse, bitterly.

"Unpalatable truths, dear boy, but necessary antidotes to that sweet poison of which you have already tasted too much."

"What would you have me to do, my mother?"

"Guard your acts and words, and even thoughts; forbear to look at, or speak to, or think of Clara, except when it is unavoidable—or if you do, regard her as she is—one so far beyond your sphere as to be forever unattainable!"

"Oh, mother, I never once dreamed of such presumption as to think of—of"— The youth paused and a deep blush again overspread his face.

"I know you have not indulged presumptuous thoughts as yet, my boy, and it is to warn you against them, while yet your heart is in some measure within your own keeping, that I speak to you. Indulge your imagination in no more sweet reveries about Miss Day, for the end thereof will be bitter humiliation and disappointment. Remember also that in so doing you would indulge a sort of treachery against your patron, who in his great faith in your integrity has received you in the bosom of his family and admitted you to an almost brotherly intimacy with his daughter. Honor his trust in you, and treat his daughter with the distant respect due to a princess."

"I will, mother! It will be hard, but I will! Oh, an hour ago I did not dream how miserable I should be now!" said Traverse, in a choking voice.

"Because I have pointed out to you the gulf toward which you were walking blindfolded!"

"I know it! I know it now, mother," said Traverse, as he arose and pressed his mother's hand and hurried to his own room.

The poor youth did his best to follow out the line of conduct prescribed for him by his mother. He devoted himself to his studies and to the active service of his patron. He avoided Clara as much as possible, and when obliged to be in her company, he treated her with the most respectful reserve.

Clara saw and wondered at his change of manner, and began to cast about in her own mind for the probable cause of his conduct.

"I am the young mistress of the house," said Clara to herself, "and I know I owe to every inmate of it consideration and courtesy; perhaps I may have been unconsciously lacking in these toward Traverse, whose situation would naturally render him very sensitive to neglect. I must endeavor to convince him that none was intended." And so resolving, Clara redoubled all her efforts to make Traverse, as well as others, happy and comfortable.

But happiness and comfort seemed for the time to have departed from the youth. He saw her generous endeavors to cheer him, and while adoring her amiability, grew still more reserved.

This pained the gentle girl, who, taking herself seriously to task, said:

"Oh, I must have deeply wounded his feelings in some unconscious way! And if so, how very cruel and thoughtless of me! How could I have done it? I cannot imagine! But I know I shall not allow him to continue unhappy if I can prevent it! I will speak to him about it."

And then in the candor, innocence and humility of her soul, she followed him to the window where he stood in a moody silence, and said pleasantly:

"Traverse, we do not seem to be so good friends as formerly. If I have done anything to offend you, I know that you will believe me when I say that it was quite unintentional on my part and that I am very sorry for it, and hope you will forget it."

"You—you—Miss Day! You say anything to displease anybody! Any one become displeased with you!" exclaimed the youth in a tremulous enthusiasm that shook his voice and suffused his cheeks.

"Then if you are not displeased, Traverse, what is the matter, and why do you call me Miss Day instead of Clara?"

"Miss Day, because it is right that I should. You are a young lady—the only daughter and heiress of Doctor Day of Willow Heights, while I am——"

"His friend," said Clara.

"The son of his housekeeper," said Traverse, walking away.

Clara looked after him in dismay for a moment, and then sat down and bent thoughtfully over her needlework.

From that day Traverse grew more deeply in love and more reserved than before. How could it be otherwise, domesticated as he was, with this lovely girl and becoming daily more sensible of her beauty, goodness and intelligence? Yet he struggled against his inevitable attachment as a great treachery. Meantime he made rapid progress in his medical studies. It was while affairs were in this state that one morning the doctor entered the study holding the morning paper in his hand. Seating himself in his leathern armchair at the table, he said:

"I see, my dear Traverse, that a full course of lectures is to be commenced at the medical college in Washington, and I think that you are sufficiently far advanced in your studies to attend them with great advantage—what say you?"

"Oh, sir!" said Traverse, upon whom the proposition had burst quite unexpectedly, "I should indeed be delighted to go if that were possible."

"There is no 'if' about it, my boy; if you wish to go, you shall do so. I have made up my mind to give you a professional education, and shall not stop half way."

"Oh, sir, the obligation—the overwhelming obligation you lay upon me!"

"Nonsense, Traverse! it is only a capital investment of funds! If I were a usurer I could not put out money to a better advantage. You will repay me by-and-by with compound interest; so just consider all that I may be able to do for you as a loan to be repaid when you shall have achieved success."

"I am afraid, sir, that that time will never — —"

"No, you are not!" interrupted the doctor, "and so don't let modesty run into hypocrisy. Now put up your books and go and tell your good little mother to get your clothes all ready for you to go to Washington, for you shall start by the next coach."

Much surprise was created in the little household by the news that Traverse was going immediately to Washington to attend the medical lectures. There were but two days to prepare his wardrobe for the journey. Mrs. Rocke went cheerfully to work; Clara lent her willing and skilful aid, and at the end of the second day his clothes, in perfect order, were all neatly packed in his trunk.

And on the morning of the third day Traverse took leave of his mother and Clara, and for the first time left home to go into the great world. Doctor Day accompanied him in the old green gig as far as Staunton, where he took the stage.

As soon as they had left the house Marah Rocke went away to her own room to drop a few natural tears over this first parting with her son. Very lonely and desolate the mother felt as she stood weeping by the window, and straining her eyes to catch a distant view of the old green gig that had already rolled out of sight.

While she stood thus in her loneliness and desolation, the door silently opened, a footstep softly crossed the floor, a pair of arms was put around her neck, and Clara Day dropped her head upon the mother's bosom and wept softly.

Marah Rocke pressed that beautiful form to her breast, and felt with dismay that the doctor's sweet daughter already returned her boy's silent love!

CHAPTER XXIV.

CAPITOLA'S MOTHER.

A woman like a dew-drop she was purer than the purest,
And her noble heart the noblest, yes, and her sure faith the sur-
est;
And her eyes were dark and humid like the depth in depth of
lustre
Hid i' the harebell, while her tresses, sunnier than the wild
grape's cluster,
Gushed in raven-tinted plenty down her cheeks' rose-tinted
marble;
Then her voice's music—call it the well's bubbling, the bird's
warble.

—BROWNING.

"Cap?"

"Sir!"

"What the blazes is the matter with you?"

"What the blazes! You better say what the dust and ashes! I'm bored to death! I'm blue as indigo! There never was such a rum old place as this or such a rum old uncle as you!"

"Cap, how often have I told you to leave off this Bowery boy talk? Rum! pah!" said Old Hurricane.

"Well, it is rum, then! Nothing ever happens here! The silence deafens me! the plenty takes away my appetite! the safety makes me low!"

"Hum! you are like the Bowery boys in times of peace, 'spoiling for a fight.'"

"Yes. I am! just decomposing above ground for want of having my blood stirred, and I wish I was back in the Bowery! Something was always happening there! One day a fire, next day a fight, another day a fire and a fight together."

"Umph! and you to run with the engine!"

"Don't talk about it, uncle; it makes me homesick—every day something glori-ous to stir one's blood! Here nothing ever happens, hardly! It has been three days since I caught Black Donald; ten days since you blowed up the whole household! Oh! I wish the barns would catch on fire! I wish thieves would break in and steal.

I wish Demon's Run would rise to a flood and play the demon for once! Ohyah!—oo!" said Cap, opening her mouth with a yawn wide enough to threaten the dislocation of her jaws.

"Capitola," said the old man, very gravely, "I am getting seriously uneasy about you. I know I am a rough old soldier, quite unfit to educate a young girl, and that Mrs. Condiment can't manage you, and—I'll consult Mr. Goodwin!" he concluded, getting up and putting on his hat, and walking out of the breakfast-room, where this conversation had taken place.

Cap laughed to herself. "I hope it is not a sin. I know I should die of the blues if I couldn't give vent to my feelings and—tease uncle!"

Capitola had scarcely exaggerated her condition. The monotony of her life affected her spirits; the very absence of the necessity of thinking and caring for herself left a dull void in her heart and brain, and as the winter waned the annual spring fever of lassitude and dejection to which mercurial organizations like her own are subject, tended to increase the malady that Mrs. Condiment termed "a lowness of spirits."

At his wits' end, from the combined feelings of his responsibility and his helplessness in his ward's case, Old Hurricane went and laid the matter before the Rev. Mr. Goodwin.

Having reached the minister's house and found him alone and disengaged in his library, Old Hurricane first bound him over to strict secrecy and then "made a clean breast of it;" told him where Capitola had been brought up and under what circumstances he had found her.

The honest country clergyman was shocked beyond all immediate power of recovering himself—so shocked, in fact, that Old Hurricane, fearing he had gone too far, hastened to say:

"But mind, on my truth as a man, my honor as a soldier, and my faith as a Christian, I declare that that wild, reckless, desolate child has passed unscathed through the terrible ordeal of destitution, poverty and exposure. She has, sir! She is as innocent as the most daintily sheltered young heiress in the country! She is, sir! And I'd cut off the tongue and ears of any man that said otherwise."

"I do not say otherwise, my friend; but I say that she has suffered a frightful series of perils."

"She has come out of them safe, sir! I know it by a thousand signs; what I fear for her is the future. I can't manage her. She won't obey me, except when she likes. She has never been taught obedience nor been accustomed to subordination, and I don't understand either. She rides and walks out alone in spite of all I can do or say. If she were a boy I'd thrash her; but what can I do with a girl?" said Old Hurricane, in despair.

"Lock her up in her chamber until she is brought to reason," suggested the minister.

"Demmy, she'd jump out of the window and break her neck! or hang herself with her garters! or starve herself to death! You don't know what an untamable thing she is. Some birds, if caged, beat themselves to death against the bars of their prison. She is just such a wild bird as that."

"Humph! it is a difficult case to manage; but you should not shrink from responsibility; you should be firm with her."

"That's just what I can't be with the witch, confound her! she is such a wag, such a drole, such a mimic; disobeys me in such a mocking, cajoling, affectionate way. I could not give her pain if her soul depended on it!"

"Then you should talk to her; try moral suasion."

"Yes; if I could only get her to be serious long enough to listen to me! But you see Cap isn't sentimental, and if I try to be she laughs in my face."

"But, then, is she so insensible to all the benefits you have conferred upon her? Will not gratitude influence her?"

"Yes; so far as repaying me with a genuine affection, fervent caresses and careful attention to my little comforts can go; but Cap evidently thinks that the restriction of her liberty is too heavy a price to pay for protection and support. The little rogue! Think of her actually threatening, in her good-humored way, to cite me before the nearest justice to show cause why I detained her in my house!"

"Well, you could easily do that, I suppose, and she could no longer oppose your authority."

"No; that is just what I couldn't do; I couldn't show any legal rights to detain Capitola."

"Humph! That complicates the case very much!"

"Yes; and much more than you think; for I wish to keep Capitola until she is of legal age. I do not wish that she should fall into the hands of her perfidious guardian until I shall be able to bring legal proof of his perfidy."

"Then it appears that this girl has received foul play from her friends?"

"Foul play! I should think so! Gabriel Le Noir has very nearly put his neck into a halter."

"Gabriel Le Noir! Colonel Le Noir, our neighbor!" exclaimed the minister.

"Exactly so. Parson, you have given me your word as a Christian minister to be silent forever concerning this interview, or until I give you leave to speak of it."

"Yes, major, and I repeat my promise; but, indeed, sir, you astound me!"

"Listen, and let astonishment rise to consternation. I will tell you who Capitola is. You, sir, have been in this neighborhood only ten years, and, consequently, you know Gabriel Le Noir only as the proprietor of Hidden House, a widower with a grown son——"

"And as a gentleman of irreproachable reputation, in good standing both in the church and in the county."

"Ex-actly! A man that pays his pew rent, gives good dinners and takes off his hat to women and clergymen! Well, sir, this gentleman of irreproachable manners and morals—this citizen of consideration in the community—this member in good standing with the church—has qualified himself for twenty years' residence in the penitentiary, even if not for the exaltation of a hangman's halter!"

"Sir, I am inexpressibly shocked to hear you say so, and I must still believe that there is some great mistake."

"Wait until I tell you! I, Ira Warfield, have known Gabriel Le Noir as a villain for the last eighteen years. I tell you so without scruple, and hold myself ready to maintain my words in field or forum, by sword or law! Well, having known him so long for such a knave, I was in no manner surprised to discover some six months ago that he was also a criminal, and only needed exposure to become a felon!"

"Sir, sir! this is strong language!"

"I am willing to back it with 'life, liberty and sacred honor,' as the Declaration of Independence has it. Listen: Some sixteen years ago, before you came to take this pastoral charge, the Hidden House was occupied by old Victor Le Noir, the father of Eugene, the heir, and of Gabriel, the present usurper. The old man died, leaving a will to this effect—the landed estate, including the coal and iron mines, the Hidden House and all the negroes, stock, furniture and other personal property upon the premises to his eldest son Eugene, with the proviso that if Eugene should die without issue, the landed estate, houses, negroes, etc., should descend to his younger brother Gabriel. To Gabriel he left his bank stock and blessing."

"An equitable will," observed the minister.

"Yes; but hear! At the time of his father's death Eugene was traveling in Europe. On receiving the news he immediately returned home, bringing with him a lovely young creature, a mere child, that he presented to his astounded neighbors as Madame Eugene Le Noir! I declare to you there was one simultaneous outcry of shame, that he should have trapped into matrimony a creature so infantile, for she was scarcely fourteen years of age!"

"It was indeed highly improper," said the minister.

"So thought all the neighborhood; but when they found out how it happened, disapproval was changed to commendation. She was the daughter of a French patriot. Her father and mother had both perished on the scaffold in the sacred cause of liberty; she was thrown helpless, friendless and penniless upon the cold charity of the world; Providence cast her in the way of our sensitive and enthusiastic young traveler; he pitied her; he loved her, and was casting about in his own mind how he could help without compromising her, when the news of his father's illness summoned him home. Then, seeing no better way of protecting her, after a little hesitation upon account of her tender age, he married her and brought with him."

"Good deeds, we know, must be rewarded in heaven, since on earth they are so often punished."

"He did not long enjoy his bride. She was just the most beautiful creature that ever was seen—with a promise of still more glorious beauty in riper years. I have seen handsome women and pretty women—but Madame Eugene Le Noir was the only perfectly beautiful woman I ever saw in my long life! My own aged eyes seemed 'enriched' only to look at her! She adored Eugene, too; any one could see that. At first she spoke English in 'broken music,' but soon her accent became as perfect as if she had been native born. How could it have been otherwise, when her teacher and inspirer was love? She won all hearts with her loveliness! Humph! hear me, an old fool—worse—an Old Hurricane—betrayed into discourses of love and beauty merely by the remembrance of Madame Eugene Le Noir! Ah, bright, exotic flower! she did not bloom long. The bride had scarcely settled down into the wife when one night Eugene Le Noir did not come home as usual. The next day his dead body, with a bullet in his brain, was found in the woods around the Hidden House. The murderer was never discovered. Gabriel Le Noir came in haste from the military post where he had been stationed. Madame Eugene was never seen abroad after the death of her husband. It was reported that she had lost her reason, a consequence that surprised no one. Eugene having died without issue, and his young widow being mad, Gabriel, by the terms of his father's will, stepped at once into the full possession of the whole property."

"Something of all this I have heard before," said the minister.

"Very likely, for these facts and falsehoods were the common property of the neighborhood. But what you have not heard before, and what is not known to any now living, except the criminals, the victims and myself, is that, three months after the death of her husband, Madame Eugene Le Noir gave birth to twins—one living, one dead. The dead child was privately buried; the living one, together with the nurse that was the sole witness of the birth, was abducted."

"Great heavens! can this be true?" exclaimed the minister, shocked beyond all power of self-control.

"True as gospel! I have proof enough to carry conviction to any honest breast—to satisfy any caviller—except a court of justice. You shall hear. You remember the dying woman whom you dragged me out in the snow-storm to see—blame you!"

"Yes."

"She was the abducted nurse, escaped and returned. It was to make a deposition to the facts I am about to relate that she sent you to fetch me," said Old Hurricane; and with that he commenced and related the whole dark history of crime comprised in the nurse's dying deposition. They examined the instrument together, and Old Hurricane again related, in brief, the incidents of his hurried journey to New York; his meeting and identifying Capitola and bringing her home in safety to his house.

"And thus," said the old man, "you perceive that this child whose birth was feloniously concealed, and who was cast away to perish among the wretched beggars, thieves and street-walkers of New York, is really the only living child of the late Eugene Le Noir, and the sole inheritrix of the Hidden House, with its vast acres of fields, forests, iron and coal mines, water power, steam mills, furnaces and foundries—wealth that I would not undertake to estimate within a million of dollars—all of which is now held and enjoyed by that usurping villain, Gabriel Le

Noir!"

"But," said the minister, gravely, "you have, of course, commenced proceedings on the part of your protégé."

"Listen; I will tell you what I have done. When I first brought Cap home I was moved not only by the desire of wreaking vengeance upon a most atrocious miscreant who had done me an irreparable injury, but also by sympathy for the little witch who had won my heart at first sight. Therefore, you may judge I lost no time in preparing to strike a double blow which should ruin my own mortal enemy and reinstate my favorite in her rights. With this view, immediately on my return home, I sent for Breefe, my confidential attorney, and laid the whole matter before him."

"And he——"

"To my dismay he told me that, though the case was clear enough, it was not sufficiently strong, in a legal point of view, to justify us in bringing suit; for that the dying deposition of the mulatto nurse could not be received as evidence in our county courts."

"You knew that before, sir, I presume."

"Of course I did; but I thought it was a lawyer's business to get over such difficulties; and I assure you, parson, that I flew into a passion and cursed court and county law and lawyers to my heart's content. I would have quarreled with old Breefe then and there, only Breefe won't get excited. He very coolly advised me to keep the matter close and my eyes open, and gather all the corroborative testimony I could find, and that, in the meantime, he would reflect upon the best manner of proceeding."

"I think, Major Warfield, that his counsel was wise and disinterested. But tell me, sir, of the girl's mother. Is it not astonishing—in fact, is it not perfectly incomprehensible—that so lovely a woman as you have represented her to be should have consented to the concealment, if not to the destruction, of her own legitimate offspring?"

"Sir, to me it is not incomprehensible at all. She was at once an orphan and a widow; a stranger in a strange land; a poor, desolate, broken-hearted child, in the power of the cunningest and most unscrupulous villain that the Lord ever suffered to live! I wonder at nothing that he might have deceived or frightened her into doing."

"Heaven forgive us! Have I known that man for ten years to hear this account of him at last? But tell me, sir, have you really any true idea of what has been the fate of the poor young widow?"

"No; not the slightest. Immediately after his brother's funeral, Gabriel Le Noir gave out that Madame Eugene had lost her reason through excessive grief, soon after which he took her with him to the North, and, upon his return alone, reported that he had left her in a celebrated lunatic asylum. The story was probable enough, and received universal belief. Only now I do not credit it, and do not know whether the widow be living or dead; or, if living, whether she be mad or sane; if dead, whether she came to her end by fair means or foul!"

"Merciful heaven, sir! you do not mean to say——"

"Yes; I do mean to say; and if you would like to know what is on my private mind I'll tell you. I believe that Madame Eugene Le Noir has been treacherously made away with by the same infernal demon at whose instigation her husband was murdered and her child stolen."

The minister seemed crushed beneath the overwhelming weight of this communication; he passed his hand over his brow and thence down his face and sighed deeply. For a few moments he seemed unable to reply, and when he spoke it was only to say:

"In this matter, Major Warfield, I can offer you no counsel better than that of your confidential attorney—follow the light that you have until it lead you to the full elucidation of this affair; and may heaven grant that you may find Colonel Le Noir less guilty than you apprehend."

"Parson, humbug! When charity drivels it ought to be turned off by justice! I will follow the little light I have. I suspect, from the description, that the wretch who at Le Noir's instance carried off the nurse and child was no other than the notorious Black Donald. I have offered an additional thousand dollars for his apprehension, and if he is taken he will be condemned to death, make a last dying speech and confession and give up his accomplices, the accomplished Colonel Le Noir among the rest!"

"If the latter really was an accomplice, there could be no better way of discovering the fact than to bring this Black Donald to justice; but I greatly fear that there is little hope of that," said the minister.

"Aye, but there is! Listen! The long impunity enjoyed by this desperado has made him daring to fatuity. Why, I was within a hair's breadth of capturing him myself a few days ago."

"Ha! is it possible?" asked the minister, with a look of surprise and interest.

"Aye, was I; and you shall hear all about it," said Old Hurricane. And upon that he commenced and told the minister the adventure of Capitola with Black Donald at Hurricane Hall.

The minister was amazed, yet could not forbear to say:

"It seems to me, however, that it was Capitola who was in a hair's breadth of capturing this notorious desperado."

"Pooh! she clung to him like the reckless lunatic that she is; but Lord, he would have carried her off on his back if it had not been for me."

The minister smiled a little to himself and then said:

"This protégé of yours is a very remarkable girl, as interesting to me in her character as she is in her history; her very spirit, courage and insubordination make her singularly hard to manage and apt to go astray. With your permission I will make her acquaintance, with the view of seeing what good I can do her."

"Pray do so, for then you will be better able to counsel me how to manage the capricious little witch who, if I attempt to check her in her wild and dangerous freedom of action, tells me plainly that liberty is too precious a thing to be exchanged for food and clothing, and that, rather than live in bondage, she will throw herself upon the protection of the court. If she does that the game is up. Le Noir, against whom we can as yet prove nothing, would claim her as his niece and ward, and get her into his power for the purpose of making way with her, as he did with her father and mother."

"Oh, for heaven's sake, sir! no more of that until we have further evidence," said the minister, uneasily, adding, "I will see your very interesting protégé to-morrow."

"Do, do! to-morrow, to-day, this hour, any time!" said Major Warfield, as he cordially took leave of the pastor.

CHAPTER XXV.

CAP'S TRICKS AND PERILS.

I'll be merry and free,
I'll be sad for naebody;
Naebody cares for me,
I care for naebody.

—Burns.

The next day, according to agreement, the pastor came and dined at Hurricane Hall. During the dinner he had ample opportunity of observing Capitola.

In the afternoon Major Warfield took an occasion of leaving him alone with the contumacious young object of his visit.

Cap, with her quick perceptions, instantly discovered the drift and purpose of this action, which immediately provoked all the mischievous propensities of her elfish spirit.

"Uncle means that I shall be lectured by the good parson. If he preaches to me, won't I humor him 'to the top of his bent?' — that's all," was her secret resolution, as she sat demurely, with pursed-up lips, bending over her needlework.

The honest and well-meaning old country clergyman hitched his chair a little nearer to the perverse young rebel, and gingerly—for he was half afraid of his questionable subject—entered into conversation with her.

To his surprise and pleasure, Capitola replied with the decorum of a young nun.

Encouraged by her manner, the good minister went on to say how much interested he felt in her welfare; how deeply he compassionated her lot in never having possessed the advantage of a mother's teaching; how anxious he was by his counsels to make up to her as much as possible such a deficiency.

Here Capitola put up both her hands and dropped her face upon them.

Still farther encouraged by this exhibition of feeling, Mr. Goodwin went on. He told her that it behooved her, who was a motherless girl, to be even more circumspect than others, lest, through very ignorance, she might err; and in particular he warned her against riding or walking out alone, or indulging in any freedom of manners that might draw upon her the animadversions of their very strict community.

"Oh, sir, I know I have been very indiscreet, and I am very miserable," said Capitola, in a heart-broken voice.

"My dear child, your errors have hitherto been those of ignorance only, and I am very much pleased to find how much your good uncle has been mistaken, and how ready you are to do strictly right when the way is pointed out," said the minister, pleased to his honest heart's core that he had made this deep impression.

A heavy sigh burst from the bosom of Capitola.

"What is the matter, my dear child?" he said, kindly.

"Oh, sir, if I had only known you before!" exclaimed Capitola, bitterly.

"Why, my dear? I can do just as much good now."

"Oh, no, sir; it is too late; it is too late!"

"It is never to late to do well."

"Oh, yes, sir; it is for me! Oh, how I wish I had had your good counsel before; it would have saved me from so much trouble."

"My dear child, you make me seriously uneasy; do explain yourself," said the old pastor, drawing his chair closer to hers and trying to get a look at the distressed little face that was bowed down upon her hands and veiled with her hair; "do tell me, my dear, what is the matter."

"Oh, sir, I am afraid to tell you; you'd hate and despise me; you'd never speak to me again," said Capitola, keeping her face concealed.

"My dear child," said the minister, very gravely and sorrowfully, "whatever your offense has been, and you make me fear that it has been a very serious one, I invite you to confide it to me, and, having done so, I promise, however I may mourn the sin, not to 'hate,' or 'despise,' or forsake the sinner. Come, confide in me."

"Oh, sir, I daren't! indeed I daren't!" moaned Capitola.

"My poor girl!" said the minister, "if I am to do you any good it is absolutely necessary that you make me your confidant."

"Oh, sir, I have been a very wicked girl; I daren't tell you how wicked I have been!"

"Does your good uncle know or suspect this wrongdoing of yours?"

"Uncle! Oh, no, sir! He'd turn me out of doors! He'd kill me! Indeed he would, sir! Please don't tell him!"

"You forget, my child, that I do not yet know the nature of your offense," said the minister, in a state of painful anxiety.

"But I am going to inform you, sir; and oh! I hope you will take pity on me and tell me what to do; for though I dread to speak, I can't keep it on my conscience any longer, it is such a heavy weight on my breast!"

"Sin always is, my poor girl," said the pastor, with a deep moan.

"But, sir, you know I had no mother, as you said yourself."

"I know it, my poor girl, and am ready to make every allowance," said the old pastor, with a deep sigh, not knowing what next to expect.

"And—and—I hope you will forgive me, sir; but—but he was so handsome I couldn't help liking him!"

"Miss Black!" cried the horrified pastor.

"There! I knew you'd just go and bite my head off the very first thing! Oh, dear, what shall I do?" sobbed Capitola.

The good pastor, who had started to his feet, remained gazing upon her in a panic of consternation, murmuring to himself:

"Good angel! I am fated to hear more great sins than if I were a prison chaplain!" Then, going up to the sobbing delinquent he said:

"Unhappy girl! who is this person of whom you speak?"

"H—h—h—him that I met when I went walking in the woods," sobbed Capitola.

"Heaven of heavens! this is worse than my very worst fears! Wretched girl! Tell me instantly the name of this base deceiver!"

"He—he—he's no base deceiver; he—he—he's very amiable and good-looking; and—and—and that's why I liked him so much; it was all my fault, not his, poor, dear fellow!"

"His name?" sternly demanded the pastor.

"Alf—Alf—Alfred," wept Capitola.

"Alfred whom?"

"Alfred Blen—Blen—Blenheim!"

"Miserable girl! how often have you met this miscreant in the forest?"

"I—don't—know!" sobbed Capitola.

"Where is the wretch to be found now?"

"Oh, please don't hurt him, sir! Please don't! He—he—he's hid in the closet in my room."

A groan that seemed to have rent his heart in twain burst from the bosom of the minister, as he repeated in deepest horror:

"In your room! (Well, I must prevent murder being done!) Did you not know, you poor child, the danger you ran by giving this young man private interviews; and, above all, admitting him to your apartment? Wretched girl! better you'd never been born than ever so to have received a man!"

"Man! man! man!—I'd like to know what you mean by that, Mr. Goodwin!" exclaimed Capitola, lifting her eyes flashing through their tears.

"I mean the man with whom you have given these private interviews."

"I!—I give private interviews to a man! Take care what you say, Mr. Goodwin; I won't be insulted; no, not even by you!"

"Then, if you are not talking of a man, who or what in the world are you talking about?" exclaimed the amazed minister.

"Why, Alfred, the Blenheim poodle that strayed away from some of the neighbors' houses, and that I found in the woods and brought home and hid in my closet, for fear he would be inquired after, or uncle would find it out and make me give him up. I knew it was wrong, but then he was so pretty——"

Before Capitola had finished her speech Mr. Goodwin had seized his hat and rushed out of the house in indignation, nearly overturning Old Hurricane, whom he met on the lawn, and to whom he said:

"Thrash that girl as if she were a bay boy, for she richly deserves it!"

"There! what did I say? Now you see what a time I have with her; she makes me sweat, I can tell you," said Old Hurricane, in triumph.

"Oh! oh! oh!" groaned the sorely-tried minister.

"What's it now?" inquired Old Hurricane.

The pastor took the major's arm and, while they walked up and down before the house, told how he had been "sold" by Capitola, ending by saying:

"You will have to take her firmly in hand."

"I'll do it," said Old Hurricane. "I'll do it."

The pastor then called for his horse and, resisting all his host's entreaties to stay to tea, took his departure.

Major Warfield re-entered the house, resolving to say nothing to Capitola for the present, but to seize the very first opportunity of punishing her for her flippancy.

The village fair had commenced on Monday. It had been arranged that all Major Warfield's family should go, though not all upon the same day. It was proposed that on Thursday, when the festival should be at its height, Major Warfield, Capitola and the house servants should go. And on Saturday Mrs. Condiment, Mr. Ezy and the farm servants should have a holiday for the same purpose.

Therefore, upon Thursday morning all the household be-stirred themselves at an unusually early hour, and appeared before breakfast in their best Sunday's suit.

Capitola came down to breakfast in a rich blue silk carriage dress, looking so fresh, blooming and joyous that it went to the old man's heart to disappoint her; yet Old Hurricane resolved, as the pastor had told him, to "be firm," and, once for all, by inflicting punishment, to bring her to a sense of her errors.

"There, you need not trouble yourself to get ready, Capitola; you shall not go to the fair with us," he said, as Cap took her seat.

"Sir!" exclaimed the girl, in surprise.

"Oh, yes; you may stare; but I'm in earnest. You have behaved very badly; you have deeply offended our pastor; you have no reverence, no docility, no propriety, and I mean to bring you to a sense of your position by depriving you of some of your indulgences; and, in a word, to begin I say you shall not go to the fair to-day."

"You mean, sir, that I shall not go with you, although you promised that I should," said Cap, coolly.

"I mean you shall not go at all, demmy!"

"I'd like to know who'll prevent me," said Cap.

"I will, Miss Vixen! Demmy, I'll not be set at naught by a beggar! Mrs. Condiment, leave the room, mum, and don't be sitting there listening to every word I have to say to my ward. Wool, be off with yourself, sir; what do you stand there gaping and staring for? Be off, or——" the old man looked around for a missile, but before he found one the room was evacuated except by himself and Capitola.

"Now, minion," he began, as soon as he found himself alone with the little rebel, "I did not choose to mortify you before the servants, but, once for all, I will have you to understand that I intend to be obeyed." And Old Hurricane "gathered his brows like a gathering storm."

"Sir, if you were really my uncle, or my father, or my legal guardian, I should have no choice but obey you; but the same fate that made me desolate made me free—a freedom that I would not exchange for any gilded slavery," said Cap, gaily.

"Pish! tush! pshaw! I say I will have no more of this nonsense. I say I will be obeyed," cried Old Hurricane, striking his cane down upon the floor, "and in proof of it I order you immediately to go and take off that gala dress and settle yourself down to your studies for the day."

"Uncle, I will obey you as far as taking off this dress goes, for, since you won't give me a seat in your carriage, I shall have to put on my habit and ride Gyp," said Cap, good humoredly.

"What! Do you dare to hint that you have the slightest idea of going to the fair against my will?"

"Yes, sir," said Cap, gaily. "Sorry it's against your will, but can't help it; not used to being ordered about and don't know how to submit, and so I'm going."

"Ungrateful girl; actually meditating disobedience on the horse I gave her!"

"Easy now, uncle—fair and easy. I did not sell my free will for Gyp! I wouldn't for a thousand Gyps! He was a free gift," said Capitola, beginning an impatient little dance about the floor.

"Come here to me; come—here—to—me!" exclaimed the old man peremptorily, rapping his cane down upon the floor with every syllable.

Capitola danced up to him and stood half smiling and fingering and arranging the lace of her under sleeves.

"Listen to me, you witch! Do you intend to obey me or not?"

"Not," said Cap, good-humoredly adjusting her cameo bracelet and holding up her arm to see its effect.

"You will not! Then, demmy, miss, I shall know how to make you!" thundered Old Hurricane, bringing the point of his stick down with a sharp rap.

"Eh!" cried Capitola, looking up in astonishment.

"Yes, miss; that's what I said—make you!"

"I should like to know how," said Cap, returning to her cool good humor.

"You would, would you? Demmy, I'll tell you! I have broken haughtier spirits than yours in my life. Would you know how?"

"Yes," said Cap, indifferently, still busied with her bracelets.

"Stoop and I will whisper the mystery."

Capitola bent her graceful head to hear.

"With the rod!" hissed Old Hurricane, maliciously.

Capitola sprang up as if she had been shot, wave after wave of blood tiding up in burning blushes over neck, face and forehead; then, turning abruptly, she walked off to the window.

Old Hurricane, terrified at the effect of his rude, rash words, stood excommunicating himself for having been provoked to use them; nor was the next aspect of Capitola one calculated to reassure his perturbed feelings.

She turned around. Her face was as white as marble, excepting her glittering eyes; they, half sheathed under their long lashes, flashed like stilettoes. Raising her hand and keeping her eyes fixed upon him, with a slow and gliding motion, and the deep and measured voice that scarcely seemed to belong to a denizen of earth, she approached and stood before him and spoke these words:

"Uncle, in all the sorrows, shames and sufferings of my destitute childhood, no one ever dishonored my person with a blow; and if ever you should have the misfortune to forget your manhood so far as to strike me—" She paused, drew her breath hard between her set teeth, grew a shade whiter, while her dark eyes dilated until a white ring flamed around the iris.

"Oh, you perilous witch! what then!" cried Old Hurricane, in dismay.

"Why, then," said Capitola, speaking in a low, deep and measured tone, and keeping her gaze upon his astonished face, "the—first—time—I— should—find— you—asleep—I—would—take—a—razor—and— —"

"Cut my throat! I feel you would, you terrible termagant!" shuddered Old Hurricane.

"Shave your beard off smick, smack, smoove!" said Cap, bounding off and laughing merrily as she ran out of the room.

In an instant she came bounding back, saying, "Uncle, I will meet you at the fair; *au revoir, au revoir!*" and, kissing her hand, she dashed away and ran off to her room.

"She'll kill me; I know she will. If she don't do it one way she will in another. Whew! I'm perspiring at every pore. Wool! Wool, you scoundrel!" exclaimed the old man, jerking the bell-rope as if he would have broken the wires.

"Yes, sir; here I am, marse," exclaimed that worthy, hastening in in a state of perturbation, for he dreaded another storm.

"Wool, go down to the stables and tell every man there that if either of them allows a horse to be brought out for the use of Miss Black to-day. I'll flay them alive and break every bone in their skins. Away with you."

"Yes, sir," cried the shocked and terrified Wool, hurrying off to convey his panic to the stables.

Old Hurricane's carriage being ready, he entered it and drove off for the fair.

Next the house servants, with the exception of Pitapat, who was commanded to remain behind and wait upon her mistress, went off in a wagon.

When they were all gone, Capitola dressed herself in her riding-habit and sent Pitapat down to the stables to order one of the grooms to saddle Gyp and bring him up for her.

Now, when the little maid delivered this message, the unfortunate grooms were filled with dismay—they feared their tyrannical little mistress almost as much as their despotic old master, who, in the next change of his capricious temper, might punch all their heads for crossing the will of his favorite, even though in doing so they had followed his directions. An immediate private consultation was the consequence, and the result was that the head groom came to Pitapat, told her that he was sorry, but that Miss Black's pony had fallen lame.

The little maid went back with the answer.

When she was gone the head groom, calling to his fellows, said:

"That young gal ain't a-gwine to be fooled either by ole marse or we. She'll be down here herself nex' minute and have the horse walked out. Now we must make him lame a little. Light a match here, Jem, and I'll burn his foot."

This was immediately done. And, sure enough, while poor Gyp was still smarting with his burn, Capitola came, holding up her riding train and hurrying to the scene, and asking indignantly:

"Who dares to say that my horse is lame? Bring him out here this instant, that I may see him!"

The groom immediately took poor Gyp and led him limping to the presence of his mistress.

At the sight Capitola was almost ready to cry with grief and indignation.

"He was not lame last evening. It must have been your carelessness, you good-for-nothing loungers; and if he is not well enough to take me to the fair to-morrow, at least, I'll have the whole set of you lamed for life!" she exclaimed, angrily, as she turned off and went up to the house—not caring so much, after all, for her own personal disappointment as for Old Hurricane's triumph.

Cap's ill humor did not last long. She soon exchanged her riding-habit for a morning wrapper, and took her needlework and sat down to sew by the side of Mrs. Condiment in the housekeeper's room.

The day passed as usual, only that just after sunset Mrs. Condiment, as a matter of precaution, went all over the house securing windows and doors before nightfall. Then, after an early tea, Mrs. Condiment, Capitola and the little maid Pitapat gathered around the bright little wood fire that the chilly spring evening made necessary in the housekeeper's room. Mrs. Condiment was knitting, Capitola stitching a bosom for the major's shirts and Pitapat winding yarn from a reel.

The conversation of the three females left alone in the old house naturally turned upon subjects of fear—ghosts, witches and robbers.

Mrs. Condiment had a formidable collection of accredited stories of apparitions, warnings, dreams, omens, etc., all true as gospel. There was a haunted house, she said, in their own neighborhood—The Hidden House. It was well authenticated that ever since the mysterious murder of Eugene Le Noir unaccountable sights and sounds had been seen and heard in and about the dwelling. A traveler, a brother officer of Colonel Le Noir, had slept there once, and, "in the dead waste and middle of the night," had had his curtains drawn by a lady, pale and passing fair, dressed in white, with flowing hair, who, as soon as he attempted to speak to her, fled. And it was well known that there was no lady about the premises.

Another time old Mr. Ezy himself, when out after coons, and coming through the woods near the house, had been attracted by seeing a window near the roof lighted up by a strange blue flame; drawing near, he saw within the lighted room a female clothed in white passing and repassing the window.

Another time, when old Major Warfield was out with his dogs, the chase led him past the haunted house, and as he swept by he caught a glimpse of a pale, wan, sorrowful female face pressed against the window pane of an upper room, which vanished in an instant.

"But might not that have been some young woman staying at the house?" asked Capitola.

"No, my child; it is well ascertained that, since the murder of Eugene Le Noir and the disappearance of his lovely young widow, no white female has crossed the threshold of that fatal house," said Mrs. Condiment.

"'Disappearance,' did you say? Can a lady of condition disappear from a neighborhood and no inquiry be made for her?"

"No, my dear; there was inquiry, and it was answered plausibly—that Madame Eugene was insane and sent off to a lunatic asylum: but there are those who believe that the lovely lady was privately made away with," whispered Mrs. Condiment.

"How dreadful! I did not think such things happened in a quiet country neighborhood. Something like that occurred, indeed, in New York, within my own recollection, however," said Capitola, who straightway commenced and related the story of Mary Rogers and all other stories of terror that memory supplied her with.

As for poor little Pitapat, she did not presume to enter into the conversation; but, with her ball of yarn suspended in her hand, her eyes started until they threatened to burst from their sockets, and her chin dropped until her mouth gaped wide open, she sat and swallowed every word, listening with a thousand audience power.

By the time they had frightened themselves pretty thoroughly the clock struck eleven and they thought it was time to retire.

"Will you be afraid, Mrs. Condiment?" asked Capitola.

"Well, my dear, if I am I must try to trust in the Lord to overcome it, since it is no use to be afraid. I have fastened up the house well, and I have brought in Growler, the bull-dog, to sleep on the mat outside of my bedroom door, so I shall say my prayers and try to go to sleep. I dare say there is no danger, only it seems lonesome like for us three women to be left in this big house by ourselves."

"Yes," said Capitola; "but, as you say, there is no danger; and as for me, if it will give you any comfort or courage to hear me say it, I am not the least afraid, although I sleep in such a remote room and have no one but Patty, who, having no more heart that a hare, is not near such a powerful protector as Growler." And, bidding her little maid take up the night lamp, Capitola wished Mrs. Condiment good-night and left the housekeeper's room.

CHAPTER XXVI.

THE PERIL AND THE PLUCK OF CAP.

"Who that had seen her form so light
For swiftness only turned,
Would e'er have thought in a thing so slight
Such a fiery spirit burned?"

Very dreary looked the dark and silent passages as they went on toward Capitola's distant chamber.

When at last they reached it, however, and opened the door, the cheerful scene within quite reanimated Capitola's spirits. The care of her little maid had prepared a blazing wood fire that lighted up the whole room brightly, glowing on the crimson curtains of the bed and the crimson hangings of the windows opposite and flashing upon the high mirror between them.

Capitola, having secured her room in every way, stood before her dressing bureau and began to take off her collar, under sleeves and other small articles of dress. As she stood there her mirror, brilliantly lighted up by both lamp and fire, reflected clearly the opposite bed, with its warm crimson curtains, white coverlet and little Pitapat flitting from post to post as she tied back the curtains or smoothed the sheets.

Capitola stood unclasping her bracelets and smiling to herself at the reflected picture—the comfortable nest in which she was so soon to curl herself up in sleep. While she was smiling thus she tilted the mirror downwards a little for her better convenience, and, looking into it again— —

Horror! What did she see reflected there? Under the bed a pair of glaring eyes watching her from the shadows!

A sick sensation of fainting came over her; but, mastering the weakness, she tilted the glass a little lower, until it reflected all the floor, and looked again.

Horror of horrors there were three stalwart ruffians, armed to the teeth, lurking in ambush under her bed!

The deadly inclination to swoon returned upon her; but with a heroic effort she controlled her fears and forced herself to look.

Yes, there they were! It was no dream, no illusion, no nightmare—there they were, three powerful desperadoes armed with bowie knives and revolvers, the nearest one crouching low and watching her with his wolfish eyes, that shone like phosphorus in the dark.

What should she do? The danger was extreme, the necessity of immediate action imminent, the need of perfect self-control absolute! There was Pitapat flitting about the bed in momentary danger of looking under it! If she should their lives would not be worth an instant's purchase! Their throats would be cut before they should utter a second scream! It was necessary, therefore, to call Pitapat away from the bed, where her presence was as dangerous as the proximity of a lighted candle to an open powder barrel!

But how to trust her voice to do this? A single quaver in her tones would betray her consciousness of their presence to the lurking robbers and prove instantly fatal!

Happily Capitola's pride in her own courage came to her aid.

"Is it possible," she said to herself, "that after all I am a coward and have not even nerve and will enough to command the tones of my own voice? Fie on it! Cowardice is worse than death!"

And summoning all her resolution she spoke up, glibly:

"Patty, come here and unhook my dress."

"Yes, miss, I will just as soon as I get your slippers from unnerneaf of de bed!"

"I don't want them! Come here this minute and unhook my dress—I can't breathe! Plague take these country dress-makers—they think the tighter they screw one up the more fashionable they make one appear! Come, I say, and set my lungs at liberty."

"Yes, miss, in one minute," said Pitapat; and to Capitola's unspeakable horror the little maid stooped down and felt along under the side of the bed, from the head post to the foot post, until she put her hands upon the slippers and brought them forth! Providentially, the poor little wretch had not for an instant put her stupid head under the bed, or used her eyes in the search—that was all that saved them from instant massacre!

"Here dey is, Caterpillar! I knows how yer foots mus' be as much out of breaf wid yer tight gaiters as your waist is long of yer tight dress."

"Unhook me!" said Capitola, tilting up the glass lest the child should see what horrors were reflected there.

The little maid began to obey and Capitola tried to think of some plan to escape their imminent danger. To obey the natural impulse—to fly from the room would be instantly fatal—they would be followed and murdered in the hall before they could possibly give the alarm! And to whom could she give the alarm when there was not another creature in the house except Mrs. Condiment?

While she was turning these things over in her mind it occurred to her that "man's extremity is God's opportunity." Sending up a silent prayer to heaven for help at need, she suddenly thought of a plan—it was full of difficulty, uncertainty and peril, affording not one chance in fifty of success, yet the only possible plan of escape! It was to find some plausible pretext for leaving the room without exciting suspicion, which would be fatal. Controlling her tremors, and speaking cheerfully, she asked:

"Patty, do you know whether there were any of those nice quince tarts left from dinner?"

"Lor', yes, miss, a heap on 'em! Ole Mis' put 'em away in her cubberd."

"Was there any baked custard left?"

"Lor', yes Miss Caterpillar; dere was nobody but we-dens three, and think I could eat up all as was left?"

"I don't know but you might! Well, is there any pear sauce?"

"Yes, miss, a big bowl full."

"Well, I wish you'd go down and bring me up a tart, a cup of custard and a spoonful of pear sauce. Sitting up so late makes me as hungry as a wolf! Come, Patty, go along!"

"Deed, miss, I'se 'fraid!" whimpered the little maid.

"Afraid of what, you goose?"

"'Fraid of meeting of a ghose in the dark places!"

"Pooh! you can take the light with you! I can stay here in the dark well enough."

"'Deed, miss, I'se 'fraid!"

"What! with the candle, you blockhead?"

"Lors, miss, de candle wouldn't be no 'tection! I'd see de ghoses all de plainer wid de candle!"

"What a provoking, stupid dolt! You're a proper maid—afraid to do my bidding! Afraid of ghosts, forsooth. Well, I suppose I shall have to go myself—plague on you for an aggravating thing! There—take the candle and come along!" said Capitola, in a tone of impatience.

Pitapat took up the light and stood ready to accompany her mistress, Capitola, humming a gay tune, went to the door and unlocked and opened it.

She wished to withdraw the key, so as to lock it on the other side and secure the robbers and insure the safety of her own retreat; but to do this without betraying her purpose and destroying her own life seemed next to impossible. Still singing gayly she ran over in her mind with the quickness of lightning every possible means by which she might withdraw the key silently, or without attracting the attention of the watchful robbers. It is difficult to say what she would have done, had not chance instantly favored her.

At the same moment that she unlocked and opened the door and held the key in her hand fearful of withdrawing it, Pitapat, who was hurrying after her with the candle, tripped and fell against a chair, with a great noise, under cover of which Capitola drew forth the key.

Scolding and pushing Pitapat out before her, she closed the door with a bang. With the quickness of lightning she slipped the key in the key-hole and turned the lock, covering the whole with loud and angry railing against poor Pitapat, who silently wondered at this unhappy change in her mistress's temper, but ascribed it all to hunger, muttering to herself:

"I'se offen hern tell how people's cross when dere empty! Lors knows ef I don't fetch up a whole heap o' wittels ebery night for Miss Caterpillar from dis time forred, so I will—'deed me!"

So they went on through the long passages and empty rooms. Capitola carefully locking every door behind her until she got down-stairs into the great hall.

"Now, Miss Caterpillar, ef you wants quint tart, an' pear sass, and baked cussets, an' all dem, you'll jest has to go an' wake Ole Mis' up, case dey's in her cubbed an' she's got the keys," said Pitapat.

"Never mind, Patty, you follow me," said Capitola, going to the front hall door and beginning to unlock it and take down the bars and withdraw the bolts.

"Lors, miss, what is yer a-doin' of?" asked the little maid, in wonder, as Capitola opened the door and looked out.

"I am going out a little way and you must go with me!"

"Deed, miss, I'se 'fraid!"

"Very well, then, stay here in the dark until I come back, but don't go to my room, because you might meet a ghost on the way!"

"Oh, Miss, I daren't stay here—indeed I daren't!"

"Then you'll have to come along with me, and so no more about it," said Capitola, sharply, as she passed out from the door. The poor little maid followed, bemoaning the fate that bound her to so capricious a mistress.

Capitola drew the key from the hall door and locked it on the outside. Then clasping her hands and raising her eyes to heaven, she fervently ejaculated:

"Thank God—oh, thank God that we are safe!"

"Lors, miss, was we in danger?"

"We are not now at any rate, Pitapat! Come along!" said Capitola, hurrying across the lawn toward the open fields.

"Oh, my goodness, miss, where is yer-a-goin' of? Don't less us run so fur from home dis lonesome, wicked, onlawful hour o' de night!" whimpered the distressed little darkey, fearing that her mistress was certainly crazed.

"Now, then, what are you afraid of?" asked Capitola, seeing her hold back.

"Lors, miss, you knows—eberybody knows—Brack Dunnel!"

"Patty, come close—listen to me—don't scream—Black Donald and his men are up there at the house—in my chamber, under the bed," whispered Capitola.

Pitapat could not scream, for though her mouth was wide open, her breath was quite gone. Shivering with fear, she kept close to her mistress's heels as Capitola scampered over the fields.

A run of a quarter of a mile brought them to the edge of the woods, where in its little garden stood the overseer's house.

Capitola opened the gate, hurried through the little front yard and rapped loudly at the door.

This startled the house dog into furious barking and brought old Mr. Ezy, with his night-capped head, to the window to see what was the matter.

"It is I—Capitola, Mr. Ezy—Black Donald and his men are lurking up at the house," said our young heroine, commencing in an eager and hurried voice, and giving the overseer an account of the manner in which she had discovered the presence of the robbers, and left the room without alarming them.

The old man heard with many cries of astonishment, ejaculations of prayer, and exclamations of thanksgiving. And all the while his head was bobbing in and out of the window, as he pulled on his pantaloons or buttoned his coat.

"And oh!" he said, at last, as he opened the door to Capitola, "how providential that Mr. Herbert Greyson is arrove!"

"Herbert Greyson! Herbert Greyson arrived! Where is he, then?" exclaimed Capitola, in surprise and joy.

"Yes, sartain! Mr. Herbert arrove about an hour ago, and thinking you all abed and asleep at the Hall, he just stopped in with us all night! I'll go and see—I doubt if he's gone to bed yet," said Mr. Ezy, withdrawing into the house.

"Oh, thank heaven! thank heaven!" exclaimed Capitola, just as the door opened and Herbert sprang forward to greet her with a—

"Dear Capitola! I am so glad to come to see you!"

"Dear Herbert, just fancy you have said that a hundred times over and that I have replied to the same words a hundred times—for we haven't a moment to spare," said Capitola, shaking his hands, and then, in an eager, vehement manner, recounting her discovery and escape from the robbers whom she had locked up in the house.

"Go, now," she said, in conclusion, "and help Mr. Ezy to rouse up and arm the farm hands and come immediately to the house! I am in agony lest my prolonged absence should excite the robbers' suspicion of my ruse, and that they should break out and perhaps murder poor Mrs. Condiment. Her situation is awful, if she did but know it! For the love of mercy, hasten!"

Not an instant more of time was lost. Mr. Ezy and Herbert Greyson, accompanied by Capitola and Patty, hurried at once to the negro quarters, roused up and armed the men with whatever was at hand, and, enjoining them to be as stealthy as cats in their approach, set out swiftly for the Hall, where they soon arrived.

"Take off all your shoes and walk lightly in your stocking feet—do not speak—do not breathe—follow me as silent as death," said Herbert Greyson, as he softly unlocked the front door and entered the house.

Silently and stealthily they passed through the middle hall, up the broad staircase, and through the long, narrow passages and steep stairs that led to Capitola's remote chamber.

There at the door they paused awhile to listen.

All was still within.

Herbert Greyson unlocked the door, withdrew the key, and opened it and entered the room, followed by all the men. He had scarcely time to close the door and lock it on the inside, and withdraw the key, before the robbers, finding themselves surprised, burst out from their hiding place and made a rush for the passage; but their means of escape had been already cut off by the forethought of Herbert Greyson.

A sharp conflict ensued.

Upon first being summoned to surrender the robbers responded by a hailstorm of bullets from their revolvers, followed instantly by a charge of bowie knives. This was met by an avalanche of blows from pick-axes, pokers, pitchforks, sledge-hammers, spades and rakes, beneath which the miscreants were quickly beaten down and overwhelmed.

They were then set upon and bound with strong ropes brought for the purpose by Mr. Ezy.

When they were thus secured, hand and foot, Capitola, who had been a spectator of the whole scene, and exposed as much as any other to the rattle of the bullets, now approached and looked at the vanquished.

Black Donald certainly was not one of the party, who were no other than our old acquaintances—Hal, Steve and Dick—of the band!

Each burglar was conveyed to a separate apartment and a strong guard set over him.

Then Herbert Greyson, who had received a flesh wound in his left arm, returned to the scene of the conflict to look after the wounded. Several of the negroes had received gun-shot wounds of more or less importance. These were speedily attended to. Mrs. Condiment, who had slept securely through all the fight, was now awakened by Capitola, and cautiously informed of what had taken place and assured that all danger was now over.

The worthy woman, as soon as she recovered from the consternation into which the news had plunged her, at once set about succoring the wounded. Cots and mattresses were made up in one of the empty rooms and bandages and balsams prepared.

And not until all who had been hurt were made comfortable, did Herbert Greyson throw himself upon horseback, and ride off to the county seat to summon the authorities, and to inform Major Warfield of what had happened.

No one thought of retiring to bed at Hurricane Hall that night.

Mrs. Condiment, Capitola and Patty sat watching by the bedsides of the wounded.

Bill Ezy and the men who had escaped injury mounted guard over the prisoners.

Thus they all remained until sunrise, when the Major, attended by the Deputy Sheriff and half a dozen constables, arrived. The night ride of several miles had not sufficed to modify the fury into which Old Hurricane had been thrown by the news Herbert Greyson had aroused him from sleep to communicate. He reached Hurricane Hall in a state of excitement that his factotum Wool characterized as "boiling." But "in the very torrent, tempest and whirlwind of his passion" he remembered that to rail at the vanquished, wounded and bound was unmanly, and so he did not trust himself to see or speak to the prisoners.

They were placed in a wagon and under a strong escort of constables were conveyed by the Deputy Sheriff to the county seat, where they were securely lodged in jail.

But Old Hurricane's emotions of one sort or another were a treat to see! He bemoaned the sufferings of his poor wounded men; he raved at the danger to which his "women-kind" had been exposed, and he exulted in the heroism of Capitola, catching her up in his arms and crying out:

"Oh, my dear Cap! My heroine! My queen! And it was you against whom I was plotting treason—ninny that I was! You that have saved my house from pillage and my people from slaughter! Oh, Cap, what a jewel you are—my dear!"

To all of which Capitola, extricating her curly head from his embrace, cried only:

"Bother!"

Utterly refusing to be made a lioness of, and firmly rejecting the grand triumph.

The next day Major Warfield went up to the county seat to attend the examination of the three burglars, whom he had the satisfaction of seeing fully committed to prison to await their trial at the next term of the Criminal Court, which would not sit until October; consequently the prisoners had the prospect of remaining in jail some months, which Old Hurricane declared to be "some satisfaction."

CHAPTER XXVII.

SEEKING HIS FORTUNE.

A wide future smiles before him,
His heart will beat for fame,
And he will learn to breathe with love
The music of a name,
Writ on the tablets of his heart
In characters of flame.

—SARGENT.

When the winter's course of medical lectures at the Washington College was over, late in the spring, Traverse Rocke returned to Willow Heights.

The good doctor gave him a glad welcome, congratulating him upon his improved appearance and manly bearing.

Clara received him with blushing pleasure, and Marah Rocke with all the mother's love for her only child.

He quickly fell into the old pleasant routine of his country life, resumed his arduous studies in the doctor's office, his work in the flower garden, and his morning rides and evening talk with the doctor's lovely child.

Not the least obstacle was set in the way of his association with Clara, yet Traverse, grown stronger and wiser than his years would seem to promise, controlled both his feelings and his actions, and never departed from the most respectful reserve, or suffered himself to be drawn into that dangerous familiarity to which their constant companionship might tempt him.

Marah Rocke, with maternal pride, witnessed his constant self-control and encouraged him to persevere. Often in the enthusiasm of her heart, when they were alone, she would throw her arm around him, and push the dark, clustering curls from his fine forehead, and, gazing fondly on his face, exclaim:

"That is my noble-hearted boy! Oh, Traverse, God will bless you! He only tries you now to strengthen you!"

Traverse always understood these vague words and would return her embrace with all his boyish ardor and say:

"God does bless me now, mother! He blesses me so much, in so many, many ways, that I should be worse than a heathen not to be willing to bear cheerfully one trial?"

And so Traverse would "reck his own rede" and cultivate cheerful gratitude as a duty to God and man.

Clara, also, now, with her feminine intuition, comprehended her reserved lover, honored his motives and rested satisfied with being so deeply loved, trusting all their unknown future to heaven.

The doctor's appreciation and esteem for Traverse increased with every new unfolding of the youth's heart and intellect, and never did master take more pains with a favorite pupil, or father with a beloved son, than did the doctor to push Traverse on in his profession. The improvement of the youth was truly surprising.

Thus passed the summer in healthful alternation of study and exercise.

When the season waned, late in the autumn, he went a second time to Washington to attend the winter's course of lectures at the Medical College.

The doctor gave him letters recommending him as a young man of extraordinary talents and of excellent moral character, to the particular attention of several of the most eminent professors.

His mother bore this second parting with more cheerfulness, especially as the separation was enlivened by frequent letters from Traverse, full of the history of the present and the hopes of the future.

The doctor did not forget from time to time to jog the memories of his friends, the professors of the medical college, that they might afford his protégé every facility and assistance in the prosecution of his studies.

Toward spring Traverse wrote to his friends that his hopes were sanguine of obtaining his diploma at the examination to be held at the end of the session. And when Traverse expressed this hope, they who knew him so well felt assured that he had made no vain boast.

And so it proved, for early in April Traverse Rocke returned home with a diploma in his pocket.

Sincere was the joyful sympathy that met him.

The doctor shook him cordially by the hands, declaring that he was the first student he ever knew to get his diploma at the end of only three years' study.

Clara, amid smiles and blushes, congratulated him.

And Mrs. Rocke, as soon as she had him alone, threw her arms around his neck and wept for joy.

A few days Traverse gave up solely to enjoyment of his friends' society, and then, growing restless, he began to talk of opening an office and hanging out a sign in Staunton.

He consulted the doctor upon this subject. The good doctor heard him out and then, caressing his own chin and looking over the tops of his spectacles, with good-humored satire, he said:

"My dear boy, you have confidence enough in me by this time to bear that I should speak plainly to you?"

"Oh, Doctor Day, just say whatever you like!" replied the young man, fervently.

"Very well, then. I shall speak very plainly—to wit—you'll never succeed in Staunton! No, not if you had the genius of Galen and Esculapius, Abernethy and Benjamin Rush put together!"

"My dear sir—why?"

"Because, my son, it is written that 'a prophet hath no honor in his own city!' Of our blessed Lord and Saviour the contemptuous Jews said, 'Is not this Jesus, the carpenter's son?'"

"Oh, I understand you, sir!" said Traverse, with a deep blush. "You mean that the people who used some years ago to employ me to put in their coal and saw their wood and run their errands, will never trust me to look at their tongues and feel their pulses and write prescriptions!"

"That's it, my boy! You've defined the difficulty! And now I'll tell you what you are to do, Traverse! You must go to the West, my lad!"

"Go to the West, sir—leave my mother—leave you—leave"—he hesitated and blushed.

"Clara? Yes, my son, you must go to the West, leave your mother, leave me and leave Clara! It will be best for all parties! We managed to live without our lad, when he was away at his studies in Washington, and we will try to dispense with him longer if it be for his own good."

"Ah, sir; but then absence had a limitation, and the hope of return sweetened every day that passed; but if I go to the West to settle it will be without the remotest hope of returning!"

"Not so, my boy—not so—for just as soon as Doctor Rocke has established himself in some thriving western town and obtained a good practice, gained a high reputation and made himself a home—which, as he is a fast young man, in the best sense of the phrase—he can do in a very few years—he may come back here and carry to his western home—his mother," said the doctor, with a mischievous twinkle of his eyes.

"Doctor Day, I owe you more than a son's honor and obedience! I will go wherever you think it best that I should," said Traverse, earnestly.

"No more than I expected from all my previous knowledge of you, Traverse! And I, on my part, will give you only such counsel as I should give my own son, had heaven blessed me with one. And now, Traverse, there is no better season for emigration than the spring, and no better point to stop and make observations at than St. Louis! Of course, the place of your final destination must be left for future consideration. I have influential friends at St. Louis to whom I will give you letters."

"Dear sir, to have matured this plan so well you must have been kindly thinking of my future this long time past!" said Traverse, gratefully.

"Of course—of course! Who has a better right? Now go and break this plan to your mother."

Traverse pressed the doctor's hand and went to seek his mother. He found her in his room busy among his clothing. He begged her to stop and sit down while he talked to her. And when she had done so, he told her the doctor's plan. He had almost feared that his mother would meet this proposition with sighs and tears.

To his surprise and pleasure, Mrs. Rocke received the news with an encouraging smile, telling him that the doctor had long prepared her to expect that her boy would very properly go and establish himself in the West; that she should correspond with him frequently, and as soon as he should be settled, come and keep house for him.

Finally she said that, anticipating this emergency, she had, during her three years' residence beneath the doctor's roof, saved three hundred dollars, which she should give her boy to start with.

The tears rushed to the young man's eyes.

"For your dear sake, mother, only for yours, may they become three hundred thousand in my hands!" he exclaimed.

Preparations were immediately commenced for Traverse's journey.

As before, Clara gladly gave her aid in getting ready his wardrobe. As he was about to make his debut as a young physician in a strange city, his mother was anxious that his dress should be faultless; and, therefore, put the most delicate needlework upon all the little articles of his outfit. Clara volunteered to mark them all. And one day, when Traverse happened to be alone with his mother, she showed him his handkerchiefs, collars and linen beautifully marked in minute embroidered letters.

"I suppose, Traverse, that you, being a young man, cannot appreciate the exquisite beauty of this work," she said.

"Indeed, but I can, mother! I did not sit by your side so many years while you worked without knowing something about it. This is wonderful! The golden thread with which the letters are embroidered is finer than the finest silk I ever saw!" said Traverse, admiringly, to please his mother, whom he supposed to be the embroideress.

"Well they may be!" said Mrs. Rocke, "for that golden thread of which you speak is Clara's golden hair, which she herself has drawn out and threaded her needle with, and worked into the letters of your name."

Traverse suddenly looked up, his color went and came, he had no words to reply.

"I told you because I thought it would give you pleasure to know it, and that it would be a comfort to you when you are far away from us; for, Traverse, I hope that by this time you have grown strong and wise enough to have conquered yourself, and to enjoy dear Clara's friendship aright!"

"Mother!" he said, sorrowfully, and then his voice broke down, and without another word he turned and left the room.

To feel how deeply and hopelessly he loved the doctor's sweet daughter—to feel sure that she perceived and returned his dumb, despairing love—and to know that duty, gratitude, honor commanded him to be silent, to tear himself away from her and make no sign, was a trial almost too great for the young heart's integrity. Scarcely could he prevent the internal struggle betraying itself upon his countenance. As the time drew near for his departure self-control grew difficult and almost impossible. Even Clara lost her joyous spirits and despite all her efforts to be cheerful, grew so pensive that her father, without seeming to understand the cause, gayly rallied her upon her dejection.

Traverse understood it and almost longed for the day to come when he should leave this scene of his love and his sore trial.

One afternoon, a few days before he was to start, Doctor Day sent for Traverse to come to him in his study. And as soon as they were seated comfortably together at the table the doctor put into the young man's hand a well-filled pocketbook; and when Traverse, with a deep and painful blush, would have given it back, he forced it upon him with the old argument:

"It is only a loan, my boy! Money put out at interest! Capital well and satisfactorily invested! And now listen to me! I am about to speak to you of that which is much nearer your heart— —"

Traverse became painfully embarrassed.

"Traverse," resumed the doctor, "I have grown to love you as a son, and to esteem you as a man. I have lived long enough to value solid integrity far beyond wealth or birth, and when that integrity is adorned and enriched by high talents, it forms a character of excellence not often met with in this world. I have proved both your integrity and your talents, Traverse, and I am more than satisfied with you—I am proud of you, my boy."

Traverse bowed deeply, but still blushed.

"You will wonder," continued the doctor, "to what all this talk tends. I will tell you. Traverse, I have long known your unspoken love for Clara, and I have honored your scruples in keeping silent, when silence must have been so painful. Your trial is now over, my son! Go and open for yourself an honorable career in the profession you have chosen and mastered, and return, and Clara shall be yours!"

Traverse, overwhelmed with surprise and joy at this incredible good fortune, seized the doctor's hand, and in wild and incoherent language tried to express his gratitude.

"There—there," said the doctor, "go and tell Clara all this and bring the roses back to her cheeks, and then your parting will be the happier for this hope before you."

"I must speak! I must speak first!" said the young man, in a choking voice. "I must tell you some little of the deep gratitude I feel for you, sir. Oh, when I forget all that you have done for me, 'may my right hand forget her cunning!' may God and man forget me! Doctor Day, the Lord helping me for your good sake, I will be all that you have prophesied, and hope and expect of me! For your sake, for Clara's and my mother's, I will bend every power of my mind, soul and body to attain the eminence you desire for me! In a word, the Lord giving me grace, I will become worthy of being your son and Clara's husband."

"There, there, my dear boy, go and tell Clara all that!" said the doctor, pressing the young man's hand and dismissing him.

Traverse went immediately to seek Clara, whom he found sitting alone in the parlor.

She was bending over some delicate needlework that Traverse knew by instinct was intended for himself.

Now, had Traverse foreseen from the first the success of his love, there might possibly have been the usual shyness and hesitation in declaring himself to the object of his affection. But although he and Clara had long deeply and silently loved and understood each other, yet neither had dared to hope for so improbable an event as the doctor's favoring their attachment, and now, under the exciting influence of the surprise, joy and gratitude with which the doctor's magnanimity had filled his heart, Traverse forgot all shyness and hesitation, and, stepping quickly to Clara's side, and dropping gently upon one knee, he took her hand, and, bowing his head upon it, said:

"Clara, my own, own Clara, your dear father has given me leave to tell you at last how much and how long I have loved you!" and then he arose and sat down beside her.

The blush deepened upon Clara's cheek, tears filled her eyes, and her voice trembled as she murmured: "Heaven bless my dear father! He is unlike every other man on earth!"

"Oh, he is—he is!" said Traverse, fervently, "and, dear Clara, never did a man strive so hard for wealth, fame, or glory, as I shall strive to become 'worthy to be called his son!'"

"Do, Traverse—do, dear Traverse! I want you to honor even his very highest drafts upon your moral and intellectual capacities! I know you are 'worthy' of his high regard now, else he never would have chosen you as his son—but I am ambitious for you, Traverse! I would have your motto be, 'Excelsior!'—higher!" said the doctor's daughter.

"And you, dear Clara, may I venture to hope that you do not disapprove of your father's choice, or reject the hand that he permits me to offer you?" said Traverse, for though he understood Clara well enough, yet like all honest men, he wanted some definite and practical engagement.

"There is my hand—my heart was yours long ago," murmured the maiden, in a tremulous voice.

He took and pressed that white hand to his heart, looked hesitatingly and pleadingly in her face for an instant, and then, drawing her gently to his bosom, sealed their betrothal on her pure lips.

Then they sat side by side, and hand in hand, in a sweet silence for a few moments, and then Clara said:

"You have not told your mother yet! Go and tell her, Traverse; it will make her so happy! And Traverse, I will be a daughter to her, while you are gone. Tell her that, too."

"Dear girl, you have always been as kind and loving to my mother as it was possible to be. How can you ever be more so than you have been?"

"I shall find a way!" smiled Clara.

Again he pressed her hand to his heart and to his lips, and left the room to find his mother. He had a search before he discovered her at last in the drawing-room, arranging it for their evening fireside gathering.

"Come, mother, and sit down by me on this sofa, for I have glorious tidings for your ear! Dear Clara sent me from her own side to tell you!"

"Ah, still thinking—always thinking, madly thinking of the doctor's daughter! Poor, poor boy!" said Mrs. Rocke.

"Yes, and always intend to think of her to the very end of my life, and beyond, if possible! But come, dear mother, and hear me explain!" said Traverse, and as soon as Mrs. Rocke had taken the indicated seat, Traverse commenced and related to her the substance of the conversation between the doctor and himself in the library, in which the former authorized his addresses to his daughter, and also his own subsequent explanation and engagement with Clara.

Mrs. Rocke listened to all this, in unbroken silence, and when, at length, Traverse had concluded his story, she clasped her hands and raised her eyes, uttering fervent thanksgivings to the fountain of all mercies.

"You do not congratulate me, dear mother."

"Oh, Traverse, I am returning thanks to heaven on your behalf! Oh, my son! my son; but that such things as these are Providential, I should tremble to see you so happy! So I will not presume to congratulate! I will pray for you!"

"Dear mother, you have suffered so much in your life that you are incredulous of happiness! Be more hopeful and confiding! The Bible says, 'There remaineth now these three—Faith, Hope and Charity—but the greatest of all is Charity.' You have Charity enough, dear mother; try to have more Faith and Hope, and you will be happier! And look—there is Clara coming this way! She does not know that we are here. I will call her. Dear Clara, come in and convince my mother—she will not believe in our happiness," said Traverse, going to the door and leading his blushing and smiling betrothed into the room.

"It may be that Mrs. Rocke does not want me for a daughter-in-law," said Clara, archly, as she approached and put her hand in that of Marah.

"Not want you, my own darling!" said Marah Rocke, putting her arm around Clara's waist, and drawing her to her bosom, "not want you! You know I am just as much in love with you as Traverse himself can be! And I have longed for you, my sweet, longed for you as an unattainable blessing, ever since that day when Traverse first left us, and you came and laid your bright head on my bosom and wept with me!"

"And now if we must cry a little when Traverse leaves us, we can go and take comfort in being miserable together, with a better understanding of our relations!" said Clara with an arch smile.

"Where are you all? Where is everybody—that I am left wandering about the lonely house like a poor ghost in Hades?" said the doctor's cheerful voice in the passage without.

"Here, father—here we are—a family party, wanting only you to complete it," answered his daughter, springing to meet him.

The doctor came in smiling, pressed his daughter to his bosom, shook Traverse cordially by the hand, and kissed Marah Rocke's cheek. That was his way of congratulating himself and all others on the betrothal.

The evening was passed in unalloyed happiness.

Let them enjoy it! It was their last of comfort—that bright evening!

Over that household was already gathering a cloud heavy and dark with calamity—calamity that must have overwhelmed the stability of any faith which was not as theirs was—stayed upon God.

CHAPTER XXVIII.

A PANIC IN THE OUTLAW'S DEN.

Imagination frames events unknown,
In wild, fantastic shapes of hideous ruin,
And what it fears creates!

—HANNAH MORE.

Dark doubt and fear, o'er other spirits lower,
But touch not his, who every waking hour,
Has one fixed hope and always feels its power.

—CRABBE.

Upon the very same night, that the three robbers were surprised and captured by the presence of mind of Capitola at Hurricane Hall, Black Donald, disguised as a negro, was lurking in the woods around the mansion, waiting for the coming of his three men with their prize.

But as hour after hour passed and they came not, the desperado began heartily to curse their sloth—for to no other cause was he enabled to attribute the delay, as he knew the house, the destined scene of the outrage, to be deserted by all for the night, except by the three helpless females.

As night waned and morning began to dawn in the east, the chief grew seriously uneasy at the prolonged absence of his agents—a circumstance that he could only account for upon the absurd hypothesis that those stupid brutes had suffered themselves to be overtaken by sleep in their ambuscade.

While he was cursing their inefficiency, and regretting that he had not himself made one of the party, he wandered in his restlessness to another part of the woods, and the opposite side of the house.

He had not been long here before his attention was arrested by the tramping of approaching horsemen. He withdrew into the shade of the thicket and listened while the travelers went by.

The party proved to consist of Old Hurricane, Herbert Greyson and the Sheriff's officers, on their way from the town to Hurricane Hall to take the captured burglars into custody. And Black Donald, by listening attentively, gathered enough from their conversation to know that his men had been discovered and captured by the heroism of Capitola.

"That girl again!" muttered Black Donald, to himself. "She is doomed to be my destruction, or I hers! Our fates are evidently connected! Poor Steve! Poor Dick! Poor Hal! Little did I think that your devotion to your captain would carry you into the very jaws of death—pshaw! hang it! Let boys and women whine! I must act!"

And with this resolution Black Donald dogged the path of the horsemen until he had reached that part of the woods skirting the road opposite the park gate. Here he hid himself in the bushes to watch events. Soon from his hiding place he saw the wagon approach, containing the three men, heavily ironed and escorted by a strong guard of county constables and plantation negroes, all well armed, and under the command of the Sheriff and Herbert Greyson.

"Ha, ha, ha! They must dread an attempt on our part of rescue, or they never would think of putting such a formidable guard over three wounded and hand-cuffed men!" laughed Black Donald to himself.

"Courage, my boys," he muttered. "Your chief will free you from prison or share your captivity! I wish I could trumpet that into your ears at this moment, but prudence, 'the better part of valor,' forbids! For the same words that would encourage you would warn your captors into greater vigilance." And so saying Black Donald let the procession pass, and then made tracks for his retreat.

It was broad daylight when he reached the Old Inn. The robbers, worn out with waiting and watching for the captain and his men with the fair prize, had thrown themselves down upon the kitchen floor, and now lay in every sort of awkward attitude, stretched out or doubled up in heavy sleep. The old beldame had disappeared—doubtless she had long since sought her night lair.

Taking a poker from the corner of the fireplace, Black Donald went around among the sleeping robbers and stirred them up, with vigorous punches in the ribs and cries of:

"Wake up!—dolts! brutes! blockheads! Wake up! You rest on a volcano about to break out! You sleep over a mine about to be exploded! Wake up!—sluggards that you are! Your town is taken! Your castle is stormed! The enemy is at your throats with drawn swords! Ah, brutes, will you wake, then, or shall I have to lay it on harder?"

"What the demon?"

"How now?"

"What's this?" were some of the ejaculations of the men as they slowly and sulkily roused themselves from their heavy slumber.

"The house is on fire! The ship's sinking! The cars have run off the track! The boiler's burst, and the devil's to pay!" cried Black Donald, accompanying his words with vigorous punches of the poker into the ribs of the recumbent men.

"What the foul fiend ails you, captain? Have you got the girl and drunk too much liquor on your wedding night?" asked one of the men.

"No, Mac, I have not got the girl! On the contrary, the girl, blame her, has got three of my best men in custody! In one word, Hal, Dick and Steve are safely lodged in the county jail!"

"What?"

"Perdition!"

"My eye!"

"Here's a go!" were the simultaneous exclamations of the men as they sprang upon their feet.

"In the fiend's name, captain, tell us all about it!" said Mac, anxiously.

"I have no time to talk much, nor you to tarry long! It was all along of that blamed witch, Capitola!" said Black Donald, who then gave a rapid account of the adventure, and the manner in which Capitola entrapped and captured the burglars, together with the way in which he himself came by the information.

"I declare, one can't help liking that girl! I should admire her even if she should put a rope about my neck!" said Mac.

"She's a brick!" said another, with emphasis.

"She's some pumpkins, now, I tell you!" assented a third.

"I am more than ever resolved to get her into my possession! But in the mean time, lads, we must evacuate the Old Inn! It is getting too hot to hold us!"

"Aye, captain!"

"Aye, lads, listen! We must talk fast and act promptly; the poor fellows up there in jail are game, I know! They would not willingly peach, but they are badly wounded. If one of them should have to die, and be blessed with a psalm-singing parson to attend him, no knowing what he may be persuaded to confess! Therefore, let us quickly decide upon some new rendezvous that will be unsuspected, even by our poor caged birds! If any of you have any place in your eye, speak!"

"We would rather hear what you have to say, captain," said Mac; and all the rest assented.

"Well, then, you all know the Devil's Punch Bowl!"

"Aye, do we, captain!"

"Well, what you do not know—what nobody knows but myself is this—that about half-way down that awful chasm, in the side of the rock, is a hole, concealed by a clump of evergreens; that hole is the entrance to a cavern of enormous extent! Let that be our next rendezvous! And now, avaunt! Fly! Scatter! and meet me in the cavern to-night, at the usual hour! Listen—carry away all our arms, ammunition, disguises and provisions—so that no vestige of our presence may be left behind. As for dummy, if they can make her speak, the cutting out of her tongue was lost labor—vanish!"

"But our pals in prison!" said Mac.

"They shall be my care. We must lie low for a few days, so as to put the authorities off their guard. Then if our pals recover from their wounds, and have proved game against Church and State, I shall know what measures to take for their deliverance! No more talk now—prepare for your flitting and fly!"

The captain's orders were obeyed, and within two hours from that time no vestige of the robbers' presence remained in the deserted Old Inn.

If any Sheriff's officer had come there with a search-warrant, he would have found nothing suspicious; he would have seen only a poor old dumb woman, busy at her spinning wheel; and if he had questioned her would only have got smiles and shakes of the head for an answer, or the exhibitions of coarse country gloves and stockings of her own knitting, which she would, in dumb-show, beg him to purchase.

Days and weeks passed and the three imprisoned burglars languished in jail, each in a separate cell.

Bitterly each in his heart complained of the leader that had, apparently, deserted them in their direst need. And if neither betrayed him it was probably because they could not do so without deeply criminating themselves, and for no better motive.

There is said to be "honor among thieves." It is, on the face of it, untrue; there can be neither honor, confidence nor safety among men whose profession is crime. The burglars, therefore, had no confidence in their leader, and secretly and bitterly reproached him for his desertion of them.

Meanwhile the annual camp meeting season approached. It was rumored that a camp meeting would be held in the wooded vale below Tip-Top, and soon this report was confirmed by announcements in all the county papers. And all who intended to take part in the religious festival or have a tent on the ground began to prepare provisions—cooking meat and poultry, baking bread, cakes, pies, etc. And preachers from all parts of the country were flocking in to the village to be on the spot for the commencement.

Mrs. Condiment, though a member of another church, loved in her soul the religious excitement—"the warming up," as she called it, to be had at the camp meeting! But never in the whole course of her life had she taken part in one, except so far as riding to the preaching in the morning and returning home in the evening.

But Capitola, who was as usual in the interval between her adventures, bored half to death with the monotony of her life at Hurricane Hall—and praying not against but wishing for—fire, floods or thieves, or anything to stir her stagnant blood, heard of the camp meeting, and expressed a wish to have a tent on the camp ground and remain there from the beginning to the end, to see all that was to be seen; hear all that was to be heard; feel all that was to be felt, and learn all that was to be known!

And as Capitola, ever since her victory over the burglars, had been the queen regnant of Hurricane Hall, she had only to express this wish to have it carried into immediate effect.

Old Hurricane himself went up to Tip-Top and purchased the canvas and set two men to work under his own immediate direction to make the tent.

And as Major Warfield's campaigning experience was very valuable here, it turned out that the Hurricane Hall tent was the largest and best on the camp ground. As soon as it was set up under the shade of a grove of oak trees a wagon from Hurricane Hall conveyed to the spot the simple and necessary furniture, cooking materials and provisions. And the same morning the family carriage, driven by Wool, brought out Major Warfield, Mrs. Condiment, Capitola and her little maid Patty.

The large tent was divided into two compartments—one for Major Warfield and his man Wool—the other for Mrs. Condiment, Capitola and Patty.

As the family party stepped out of the carriage, the novelty, freshness and beauty of the scene called forth a simultaneous burst of admiration. The little snow-white tents were dotted here and there through the woods, in beautiful contrast with the greenness of the foliage, groups of well-dressed and cheerful-looking men, women and children were walking about; over all smiled a morning sky of cloudless splendor. The preachings and the prayer meetings had not yet commenced. Indeed, many of the brethren were hard at work in an extensive clearing, setting up a rude pulpit, and arranging rough benches to accommodate the women and children of the camp congregation.

Our party went into their tent, delighted with the novelty of the whole thing, though Old Hurricane declared that it was nothing new to his experience, but reminded him strongly of his campaigning days.

Wool assented, saying that the only difference was, there were no ladies in the old military camp.

I have neither time nor space to give a full account of this camp meeting. The services commenced the same evening. There were preachers of more or less fervor, of piety and eloquence of utterance. Old Christians had their "first love" revived; young ones found their zeal kindled, and sinners were awakened to a sense of their sin and danger. Every Christian there said the season had been a good one!

In the height of the religious enthusiasm there appeared a new preacher in the field. He seemed a man considerably past middle age and broken down with sickness or sorrow. His figure was tall, thin and stooping; his hair white as snow, his face pale and emaciated; his movements slow and feeble, and his voice low and unsteady! He wore a solemn suit of black, that made his thin form seem of skeleton proportions; a snow-white neck-cloth, and a pair of great round iron-rimmed spectacles, that added nothing to his good looks.

Yet this old, sickly and feeble man seemed one of fervent piety and of burning eloquence. Every one sought his society; and when it was known that Father Gray was to hold forth, the whole camp congregation turned out to hear him.

It must not be supposed that in the midst of this great revival those poor "sinners above all sinners," the burglars imprisoned in the neighboring town, were forgotten! no, they were remembered, prayed for, visited and exhorted. And no one took more interest in the fate of these men than good Mrs. Condiment, who, having seen them all on that great night at Hurricane Hall, and having with her own kind hands plastered their heads and given them possets, could not drive out of her heart a certain compassion for their miseries.

No one, either, admired Father Gray more than did the little old housekeeper of Hurricane Hall, and as her table and her accommodations were the best on the camp ground, she often invited and pressed good Father Gray to rest and refresh himself in her tent. And the old man, though a severe ascetic, yielded to her repeated solicitations, until at length he seemed to live there altogether.

One day Mrs. Condiment, being seriously exercised upon the subject of the imprisoned men, said to Father Gray, who was reposing himself in the tent:

"Father Gray, I wished to speak to you, sir, upon the subject of those poor wretched men who are to be tried for their lives at the next term of the Criminal Court. Our ministers have all been to see them, and talked to them, but not one of the number can make the least impression on them, or bring them to any sense of their awful condition!"

"Ah, that is dreadful!" sighed the aged man.

"Yes, dreadful, Father Gray! Now I thought if you would only visit them you could surely bring them to reason!"

"My dear friend, I would willingly do so, but I must confess to you a weakness—a great weakness of the flesh—I have a natural shrinking from men of blood! I know it is sinful, but indeed I cannot overcome it."

"But, my dear Father Gray, a man of your experience knows full well that if you cannot overcome that feeling you should act in direct opposition to it! And, I assure you, there is no danger! Why, even I should not be at all afraid of a robber when he is double-ironed and locked up in a cell, and I should enter guarded by a pair of turnkeys!"

"I know it, my dear lady, I know it, and I feel that I ought to overcome this weakness or do my duty in its despite."

"Yes, and if you would consent to go, Father Gray, I would not mind going with you myself, if that would encourage you any!"

"Of course it would, my dear friend; and if you will go with me, and if the brethren think that I could do any good I will certainly endeavor to conquer my repugnance and visit these imprisoned men."

It was arranged that Father Gray, accompanied by Mrs. Condiment, should go to the jail upon the following morning; and, accordingly, they set out immediately after breakfast. A short ride up the mountain brought them to Tip-Top, in the center of which stood the jail. It was a simple structure of gray stone, containing within its own walls the apartments occupied by the warden. To these Mrs. Condiment, who was the leader in the whole matter, first presented herself, introducing Father Gray as one of the preachers of the camp meeting, a very pious man, and very effective in his manner of dealing with hardened offenders.

"I have heard of the Rev. Mr. Gray and his powerful exhortations," said the warden, with a low bow; "and I hope he may be able to make some impression on these obdurate men and induce them, if possible, to 'make a clean breast of it,' and give up the retreat of their band. Each of them has been offered a free pardon on condition of turning State's evidence and each has refused."

"Indeed! have they done so, case-hardened creatures?" mildly inquired Father Gray.

"Aye, have they; but you, dear sir, may be able to persuade them to do so."

"I shall endeavor! I shall endeavor!" said the mild old man.

The warden then requested the visitors to follow him and led the way upstairs to the cells.

"I understand that the criminals are confined separately?" said Mr. Gray to the warden.

"No, sir; they were so confined at first, for better security, but as they have been very quiet, and as since those rowdies that disturbed the camp meeting have been sent to prison and filled up our cells, we have had to put those three robbers into one cell."

"I'm afraid I—" began the minister, hesitating.

"Father Gray is nervous, good Mr. Jailor; I hope there's no danger from these dreadful men—all of them together—for I promised Father Gray that he should be safe, myself," said Mrs. Condiment.

"Oh, ma'am, undoubtedly; they are double-ironed," said the warden, as he unlocked a door and admitted the visitors, into rather a darkish cell, in which were the three prisoners.

Steve the mulatto was stretched upon the floor in a deep sleep.

Hal was sitting on the side of the cot, twiddling his fingers.

Dick sat crouched up in a corner, with his head against the wall.

"Peace be with you, my poor souls," said the mild old man, as he entered the cell.

"You go to the demon!" said Dick, with a hideous scowl.

"Nay, my poor man, I came in the hope of saving you from that enemy of souls!"

"Here's another! There's three comes reg'lar! Here's the fourth! Go it, old fellow! We're gettin' used to it! It's gettin' to be entertainin'! It's the only diversion we have in this blamed hole," said Hal.

"Nay, friend, if you use profane language, I cannot stay to hear it," said the old man.

"Yaw-aw-aw-ow!" yawned Steve, half rising and stretching himself. "What's the row? I was just dreaming our captain had come to deliver us—yow-aw-aw-ooh! It's only another parson!" and with that Steve turned himself over and settled to sleep.

"My dear Mr. Jailer, do you think that these men are safe—for if you do, I think we had better leave excellent Mr. Gray to talk to them alone—he can do them so much more good if he has them all to himself," said Mrs. Condiment, who was, in spite of all her previous boasting, beginning to quail and tremble under the hideous glare of Demon Dick's eyes.

"N-no! n-no! n-no!" faltered the preacher, nervously taking hold of the coat of the warden.

"You go along out of this the whole of you! I'm not a wild beast in a cage to be stared at!" growled Demon Dick with a baleful glare that sent Mrs. Condiment and the preacher, shuddering to the cell door.

"Mr. Gray, I do assure you, sir, there is no danger! The men are double-ironed, and, malignant as they may be, they can do you no harm. And if you would stay and talk to them you might persuade them to confession and do the community much service," said the warden.

"I—I—I'm no coward, but—but—but—" faltered the old man, tremblingly approaching the prisoners.

"I understand you, sir. You are in bad health, which makes you nervous."

"Yes—yes. Heaven forgive me, but if you, Mr. Jailer, and the good lady here will keep within call, in case of accidents, I don't mind if I do remain and exhort these men, for a short time," said the old man.

"Of course we will. Come, Mrs. Condiment, mum! There's a good bench in the lobby and I'll send for my old woman and we three can have a good talk while the worthy Mr. Gray is speaking to the prisoners," said the warden, conducting the housekeeper from the cell.

As soon as they had gone the old man went to the door and peeped after them, and having seen that they went to the extremity of the lobby to a seat under an open window, he turned back to the cell, and, going up to Hal, said in a low, voice:

"Now, then, is it possible that you do not know me?"

Hal stopped twiddling his fingers and looked up at the tall, thin, stooping figure, the gray hair, the white eyebrows and the pale face, and said gruffly:

"No! May the demon fly away with me if I ever saw you before!"

"Nor you, Dick?" inquired the old man, in a mild voice, turning to the one addressed.

"No, burn you, nor want to see you now!"

"Steve! Steve!" said the old man, in a pitiful voice, waking the sleeper. "Don't you know me, either?"

"Don't bother me," said that worthy, giving himself another turn and another settle to sleep.

"Dolts! blockheads! brutes! Do you know me now?" growled the visitor, changing his voice.

"Our captain!"

"Our captain!"

"Our captain!" they simultaneously cried.

"Hush! sink your souls! Do you want to bring the warden upon us?" growled Black Donald, for it was unquestionably him in a new metamorphosis.

"Then all I have to say, captain, is that you have left us here a blamed long time!"

"And exposed to sore temptation to peach on me! Couldn't help it, lads! Couldn't help it! I waited until I could do something to the purpose!"

"Now, may Satan roast me alive if I know what you have done to turn yourself into an old man! Burn my soul, if I should know you now, captain, if it wa'n't for your voice," grumbled Steve.

"Listen, then, you ungrateful, suspicious wretches! I did for you what no captain ever did for his men before! I had exhausted all manner of disguises, so that the authorities would almost have looked for me in an old woman's gown! See, then, what I did! I put myself on a month's regimen of vegetable diet, and kept myself in a cavern until I grew as pale and thin as a hermit! Then I shaved off my hair, beard, mustaches and eyebrows! Yes, blame you, I sacrificed all my beauty to your interests! Fate helps those who help themselves! The camp meeting gathering together hosts of people and preachers gave me the opportunity of appearing without exciting inquiry. I put on a gray wig, a black suit, assumed a feeble voice, stooping gait and a devout manner, and—became a popular preacher at the camp meeting."

"Captain, you're a brick! You are indeed! I do not flatter you!" said Hal. It was a sentiment in which all agreed.

"I had no need of further machination!" continued the captain; "they actually gave me the game! I was urged to visit you here—forced to remain alone and talk with you!" laughed Black Donald.

"And now, captain, my jewel, my treasure, my sweetheart—that I love with 'a love passing the love of woman'—how is your reverence going to get us out?"

"Listen!" said the captain, diving into his pockets, "you must get yourselves out! This prison is by no means strongly fastened or well guarded! Here are files to file off your fetters! Here are tools to pick the locks, and here are three loaded revolvers to use against any of the turnkey who might discover and attempt to stop you! To-night, however, is the last of the camp meeting, and the two turnkeys are among my hearers! I shall keep them all night! Now you know what to do! I must leave you! Dick, try to make an assault on me that I may scream, but first conceal your tools and arms!"

Hal hid the instruments and Dick, with an awful roar, sprang at the visitor, who ran to the grating crying:

"Help—help!"

The warden came hurrying to the spot.

"Take 'im out o' this, then!" muttered Dick, sulkily getting back into his corner.

"Oh, what a wretch!" said Mrs. Condiment.

"I shall be glad when he's once hanged!" said the jailer.

"I—I—fear that I can do them but little good, and—and I would rather not come again, being sickly and nervous," faltered Father Gray.

"No, my dear good sir! I for one shall not ask you to risk your precious health for such a set of wretches! They are Satan's own! You shall come home to our tent and lie down to rest, and I will make you an egg-caudle that will set you up again," said Mrs. Condiment, tenderly, as the whole party left the cell.

That day the outrageous conduct of the imprisoned burglars was the subject of conversation, even dividing the interest of the religious excitement.

But the next morning the whole community was thrown into a state of consternation by the discovery that the burglars had broken jail and fled, and that the notorious outlaw Black Donald had been in their very midst, disguised as an elderly field preacher.

CHAPTER XXIX.

THE VICTORY OVER DEATH.

"Glory to God! to God!" he saith,
"Knowledge by suffering entereth,
And life is perfected in death."

—E. B. BROWNING.

One morning, in the gladness of his heart, Doctor Day mounted his horse and rode down to Staunton, gayly refusing to impart the object of his ride to any one, and bidding Traverse stay with the women until he should return.

As soon as the doctor was gone, Traverse went into the library to arrange his patron's books and papers.

Mrs. Rocke and Clara hurried away to attend to some little mystery of their own invention for the surprise and delight of the doctor and Traverse. For the more secret accomplishment of their purpose, they had dismissed all attendance, and were at work alone in Mrs. Rocke's room. And here Clara's sweet, frank and humble disposition was again manifest, for when Marah would arise from her seat to get anything, Clara would forestall her purpose and say:

"Tell me—tell me to get what you want—just as if I were your child, and you will make me feel so well—do, now!"

"You are very good, dear Miss Clara, but—I would rather not presume to ask you to wait on me," said Marah, gravely.

"Presume! What a word from you to me! Please don't use it ever again, nor call me Miss Clara. Call me 'Clara' or 'child'—do, mamma," said the doctor's daughter, then suddenly pausing, she blushed and was silent.

Marah gently took her hand and drew her into a warm embrace.

It was while the friends were conversing so kindly in Marah's room, and while Traverse was still engaged in arranging the doctor's books and papers that one of the men-servants rapped at the library door, and without waiting permission to come in, entered the room with every mark of terror in his look and manner.

"What is the matter?" inquired Traverse, anxiously rising.

"Oh, Mr. Traverse, sir, the doctor's horse has just rushed home to the stables all in foam, without his rider!"

"Good heaven!" exclaimed Traverse, starting up and seizing his hat. "Follow me immediately! Hurry to the stables and saddle my horse and bring him up instantly! We must follow on the road the doctor took to see what has happened! Stay! On your life, breathe not a word of what has occurred! I would not have Miss Day alarmed for the world!" he concluded, hastening down-stairs attended by the servant.

In five minutes from the time he left the library Traverse was in the saddle, galloping toward Staunton, and looking attentively along the road as he went. Alas! he had not gone far, when, in descending the wooded hill, he saw lying doubled up helplessly on the right side of the path, the body of the good doctor!

With an exclamation between a groan and a cry of anguish, Traverse threw himself from his saddle and kneeled beside the fallen figure, gazing in an agony of anxiety upon the closed eyes, pale features and contracted form and crying:

"Oh, heaven have mercy! Doctor Day, oh, Doctor Day! Can you speak to me?"

The white and quivering eyelids opened and the faltering tongue spoke:

"Traverse—get me home—that I may see—Clara before I die!"

"Oh, must this be so! Must this be so! Oh, that I could die for you, my friend! My dear, dear friend!" cried Traverse, wringing his hands in such anguish as he had never known before.

Then feeling the need of self-control and the absolute necessity of removing the sufferer, Traverse repressed the swelling flood of sorrow in his bosom and cast about for the means of conveying the doctor to his house. He dreaded to leave him for an instant, and yet it was necessary to do so, as the servant whom he had ordered to follow him had not yet come up.

While he was bathing the doctor's face with water from a little stream beside the path, John, the groom, came riding along, and seeing his fallen master, with an exclamation of horror, sprang from his saddle and ran to the spot.

"John," said Traverse, in a heart-broken tone, "mount again and ride for your life to the house! Have—a cart—yes—that will be the easiest conveyance—have a cart got ready instantly with a feather bed placed in it, and the gentlest horse harnessed to it, and drive it here to the roadside at the head of this path! Hasten for your life! Say not a word of what has happened lest it should terrify the ladies! Quick! quick! on your life!"

Again, as the man was hurrying away, the doctor spoke, faintly murmuring:

"For heaven's sake, do not let poor Clara be shocked!"

"No—no—she shall not be! I warned him, dear friend! How do you feel? Can you tell where you are hurt?"

The doctor feebly moved one hand to his chest and whispered:

"There, and in my back."

Traverse, controlling his own great mental agony, did all that he could to soothe and alleviate the sufferings of the doctor, until the arrival of the cart, that stopped on the road at the head of the little bridle path, where the accident happened. Then John jumped from the driver's seat and came to the spot, where he tenderly assisted the young man in raising the doctor and conveying him to the cart and laying him upon the bed. Notwithstanding all their tender care in lifting and carrying him, it was but too evident that he suffered greatly in being moved. Slowly as they proceeded, at every jolt of the cart, his corrugated brows and blanched and quivering lips told how much agony he silently endured.

Thus at last they reached home. He was carefully raised by the bed and borne into the house and up-stairs to his own chamber, where, being undressed, he was laid upon his own easy couch. Traverse sent off for other medical aid, administered a restorative and proceeded to examine his injuries.

"It is useless, dear boy—useless all! You have medical knowledge enough to be as sure of that as I am. Cover me up and let me compose myself before seeing Clara, and while I do so, go you and break this news gently to the poor child!" said the doctor, who, being under the influence of the restorative, spoke more steadily than at any time since the fall Traverse, almost broken-hearted, obeyed his benefactor and went to seek his betrothed, praying the Lord to teach him how to tell her this dreadful calamity and to support her under its crushing weight.

As he went slowly, wringing his hands, he suddenly met Clara with her dress in disorder and her hair flying, just as she had run from her room while dressing for dinner. Hurrying toward him, she exclaimed:

"Traverse, what has happened? For the good Lord's sake, tell me quickly—the house is all in confusion. Every one is pale with affright! No one will answer me! Your mother just now ran past me out of the store room, with her face as white as death! Oh, what does it all mean?"

"Clara, love, come and sit down; you are almost fainting—(oh, heaven, support her!)" murmured Traverse, as he led the poor girl to the hall sofa.

"Tell me! Tell me!" she said.

"Clara—your father——"

"My father! No, no—no—do not say any harm has happened to my father—do not, Traverse!—do not!"

"Oh, Clara, try to be firm, dear one!"

"My father! Oh, my father!—he is dead!" shrieked Clara, starting up wildly to run, she knew not whither.

Traverse sprang up and caught her arm and drawing her gently back to her seat, said:

"No, dear Clara—no, not so bad as that—he is living!"

"Oh, thank heaven for so much! What is it, then, Traverse? He is ill! Oh, let me go to him!"

"Stay, dear Clara—compose yourself first! You would not go and disturb him with this frightened and distressed face of yours—let me get you a glass of water," said Traverse, starting up and bringing the needed sedative from an adjoining room.

"There, Clara, drink that and offer a silent prayer to heaven to give you self-control."

"I will—oh, I must for his sake! But tell me, Traverse, is it—is it as I fear—as he expected—apoplexy?"

"No, dear love—no. He rode out this morning and his horse got frightened by the van of a circus company that was going into the town, and——"

"And ran away with him and threw him! Oh, heaven! Oh, my dear father!" exclaimed Clara, once more clasping her hands wildly, and starting up.

Again Traverse promptly but gently detained her, saying:

"You promised me to be calm, dear Clara, and you must be so, before I can suffer you to see your father."

Clara sank into her seat and covered her face with her hands, murmuring, in a broken voice:

"How can I be? Oh, how can I be, when my heart is with grief and fright? Traverse! Was he—was he—oh, dread to ask you! Oh, was he much hurt?"

"Clara, love, his injuries are internal! Neither he nor I yet know their full extent. I have sent off for two old and experienced practitioners from Staunton. I expect them every moment. In the mean time, I have done all that is possible for his relief."

"Traverse," said Clara, very calmly, controlling herself by an almost superhuman effort, "Traverse, I will be composed; you shall see that I will; take me to my dear father's bedside; it is there that I ought to be!"

"That is my dear, brave, dutiful girl! Come, Clara!" replied the young man, taking her hand and leading her up to the bed-chamber of the doctor. They met Mrs. Rocke at the door, who tearfully signed them to go in as she left it.

When they entered and approached the bedside, Traverse saw that the suffering but heroic father must have made some superlative effort before he could have reduced his haggard face and writhing form to its present state of placid repose, to meet his daughter's eyes and spare her feelings.

She, on her part, was no less firm. Kneeling beside his couch, she took his hand and met his eye composedly as she asked:

"Dear father, how do you feel now?"

"Not just so easy, love, as if I had laid me down here for an afternoon's nap, yet in no more pain than I can very well bear."

"Dear father, what can I do for you?"

"You may bathe my forehead and lips with cologne, my dear," said the doctor, not so much for the sake of the reviving perfume, as because he knew it would comfort Clara to feel that she was doing something, however slight, for him.

Traverse stood upon the opposite side of the bed fanning him.

In a few moments Mrs. Rocke re-entered the room, announcing that the two old physicians from Staunton, Doctor Dawson and Doctor Williams, had arrived.

"Show them up, Mrs. Rocke. Clara, love, retire while the physicians remain with me," said Doctor Day.

Mrs. Rocke left the room to do his bidding. And Clara followed and sought the privacy of her own apartment to give way to the overwhelming grief which she could no longer resist.

As soon as she was gone the doctor also yielded to the force of the suffering that he had been able to endure silently in her presence, and writhed and groaned with agony—that wrung the heart of Traverse to behold.

Presently the two physicians entered the room and approached the bed, with expressions of sincere grief at beholding their old friend in such a condition and a hope that they might speedily be able to relieve him.

To all of which the doctor, repressing all exhibitions of pain and holding out his hand in a cheerful manner, replied:

"I am happy to see you in a friendly way, old friends! I am willing also that you should try what you—what you can do for me—but I warn you that it will be useless! A few hours or days of inflammation, fever and agony, then the ease of mortification, then dissolution!"

"Tut—tut," said Doctor Williams, cheerfully. "We never permit a patient to pronounce a prognosis upon his own case!"

"Friend, my horse ran away, stumbled and fell upon me, and rolled over me in getting up. The viscera is crushed within me; breathing is difficult; speech painful; motion agonizing; but you may examine and satisfy yourselves," said Doctor Day, still speaking cheerfully, though with great suffering.

His old friends proceeded gently to the examination, which resulted in their silently and perfectly coinciding in opinion with the patient himself.

Then, with Doctor Day and Traverse, they entered into a consultation and agreed upon the best palliatives that could be administered, and begging that if in any manner, professionally or otherwise, they could serve their suffering friend, at any hour of the day or night, they might be summoned, they took leave.

As soon as they had gone, Clara, who had given way to a flood of tears, and regained her composure, rapped for admittance.

"Presently, dear daughter—presently," said the doctor, who then, beckoning Traverse to stoop low, said:

"Do not let Clara sit up with me to-night. I foresee a night of great anguish which I may not be able to repress, and which I would not have her witness! Promise you will keep her away."

"I promise," faltered the almost broken-hearted youth. "You may admit her now," said the doctor, composing his convulsed countenance as best he could, lest the sight of his sufferings should distress his daughter.

Clara entered, and resumed her post at the side of the bed.

Traverse left the room to prepare the palliatives for his patient.

The afternoon waned. As evening approached the fever, inflammation and pain arose to such a degree that the doctor could no longer forbear betraying his excessive suffering, which was, besides, momentarily increasing, so he said to Clara:

"My child, you must now leave me and retire to bed. I must be watched by Traverse alone to-night."

And Traverse, seeing her painful hesitation, between her extreme reluctance to leave him and her wish to obey him, approached and murmured:

"Dear Clara, it would distress him to have you stay; he will be much better attended by me alone."

Clara still hesitated; and Traverse, beckoning his mother to come and speak to her, left her side.

Mrs. Rocke approached her and said: "It must be so, dear girl, for you know that there are some cases in which sick men should be watched by men only, and this is one of them. I myself shall sit up to-night in the next room, within call."

"And may I not sit there beside you?" pleaded Clara.

"No, my dear love; as you can do your father no good, he desires that you should go to bed and rest. Do not distress him by refusing."

"Oh, and am I to go to bed and sleep while my dear father lies here suffering? I cannot; oh, I cannot."

"My dear, yes, you must; and if you cannot sleep you can lie awake and pray for him."

Here the doctor, whose agony was growing unendurable, called out:

"Go, Clara, go at once, my dear."

She went back to the bedside and pressed her lips to his forehead, and put her arms around him and prayed:

"Oh, my dear father, may the blessed Saviour take you in his pitying embrace and give you ease to-night. Your poor Clara will pray for you as she never prayed for herself."

"May the Lord bless you, my sweet child," said the doctor, lifting one hand painfully and laying it in benediction on her fair and graceful head.

Then she arose and left the room, saying to Mrs. Rocke as she went:

"Oh, Mrs. Rocke, only last evening we were so happy—'But if we have received good things at the hand of God, why should we not receive evil?'"

"Yes, my child; but remember nothing is really evil that comes from His good hand," said Mrs. Rocke, as she attended Clara to the door.

His daughter had no sooner gone out of hearing than the doctor gave way to his irrepressible groans.

At a sign from Traverse Mrs. Rocke went and took up her position in the adjoining room.

Then Traverse subdued the light in the sick chamber, arranged the pillows of the couch, administered a sedative and took up his post beside the bed, where he continued to watch and nurse the patient with unwearied devotion.

At the dawn of day, when Clara rapped at the door, he was in no condition to be seen by his daughter.

Clara was put off with some plausible excuse.

After breakfast his friends the physicians called and spent several hours in his room. Clara was told that she must not come in while they were there. And so, by one means and another, the poor girl was spared from witnessing those dreadful agonies which, had she seen them, must have so bitterly increased her distress.

In the afternoon, during a temporary mitigation of pain, Clara was admitted to see her father. But in the evening, as his sufferings augmented, she was again, upon the same excuse that had been used the preceding evening, dismissed to her chamber.

Then passed another night of suffering, during which Traverse never left him for an instant.

Toward morning the fever and pain abated, and he fell into a sweet sleep. About sunrise he awoke quite free from suffering. Alas! it was the ease that he had predicted—the ease preceding dissolution.

"It is gone forever now, Traverse, my boy; thank God my last hours will be sufficiently free from pain to enable me to set my house in order. Before calling Clara in I would talk to you alone. You will remain here until all is over?"

"Oh, yes, sir, yes; I would do anything on earth—anything for you! I would lay down my life this hour if I could do so to save you from this bed of death."

"Nay, do not talk so; your young life belongs to others—to Clara and your mother. 'God doeth all things well.' Better the ripened ear should fall than the budding germ. I do not feel it hard to die, dear Traverse. Though the journey has been very pleasant the goal is not unwelcome. Earth has been very sweet to me, but heaven is sweeter."

"Oh, but we love you so! we love you so! you have so much to live for!" exclaimed Traverse, with an irrepressible burst of grief.

"Poor boy, life is too hopeful before you to make you a comforter by a deathbed. Yes, Traverse, I have much to live for but more to die for. Yet not voluntarily would I have left you, though I know that I leave you in the hands of the Lord, and with every blessing and promise of His bountiful providence. Your love will console my child. My confidence in you makes me easy in committing her to your charge."

"Oh, Doctor Day, may the Lord so deal with my soul eternally as I shall discharge this trust," said Traverse, earnestly.

"I know that you will be true; I wish you to remain here with Clara and your mother for a few weeks, until the child's first violence of grief shall be over. Then you had best pursue the plan we laid out. Leave your good mother here to take care of Clara, and you go to the West, get into practice there, and, at the end of a few years, return and marry Clara. Traverse, there is one promise I would have of you."

"I give it before it is named, dear friend," said Traverse, fervently.

"My child is but seventeen; she is so gentle that her will is subject to that of all she loves, especially to yours. She will do anything in conscience that you ask her to do. Traverse, I wish you to promise me that you will not press her to marriage until she shall be at least twenty years old. And——"

"Oh, sir, I promise! Oh, believe me, my affection for Clara is so pure and so constant, as well as so confiding in her faith and so solicitous for her good, that, with the assurance of her love and the privilege of visiting her and writing to her, I could wait many years if needful."

"I believe you, my dear boy. And the very promise I have asked of you is as much for your sake as for hers. No girl can marry before she is twenty without serious risk of life, and almost certain loss of health and beauty; that so many do so is one reason why there are such numbers of sickly and faded young wives. If Clara's constitution should be broken down by prematurely assuming the cares and burdens of matrimony, you would be as unfortunate in having a sickly wife as she would be in losing her health."

"Oh, sir, I promise you that, no matter how much I may wish to do so, I will not be tempted to make a wife of Clara until she has attained the age you have prescribed. But at the same time I must assure you that such is my love for her that, if accident should now make her an invalid for life, she would be as dear—as dear—yes, much dearer to me, if possible, on that very account; and if I could not marry her for a wife, I should marry her only for the dear privilege of waiting on her night and day. Oh, believe this of me, and leave your dear daughter with an easy mind to my faithful care," said Traverse, with a boyish blush suffusing his cheeks and tears filling his eyes.

"I do, Traverse, I do; and now to other things."

"Are you not talking too much, dear friend?"

"No, no; I must talk while I have time. I was about to say that long ago my will was made. Clara, you know, is the heiress of all I possess. You, as soon as you become her husband, will receive her fortune with her. I have made no reservation in her favor against you; for he to whom I can entrust the higher charge of my daughter's person, happiness and honor I can also intrust her fortune."

"Dear sir, I am glad for Clara's sake that she has a fortune; as for me, I hope you will believe me that I would have gladly dispensed with it and worked for dear Clara all the days of my life."

"I do believe it; but this will was made, Traverse, three years ago, before any of us anticipated the present relations between you and my daughter, and while you were both still children. Therefore, I appointed my wife's half-brother, Clara's only male relative, Colonel Le Noir, as her guardian. It is true we have never been very intimate, for our paths in life widely diverged; nor has my Clara seen him within her recollection; for, since her mother's death, which took place in her infancy, he has never been at our house, but he is a man of high reputation and excellent character. I have already requested Doctor Williams to write for him, so that I expect he will be here in a very few days. When he comes Traverse, you will tell him that it is my desire that my daughter shall continue to reside in her present home, retaining Mrs. Rocke as her matronly companion. I have also requested Doctor Williams to tell him the same thing, so that in the mouths of two witnesses my words may be established."

Now, Traverse had never in his life before heard the name of Colonel Le Noir; and, therefore, was in no position to warn the dying father who placed so much confidence in the high reputation of his brother-in-law that his trust was miserably misplaced; that he was leaving his fair daughter and her large fortune to the tender mercies of an unscrupulous villain and a consummate hypocrite. So he merely promised to deliver the message with which he was charged by the dying father for his daughter's guardian, and added that he had no doubt but Clara's uncle would consider that message a sacred command and obey it to the letter.

As the sun was now well up, the doctor consented that Mrs. Rocke and his daughter should be admitted.

Marah brought with her some wine-whey that her patient drank, and from which he received temporary strength.

Clara was pale but calm; one could see at a glance that the poor girl was prepared for the worst, and had nerved her gentle heart to bear it with patience.

"Come hither, my little Clara," said the doctor, as soon as he had been revived by the whey.

Clara came and kissed his brow and sat beside him with her hands clasped in his.

"My little girl, what did our Saviour die for? First to redeem us, and also to teach us by His burial and resurrection that death is but a falling asleep in this world and an awakening in the next. Clara, after this, when you think of your father, do not think of him as lying in the grave, for he will not be there in his vacated body, no more than he will be in the trunk with his cast-off entries. As the coat is the body's covering, so the body is the soul's garment, and it is the soul that is the innermost and real man; it is my soul that is me; and that will not be in the earth, but in heaven; therefore, do not think of me gloomily as lying in the grave, but cheerfully as living in heaven—as living there with God and Christ and His saints, and with your mother, Clara, the dear wife of my youth, who has been waiting for me these many years. Think of me as being happy in that blessed society. Do not fancy that it is your duty to grieve, but, on the contrary, know that it is your duty to be as cheerful and happy as possible. Do you heed me, my daughter?"

"Oh, yes, yes, dear father!" said Clara, heroically repressing her grief.

"Seek for yourself, dear child, a nearer union with Christ and God. Seek it, Clara, until the spirit of God shall bear witness with your spirit that you are as a child of God; so shall you, as you come to lie where I do now, be able to say of your life and death, as I say with truth of mine: The journey has been pleasant, but the goal is blessed."

The doctor pressed his daughter's hand and dropped suddenly into an easy sleep.

Mrs. Rocke drew Clara away, and the room was very still.

Sweet, beautiful and lovely as is the death-bed of a Christian, we will not linger too long beside it.

All day the good man's bodily life ebbed gently away. He spoke at intervals, as he had strength given him, words of affection, comfort and counsel to those around him.

Just as the setting sun was pouring his last rays into the chamber Doctor Day laid his hand upon his child's head and blessed her. Then, closing his eyes, he murmured softly: "'Lord Jesus, into thy hands I resign my spirit:'" and with that sweet, deep, intense smile that had been so lovely in life—now so much lovelier in death—his pure spirit winged its flight to the realms of eternal bliss.

CHAPTER XXX.

THE ORPHAN.

"Let me die, father! I fear, I fear
To fall in earth's terrible strife!"
"Not so, my child, for the crown must be won
In the battle-field of Life."

—Life and Death.

"He has gone to sleep again," said Clara, with a sigh of relief.

"He has gone to heaven, my child," said Marah Rocke, softly.

The orphan started, gazed wildly on the face of the dead, turned ghastly pale and, with a low moan and suffocating sob, fell fainting into the motherly arms of Mrs. Rocke.

Marah beckoned Traverse, who lifted the insensible girl tenderly in his arms and, preceded by his mother, bore her to her chamber and laid her upon the bed.

Then Marah dismissed Traverse to attend to the duties owed to the remains of the beloved departed, while she herself stayed with Clara, using every means for her restoration.

Clara opened her eyes at length, but in reviving to life also returned to grief. Dreadful to witness was the sorrow of the orphan girl. She had controlled her grief in the presence of her father and while he lingered in life, only to give way now to its overwhelming force. Marah remained with her, Holding her in her arms, weeping with her, praying for her, doing all that the most tender mother could do to soothe, console and strengthen the bleeding young heart.

The funeral of Doctor Day took place the third day from his decease, and was attended by all the gentry of the neighboring town and county in their own carriages, and by crowds who came on foot to pay the last tribute of respect to their beloved friend.

He was interred in the family burial ground, situated on a wooded hill up behind the homestead, and at the head of his last resting place was afterwards erected a plain obelisk of white marble, with his name and the date of his birth and death and the following inscription:

"He is not here, but is risen."

"When dear Clara comes to weep at her father's grave, these words will send her away comforted and with her faith renewed," had been Traverse Rocke's secret thought when giving directions for the inscription of this inspiring text.

On the morning of the day succeeding the funeral, while Clara, exhausted by the violence of her grief, lay prostrate upon her chamber couch, Mrs. Rocke and Traverse sat conversing in that once pleasant, now desolate, morning reading-room.

"You know, dear mother, that by the doctor's desire, which should be considered sacred, Clara is still to live here, and you are to remain to take care of her. I shall defer my journey West until everything is settled to Clara's satisfaction, and she has in some degree recovered her equanimity. I must also have an interview and a good understanding with her guardian, for whom I have a message."

"Who is this guardian of whom I have heard you speak more than once, Traverse?" asked Marah.

"Dear mother, will you believe me that I have forgotten the man's name; it is an uncommon name that I never heard before in my life, and, in the pressure of grief upon my mind, its exact identity escaped my memory; but that does not signify much, as he is expected hourly; and when he announces himself, either by card or word of mouth, I shall know, for I shall recognize the name the moment I see it written or hear it spoken. Let me see, it was something like Des Moines, De Vaughn, De Saule, or something of that sort. At all events, I'm sure I shall know it again the instant I see or hear it. And now, dear mother, I must ride up to Staunton to see some of the doctor's poor sick that he left in my charge for as long as I stay here. I shall be back by three o'clock. I need not ask you to take great care of that dear suffering girl up-stairs," said Traverse, taking his hat and gloves for a ride.

"I shall go and stay with her as soon as she awakes," answered Mrs. Rocke.

And Traverse, satisfied, went his way.

He had been gone perhaps an hour when the sound of a carriage was heard below in the front of the house, followed soon by a loud rapping at the hall door.

"It is dear Clara's guardian," said Marah Rocke, rising and listening.

Soon a servant entered and placed a card in her hand, saying:

"The gentleman is waiting in the hall below, and asked to see the person that was in charge here, ma'am; so I fotch the card to you."

"You did right, John. Show the gentleman up here," said Marah; and as soon as the servant had gone she looked at the card, but failed to make it out. The name was engraved in Old English text, and in such a complete labyrinth, thicket and network of ornate flourishes that no one who was not familiar at once with the name and the style could possibly have distinguished it.

"I do not think my boy would know this name at sight," was Marah's thought as she twirled the card in her hand and stood waiting the entrance of the visitor, whose step was now heard coming up the stairs. Soon the door was thrown open and the stranger entered.

Marah, habitually shy in the presence of strangers, dropped her eyes before she had fairly taken in the figure of a tall, handsome, dark-complexioned, distinguished-looking man, somewhat past middle age, and arrayed in a rich military cloak, and carrying in his hand a military cap.

The servant who had admitted him had scarcely retired when Marah looked up and her eyes and those of the stranger met—and—

"Marah Rocke!!!"

"Colonel Le Noir!!!"

Burst simultaneously from the lips of each.

Le Noir first recovered himself, and, holding out both hands, advanced toward her with a smile as if to greet an old friend.

But Marah, shrinking from him in horror, turned and tottered to the farthest window, where, leaning her head against the sash, she moaned:

"Oh, my heart: my heart! Is this the wolf to whom my lamb must be committed?"

As she moaned these words she was aware of a soft step at her side and a low voice murmuring:

"Marah Rocke, yes! the same beautiful Marah that, as a girl of fifteen—twenty years ago—turned my head, led me by her fatal charms into the very jaws of death—the same lovely Marah with her beauty only ripened by time and exalted by sorrow!"

With one surprised, indignant look, but without a word of reply, Mrs. Rocke turned and walked composedly toward the door with the intention of quitting the room.

Colonel Le Noir saw and forestalled her purpose by springing forward, turning the key and standing before the door.

"Forgive, me, Marah, but I must have a word with you before we part," he said, in those soft, sweet, persuasive tones he knew so well how to assume.

Marah remembered that she was an honorable matron and an honored mother; that, as such, fears and tremors and self-distrust in the presence of a villain would not well become her; so calling up all the gentle dignity latent in her nature, she resumed her seat and, signing to the visitor to follow her example, she said composedly:

"Speak on, Colonel Le Noir—remembering, if you please, to whom you speak."

"I do remember, Marah; remember but too well."

"They call me Mrs. Rocke who converse with me, sir."

"Marah, why this resentment? Is it possible that you can still be angry? Have I remained true to my attachment all these years and sought you throughout the world to find this reception at last?"

"Colonel Le Noir, if this is all you had to say, it was scarcely worth while to have detained me," said Mrs. Rocke calmly.

"But it is not all, my Marah! Yes, I call you mine by virtue of the strongest attachment man ever felt for woman! Marah Rocke, you are the only woman who ever inspired me with a feeling worthy to be called a passion——"

"Colonel Le Noir, how dare you blaspheme this house of mourning by such sinful words? You forget where you stand and to whom you speak."

"I forget nothing, Marah Rocke; nor do I violate this sanctuary of sorrow"— here he sank his voice below his usual low tones—"when I speak of the passion that maddened my youth and withered my manhood—a passion whose intensity was its excuse for all extravagances and whose enduring constancy is its final, full justification!"

Before he had finished this sentence Marah Rocke had calmly arisen and pulled the bell rope.

"What mean you by that, Marah?" he inquired.

Before she replied a servant, in answer to the bell, came to the door and tried the latch, and, finding it locked, rapped.

With a blush that mounted to his forehead and with a half-suppressed imprecation, Colonel Le Noir went and unlocked the door and admitted the man.

"John," said Mrs. Rocke, quietly, "show Colonel Le Noir to the apartment prepared for him and wait his orders." And with a slight nod to the guest she went calmly from the room.

Colonel Le Noir, unmindful of the presence of the servant, stood gazing in angry mortification after her. The flush on his brow had given way to the fearful pallor of rage or hate as he muttered inaudibly:

"Insolent beggar! contradiction always confirms my half-formed resolutions. Years ago I swore to possess that woman, and I will do it, if it be only to keep my oath and humble her insolence. She is very handsome still; she shall be my slave!"

Then, perceiving the presence of John, he said:

"Lead the way to my room, sirrah, and then go and order my fellow to bring up my portmanteau."

John devoutly pulled his forelocks as he bowed low and then went on, followed by Colonel Le Noir.

Marah Rocke meanwhile had gained the privacy of her own chamber, where all her firmness deserted her.

Throwing herself into a chair, she clasped her hands and sat with blanched face and staring eyes, like a marble statue of despair.

"Oh, what shall I do? what shall I do while this miscreant remains here?—this villain whose very presence desecrates the roof and dishonors me? I would instantly leave the house but that I must not abandon poor Clara.

"I cannot claim the protection of Traverse, for I would not provoke him to wrath or run him into danger; nor, indeed, would I even permit my son to dream such a thing possible as that his mother could receive insult!

"Nor can I warn Clara of the unprincipled character of her guardian, for if she knew him as he is she would surely treat him in such a way as to get his enmity—his dangerous, fatal enmity!—doubly fatal since her person and property are legally at his disposal. Oh, my dove! my dove! that you should be in the power of this vulture! What shall I do, oh, heaven?"

Marah dropped on her knees and finished her soliloquy with prayer. Then, feeling composed and strengthened, she went to Clara's room.

She found the poor girl lying awake and quietly weeping.

"Your guardian has arrived, love," she said, sitting down beside the bed and taking Clara's hand.

"Oh, must I get up and dress to see a stranger?" sighed Clara, wearily.

"No, love; you need not stir until it is time to dress for dinner; it will answer quite well if you meet your guardian at table," said Marah, who had particular reasons for wishing that Clara should first see Colonel Le Noir with other company, to have an opportunity of observing him well and possibly forming an estimate of his character (as a young girl of her fine instincts might well do) before she should be exposed in a tête-a-tête to those deceptive blandishments he knew so well how to bring into play.

"That is a respite. Oh, dear Mrs. Rocke, you don't know how I dread to see any one!"

"My dear Clara, you must combat grief by prayer, which is the only thing that can overcome it," said Marah.

Mrs. Rocke remained with her young charge as long as she possibly could, and then she went down-stairs to oversee the preparation of the dinner.

And it was at the dinner-table that Marah, with the quiet and gentle dignity for which she was distinguished, introduced the younger members of the family to the guest, in these words:

"Your ward, Miss Day, Colonel Le Noir."

The colonel bowed deeply and raised the hand of Clara to his lips, murmuring some sweet, soft, silvery and deferentially inaudible words of condolence, sympathy and melancholy pleasure, from which Clara, with a gentle bend of her head, withdrew to take her seat.

"Colonel Le Noir, my son, Doctor Rocke," said Marah, presenting Traverse.

The colonel stared superciliously, bowed with ironical depth, said he was "much honored," and, turning his back on the young man, placed himself at the table.

During the dinner he exerted himself to be agreeable to Miss Day and Mrs. Rocke, but Traverse he affected to treat with supercilious neglect or ironical deference.

Our young physician had too much self-respect to permit himself to be in any degree affected by this rudeness. And Marah, on her part, was glad, so that it did not trouble Traverse, that Le Noir should behave in this manner, so that Clara should be enabled to form some correct idea of his disposition.

When dinner was over Clara excused herself and retired to her room, whither she was soon followed by Mrs. Rocke.

"Well, my dear, how do you like your guardian?" asked Marah, in a tone as indifferent as she could make it.

"I do not like him at all!" exclaimed Clara, her gentle blue eyes flashing with indignation through her tears; "I do not like him at all, the scornful, arrogant, supercilious—Oh! I do not wish to use such strong language, or to grow angry when I am in such deep grief; but my dear father could not have known this man, or he never would have chosen him for my guardian; do you think he would, Mrs. Rocke?"

"My dear, your excellent father must have thought well of him, or he never would have intrusted him with so precious a charge. Whether your father's confidence in this man will be justified as far as you are concerned, time will show. Meanwhile, my love, as the guardian appointed by your father, you should treat him with respect; but, so far as reposing any trust in him goes, consult your own instincts."

"I shall; and I thank heaven that I have not got to go and live with Colonel Le Noir!" said Clara, fervently.

Mrs. Rocke sighed. She remembered that the arrangement that permitted Clara to live at her own home with her chosen friends was but a verbal one, not binding upon the guardian and executor unless he chose to consider it so.

Their conversation was interrupted by the entrance of a servant with a message from Colonel Le Noir, expressing a hope that Miss Day felt better from her afternoon's repose, and desiring the favor of her company in the library.

Clara returned an answer pleading indisposition, and begging upon that account to be excused.

At tea, however, the whole family met again. As before, Colonel Le Noir exerted himself to please the ladies and treated the young physician with marked neglect. This conduct offended Miss Day to such a degree that she, being a girl of truth in every thought, word and deed, could only exhibit toward the guest the most freezing politeness that was consistent with her position as hostess, and she longed for the time to come that should deliver their peaceful home and loving little circle from the unwelcome presence of this arrogant intruder.

"How can he imagine that I can be pleased with his deference and courtesy and elaborate compliments, when he permits himself to be so rude to Traverse? I hope Traverse will tell him of our engagement, which will, perhaps, suggest to him the propriety of reforming his manners while he remains under a roof of which Traverse is destined to be master," said Clara to herself, as she arose from the table and, with a cold bow, turned to retire from the room.

"And will not my fair ward give me a few hours of her company this evening?" inquired Colonel Le Noir in an insinuating voice, as he took and pressed the hand of the doctor's orphan daughter.

"Excuse me, sir; but, except at meal times, I have not left my room since" — here her voice broke down; she could not speak to him of her bereavement, or give way in his presence to her holy sorrow. "Besides, sir," she added, "Doctor Rocke, I know, has expressed to you his desire for an early interview."

"My fair young friend, Doctor Rocke, as you style the young man, will please to be so condescending as to tarry the leisure of his most humble servant," replied the colonel, with an ironical bow in the direction of Traverse.

"Perhaps, sir, when you know that Doctor Rocke is charged with the last uttered will of my dear father, and that it is of more importance than you are prepared to anticipate, you may be willing to favor us all by granting this 'young man' an early audience," said Clara.

"The last uttered will! I had supposed that the will of my late brother-in-law was regularly drawn up and executed and in the hands of his confidential attorney at Staunton."

"Yes, sir; so it is; but I refer to my father's last dying wishes, his verbal directions entrusted to his confidential friend Doctor Rocke," said Clara.

"Last verbal directions, entrusted to Doctor Rocke. Humph! Humph! this would require corroborative evidence," said the colonel.

"Such corroborative evidence can be had, sir," said Clara, coldly "and as I know that Doctor Rocke has already requested an interview for the sake of an explanation of these subjects, I must also join my own request to his, and assure you that by giving him an early opportunity of coming to an understanding with you, you will greatly oblige me."

"Then, undoubtedly, my sweet young friend, your wishes shall be commands—Eh! you—sir! Doctor—What's-your-name! meet me in the library at ten o'clock to-morrow morning," said Le Noir, insolently.

"I have engagements, sir, that will occupy me between the hours of ten and three; before or after that period I am at your disposal," said Traverse, coldly.

"Pardieu! It seems to me that I am placed at yours!" replied the colonel, lifting his eyebrows; "but as I am so placed by the orders of my fair little tyrant here, so be it—at nine to-morrow I am your most obedient servant."

"At nine, then, sir, I shall attend you," said Traverse, with a cold bow.

Clara slightly curtsied and withdrew from the room, attended by Mrs. Rocke.

Traverse, as the only representative of the host, remained for a short time with his uncourteous guest, who, totally regardless of his presence, threw himself into an armchair, lighted a cigar, took up a book and smoked and read.

Whereupon Traverse, seeing this, withdrew to the library to employ himself with finishing the arranging and tying up of certain papers left to his charge by Doctor Day.

Lector House believes that a society develops through a two-fold approach of continuous learning and adaptation, which is derived from the study of classic literary works spread across the historic timeline of literature records. Therefore, we aim at reviving, repairing and redeveloping all those inaccessible or damaged but historically as well as culturally important literature across subjects so that the future generations may have an opportunity to study and learn from past works to embark upon a journey of creating a better future.

This book is a result of an effort made by Lector House towards making a contribution to the preservation and repair of original ancient works which might hold historical significance to the approach of continuous learning across subjects.

HAPPY READING & LEARNING!

LECTOR HOUSE LLP
E-MAIL: lectorpublishing@gmail.com

9 789353 428334

CPSIA information can be obtained
at www.ICGtesting.com
Printed in the USA
LVHW111914140922
728375LV00005B/638

9 789353 428334